Edith Sitwell

EDITH SITWELL was born in Yorkshire in 1887, the first daughter of
Sir George Sitwell, 4th Baronet, and Lady Ida Emily Augusta Denison.
She had two younger brothers, Osbert (1892–1969) and Sacheverell
(1897-1988), both well-known literary figures. Her relationship with
her parents was fraught, not least because of her father attempting to
cure a presumed spinal deformity by forcing her into an iron frame.
After she left home she became a supporter of innovative trends in
English poetry, and her flat in Bayswater, London, became a meeting
place for writers she championed, including the young Dylan Thomas
and Denton Welch. She also helped to publish the poetry of Wilfred
Owen after his death. She never married, although it is said that in
1927 she fell in love with the homosexual Russian painter. Pavel
Tchelitchew. During the Second World War she moved from France to
Renishaw with her brother Osbert and his lover David Horner. The
poems she wrote during this period were much praised. 'Still Falls the
Rain', about the London Blitz, remains perhaps her best known, being
set to music by Benjamin Britten. In 1948 she toured the United States
with her brothers. Her poetry recitals were renowned, and she also
made recordings, including two of *Façade*, set to music by William
Walton, the first with Constant Lambert and the second with Peter
Pears. In 1954 she was awarded a DBE, and the following year she converted to Roman Catholicism. She died in London in 1964.

EDITH SITWELL

I LIVE UNDER
A BLACK SUN

With a foreword by Sir Reresby Sitwell

PETER OWEN
London and Chester Springs

PETER OWEN PUBLISHERS
73 Kenway Road, London SW5 0RE

Peter Owen books are distributed in the USA by
Dufour Editions Inc., Chester Springs, PA 19425–0007

First published in Great Britain 1937
© Executors of F.T.S. Sitwell (deceased) 1937
First Peter Owen edition 1953
First Peter Owen Modern Classics edition 2007
Foreword © Sir Reresby Sitwell

ISBN 978 0 7206 1225 7

A catalogue record for this book is available from
the British Library

Printed in the UK by CPI Bookmarque, Croydon, CR0 4TD

FOR JOHN SPARROW

PANDORA: "But there was such laughing. Queen Hecuba laughed that her eyes ran o'er."

CRESSIDA: "With millstones."

PANDORA: "And Cassandra laughed."

"And observing these howling contrasts in richness and poverty, Illyich would mutter through clenched teeth . . . 'Two nations.'"—*Memories of Lenin*, N. KRUPSKAYA.

Foreword

By Sir Reresby Sitwell
First published in the *Sunday Telegraph*, 6 September 1987,
to mark the centenary of Edith Sitwell's birth

Once upon a time I had two aunts – only ever one uncle – and all four grandparents lived on until I reached the age of ten. Now they are all gone, long ago: I obtained a 'senior citizen' railway pass on in April; my father clings on in his ninetieth year, the last of his generation, and my Aunt Edith Sitwell would have been a hundred years on 7 September 1987. No two women could have differed more than Edith Sitwell and Bunny Doble, my beautiful and tragic maternal aunt, an aspiring but unsuccessful actress, briefly and unhappily the wife of a bold, bad baronet, one time a fascist sympathizer and the unsuspecting mistress of Kim Philby.

To be fair, I met my Aunt Frances barely half-a-dozen times; she looked and smelled divine and smothered one with affection that, alas, failed to conceal her self-centredness. Edith, however, or 'Lely' as I called her, was a true 'Strawberry Aunt', bent on giving one a treat, despite her slender means, frail health and professional commitments. For, unlike her opposite number, she was no amateur but most dedicated to her craft: her very businesslike handwriting is a clue to her inner character; she was a better trouper, as well as a more lovable aunt. To end this comparison, Bunny relied on her diminutive Spanish charms to off-set any lack of acting ability on stage; whereas Edith, who was on show all her life, taught herself how to contend and, indeed, capitalize on her hawk-like features and ungainly figure by regaling herself in those flowing garments and hieratic jewellery, too often submitting even the smallest family audience to her Plantagenet pretensions that we might also claim to share but learned to deplore in repetition.

Dimly, very dimly, do I remember the 1930s, but, as I bash out these reminiscences on my ancient portable in the peace of my Print Room at Renishaw, the 'Great Chamber' of former centuries and Upstairs Drawing-Room of ghostly reputation in less decent times, I can recall summer evenings lying awake in the bleak nursery up on the attic floor, unable to sleep, not because of any supernatural presence that might lurk too near me but thanks to the gales of happy laughter floating up from the downstairs rooms or the garden. Edith, with her spontaneous wit and sense of fun, was as much to blame for the noise as her brothers, their friends and hangers-on, as was confirmed when, later on, I began to attend her tea-parties.

She contrived a dramatic escape from her flat in Paris before the German occupation and spent much of the Blitz ensconced with my parents at Weston, my old home in Northamptonshire; thus, during my first few holidays from Eton, I was to see more of her than at any other time. Later she moved in with my uncle Osbert at Renishaw for the rest of the Second World War and, until her last few years, the bandwagon moved from Renishaw to Motegufoni to London, where they took up separate quarters, Osbert at his house in Carlyle Square and Edith at the Sesame Club, and the period of the triumphant lecture tours of the United States began.

Soon after I married in 1952, I started as a humble 'copy detail clerk' at Colman, Prentis and Varley Advertising, in a building opposite the Sesame, where Edith held court. Often I crossed Grosvenor Street to lunch or to have a drink with her after work, and on one Sunday in August, when Penelope was snatching an extra few days sunshine and I was alone in

London, a summons came I could not resist. 'I'm afraid I'll have to bring Klaus,' said I. We walked across Hyde Park, and on arrival I tied him up in the Porter's Lodge and went in to meet Edith and her new friends. After five minutes the barking became insupportable and I had to fetch him in; slipping his lead and paying no attention to Edith, Arthur Miller or the attendant public relations person, Klaus leaped on to Marilyn Monroe's lap and plastered the sex goddess with canine kisses! *Gentlemen of England that night abed, what would you not have done to be in that dachshund's place!*

I am afraid we were not very popular on that occasion with Edith. However, I do not agree with another newspaper that she favoured one nephew more than the other. The truth is that Edith had a great sense of fairness and, suffering herself from the system of primogeniture (Sir George bequeathed her, as his only daughter, the sum of £30 per annum), and knowing that Osbert was handing over to me, she did her best to provide for her other nephew.

As the years rolled by and both she and Osbert became increasingly dependent upon their nurses, they split forces, and Edith, under the influence of her devoted Australian secretary, Elizabeth Salter, who loved Hampstead, took a flat in the modern block there, named 'Greenhill'. On returning to the West End through rush-hour traffic one had to agree with Sir Malcolm Bullock: at last we pilgrims realized the full meaning of the words in the hymn 'There Is a Green Hill Far Away'. And here it was that our infant daughter Alexandra was in her turn gently reproved for teasing Edith's cats and interrupting Cyril Connolly (I took photographs of the occasion). The final months took place near by, at Keats's Cottage, a leafy little dwelling provided by the shy and mysterious Bryher, Edith's friend and great admirer. Despite her compounding infirmities Edith enjoyed here 'in a place of her own' a certain independence and serenity she had never known.

My virgin aunt was a sad person. If her physique was somewhat freakish, her instincts were normal: it happened that the only two men she ever fancied were orientated in a different direction. She had an arrogant and also a silly side to her nature – I cannot accept the experimental verses of *Façade* as serious poetry – she took umbrage unduly and spared no quarter in her incessant literary campaigns: yet she wrote some great poetry and some good prose, she had a great heart, she was loyal and generous to the end; nobody could deny she had a great personality; to me, her nephew, she was a wonderful person.

PART I

Chapter I

THROUGH THE forest of white damson trees with the constellations of sharp and of soft flower-stars and of dew falling upon their hair and brushing their lips, with the oceans of flower smells and of light lapping about them, two young people were walking hand in hand. The airs were green among the branches, and you felt that the forest stretched for ever, far beyond this spring and the song of birds.

"Aldebaran, Sirius, Cassiopeia, falling from the branches," he said, and put out his hand to catch them as they fell. Beyond, stretching far into the distance, were the flowering cherry trees with their laughing dazzling sweet snows, not cold to touch but warm with life and the promise of future fires.

"How sad it is," she sighed, looking at the landscape of snows and of planetary systems, all dancing to the unheard music, "to think that they must grow old."

"They will be young again next spring," the young man said; "and even if they should fade, I should always see your hand waving to me through the branches."

"Sometimes, Jonathan, you seem to me like a ghost. I expect you to fade in the light. But then if you did, I should find the spring was a ghost too."

"Oh," he replied, laughing at her through the branches, "you will not find I shall fade as quickly as that. And if I *should* turn into a ghost, it would be your fault."

"It would not be my fault if the spring should fade."

"You are always afraid of something. You live in fear—fear of living, fear of not living, fear of dying. Don't be afraid.

11

See, I will give you a bouquet of clear dancing stars, I will give you the planetary system, and you can wear it in your hair or tread it under your feet, for I will pluck it down from the sky for you. Look,"—and he held up a branch with the white flowers growing thick upon it—"it seems as if it were shaking with laughter. Perhaps it is laughing at the follies of the world." He shook it till the drops of dew fell upon the grass. "You would think, wouldn't you, that every drop was a world falling. Look at them running together and then falling apart again. That is how we change—that is how the world changes in ten years."

"You said, such a little while ago, that you would not turn into a ghost. Will *you* change, too, when ten years have gone by?"

He laughed and pressed her hand, looking into her eyes that had the strange hardness, inexorability and cruelty of spring; she seemed a fabulous creature born from the spring and the forest. They brushed through the wet boughs, with the wild snows, soft and unchilling, falling upon their hair, touching their lips, and he said: "The flowers on the branches are jealous of me. They are leaning forward to touch your lips. . . ." But as the light fell upon her face through the leaves, seeing the little lines about her eyes, he thought: "In ten years' time, my dear, it will be *you* who will have changed. It will be you who will be the ghost."

Yet he gave the bouquet of white stars into her hand, and then, pausing for a moment in his walk, he said: "I have gathered the stars from the sky for you. And what will you do in return for me?"

"Barter and exchange!" And she gave her bird-voiced laugh. "Oh, what *can* a woman give a man—excepting, of course, love."

He stared at her, his straight strong eyebrows lowered over his eyes that had a look of black and sullen power. His full, sensual-looking lips were closed in an angry line. "So *that* is unimportant, too," he thought, "as unimportant as my work and

12

my future." And he said: "It is easy enough to say that one loves; that means nothing. Love is not enough without giving. Tell me, Lucy, what does love give?"

She laughed again, and said carelessly: "How should I know?"

"You don't know? Then I will tell you. Love gives the future—and power. And that is what no woman can understand. Every human being in the world needs to be believed in—and love is belief. All my life, through all the wretchedness of my poverty and its helplessness, I have never doubted my own greatness, I have always believed in my future and the power it will give me, and have known that everything I have undergone—the misery of being dependent, first on my uncle, who cared nothing for me (I was just something that had to be kept alive, out of duty), and then on whoever employed me —the humiliation of being forced to live their lives, pretend to think their thoughts—all this will have been, not worth while, oh never worth while, but at least a wretched ground on which I have built myself. I shall still be dependent, but on one thing alone. I *must* have someone who believes in me, who is ready to give up her will to me."

Throughout his life it had been his need to inhabit another being, conquer the will of another, remake the world of another personality, seeing in this victory a symbol of destiny overcome, the universe moulded to his will; only thus could he refute his poverty, forget the humiliations he had undergone— the childhood and boyhood when he had been fed as if he were a beast (reluctantly, from a sense of duty, as he had said)— in which nobody ever spoke to him, nobody ever asked him what were his thoughts, what were his hopes, so that he lived walled up in ice, alone with the growth of the black unknowable power that would be his and that at any moment might rise to such vast and uncontrollable strength that it would turn on him who had been its master and destroy him. Now he looked at the woman beside him despairingly, hopelessly, perceiving her weakness and her fear. She would never help either herself or him.

13.

"Love!" she cried. "Love does not give power. Only money can do that. Oh, how I have longed to be rich!"

He paused in his walk. He had never felt so poor, so humbled, so alone, as at that moment. Even the spring seemed dead, and all that remained of it was the coldness of the wet ground, the moisture piercing through the holes in his boots that had been patched so often that they were now as heavy as lead. Then the hopelessness in his eyes changed, the despair hardened, and he looked at her without pity. Remembering the cold and threadbare years of his loveless childhood, his helpless dependence upon the uncle who saw him only as a burden, never as a human creature suffering and hoping, longing for tenderness and a few words of comfort—with these memories in his heart, at that moment he almost hated her. She had made him realise the weight of his chains, his full helplessness. He muttered: "Rich! I have always known that a man had far better have a poor angel for a rival, than a devil—if the devil were rich!" And he wondered if the devil was not at hand, masquerading in the guise of one of the young subalterns who haunted the house of Lucy Linden's mother. It was true that they showed no signs of having any money, but he thought it doubtful if Mrs. Linden would encourage their presence if they had none. No, they must have money, only they did not know how to use it. They would never have power—not even the power that comes through possessing the soul of another being.

"Lucy," he said, "show me, prove to me, that you have a little love for me. Don't only tell me that you love me. Words are so easy, and when you say that you love me, it sounds only too often as if it were a lesson you had learnt by heart. I ask so little of you: only that you will help me by showing your faith in me, in my future, in what I am and shall be, and not weaken me by your fear. We will make our lives together, I will build you and make you what you should be. Show that you are willing to take your part in making my life! For you can, Lucy, you can—if you will take one risk, just to show me that you believe in me—if you will take the risk of marrying

14

me before I leave the country. Or if you will at least have the courage, and the loyalty towards me, to tell your family we intend to marry. If you would even do that, I should at least know that you believe in me and in my future, and it would give me power. Oh, Lucy, I am so poor in everything but power. Show me that you are not afraid of poverty."

Power! To be rushing along always at a giant's speed—to be vast as a mountain crag! She said to herself, "I am not frightened of this, it is not fear." And taking refuge in her small tenderness, she looked at his hair, so like the hair of the child who might have clung at her breast. How could she ruin her own child, how could she believe in the power of the child who had to rely upon her own making? And she said, "How *can* we marry yet? We have so little money. You may succeed —you may do everything you hope to do. But, Jonathan, what would happen to us if you did not?"

He bent his head. In a low voice he said: "I understand. I know now, which of the two you would choose if you were given the choice between love and money. And now, at last, I know the real reason for the whole of your treatment of me. *You know how poor I am.* And that is why you fail me at every turn. I have only my faith in myself, and so you let me go, without one word of belief in me, without doing the only thing which could make me believe that you have any love for me. In a fortnight from now I shall be gone, and for all you know you will never see me again. But yet you still keep up the same pretences, the same cold and cowardly evasions. You pretend to love me, sometimes, when you think you have killed my love, you even tell me that you love me, so as to renew your power over me. You are afraid to hold me honestly —you are afraid to let me go, so you behave in such a way as to make me think you are only playing with my love for you, whilst protesting all the while that you love me. All these trivial little acceptances and withdrawals, these silly, mean little coquettish evasions, are infinitely beneath people of your pride and mine. Yet you persist in them. There are moments

15

when I wish to God you had treated me in this way, had shown you cared nothing for me, from the beginning; for your love has more terrible consequences than your indifference, or even your hate; your love will complete my ruin! "

And he thought: "Why was I so foolish as to put my hopes and fears into the power of another? A man should live and think and hope alone!"

Then she said again: "But, Jonathan, do be reasonable. You *know* I love you, but how *can* we marry without money? We have to think of the future. We really must wait for a little—there is nothing else to do." And through her mind passed the endless procession of subterfuges, attempts to piece worn-out fragments together, petty economies leading to coldness, that had gone to make up her past.

He looked at her. She wore always dresses that would be fashionable next summer, so that they gave her the appearance of looking forward to something. But they were made by a dressmaker working in a dark place at a cheap rate, and the materials were thin. Soon they would be in holes and you would see little patches of still cheaper underclothes through them. "Lucy," he said, at last, "what does the future mean to you?"

She did not speak for some moments, but looked straight in front of her with hard eyes, and then, shrugging her shoulders faintly, said in a slow, uncertain voice, "The future?" But she did not answer his question. After a short pause she continued: "You really must be sensible. You know as well as I do that it isn't possible for us to marry yet. We must wait until my health is better, and until—well—until you have some sort of assured position."

"So you have no faith in me!"

"Oh, Jonathan, you *know* that it isn't a question of having faith, it is a question of having a little ordinary common sense. Think what it would be like if we were poor, and you had a wife who is always ill. I am thinking of you just as much as of myself. You know perfectly well that my health . . ."

16

"And *you* know that a little ordinary courage, one decent and honest action, would do more to give you back your health than all the doctors and medicines in the world; *you* know that if you showed me the most ordinary justice the whole of our lives would be changed; we should be happy, we should be able to build the future together. Your ill-health is only a form of cowardice, and an excuse for cowardice. And so you won't put it aside. You hesitate, and make excuses, and give false reasons and tell half-lies. Have you no generosity in the whole of your nature? Once again I have the chance of a great future before me (political, I mean, apart from my life as a writer). Yet I have even offered to give up that chance for your sake. I don't want to touch a penny of your money. I have told you over and over again that I am perfectly willing for you to live wherever you like until we can make a home together. I meet your wishes in every way, and in return, you do nothing but make excuses and talk about your health. I can only imagine that you enjoy illness, because you have known illness longer than you have known me, and so do not want to part with an older friend." He stopped dead, and then said slowly: "You have been playing too long, Lucy, and I have grown tired of the play. I have warned you before. But now I am warning you for the last time. If you do not marry me now, in the fortnight that remains to us before I leave Ireland, or if you don't at least have the ordinary decency and courage to tell your family we are engaged—then you will never see me again. That I swear to you. I will never come back—never. There is no poverty, no misery, no destitution that I will not endure rather than return."

His voice was oddly hollow and unreal, and as she listened to him she thought: "It isn't love for me, it isn't a need for my help, it is nothing but his craze for power that is making him say this. He would sacrifice me and my whole life, he would sacrifice his own deepest feelings for that." And she said: "I have told you, dearest, it is only a question of waiting. It would be nothing but madness to rush blindly into marriage,

17

as you want us to do. What if you should change, or if I should change? There are a thousand reasons why we should wait."

Raising his arms above his head, he broke off a spray of dazzling cherry blossom, crumpled its snow in his fingers and threw the worthless thing away. That, at least, would bear no fruit, and, like his life, would never break into sweet fires. Then, in a strange, hallucinated, sleep-walking voice, he said: "Lucy, are you not afraid to lose me? Do you know what spirit you have conjured up?" (All the darkness of Africa, and the pomp of the black sun.) "It is terrible when a spirit plays or a giant dances." He paused again, and looked at her. "Lucy," he said, "I told you a moment ago, that *you* had been playing with *me*. But what if it is not so? What if it is *I* who have been playing with *you*—and now am tiring of the play? I can remember at least twenty women in my life to whom I have behaved in exactly the same way as I have with you, and for no other reason and with no other intention than that of amusing myself when I had nothing better to do, or was feeling discontented. Unflattering to the women, perhaps, but after all, what does that matter? It was perfectly innocent—nothing but a little harmless fun."

He paused, and then said, in a lower voice: "You are right, Lucy. . . . To marry would be madness. It would be to ruin oneself out of a maggot."

He had dropped her hand, and silently and alone they walked through the forest, through the planetary music unheard upon the branches.

Chapter II

UNDER THE hot gold rays of the rough fruitful sun, the wisdom and lore of the countrysides sprang from the growth and ripening and dying of the seasons, from the peaceful rhythms of their life, rising and toiling and sowing and reaping in the holy fields, loving and giving birth, growing old and sinking into sleep. This was the life they knew in the countrysides before the dawn of the day that was to change and maim the rhythm of the seasons and of all pulses.

Through the long darkness, lulled by the maternal night, the earth lay, gigantic in its slumber, breathing in a gentle sleep, and from the world of growing things a sweet breath arose, the sound that comes before the dawn. A sigh, a breath among the leaves, and the sound was gone.

Then rose the guiltless light, over the quiet countrysides, and over the cities where men have created and known fear. It filled with peace the faces of the blind from life, the man-made chasms between man and man; all men were brothers in spite of the differences of creed and speech and colour, united and made equal by the holy light. It seemed as if old tyrannies and cruelties had never been. The shallow places gained their depth again, the shadows of the cripples were made straight, all creatures praised the sun in their degrees, and all great waters and shining plains and hidden places, as the young light remade in holiness each life on earth, shining down alike upon the young lovers and the old lechers rising from their beds, laying gold in the long and unhopeful path of the beggars and in the shrunken darkness of the misers' hearts. An old rag-picker was stooping over a dustbin, searching for treasures left over by the night; her bonnet and hair were like black and filthy cobwebs, her dress seemed as if she had stolen it from the habitations of the dead. But the light, falling like snow upon her, changed her stature and the nature of her rags till she seemed tall and splendid as a queen. The light, falling on the grey waste of cokers in the dustbin had covered it with a sparkle like that of gold.

As the Governor's train passed by, the tired and harassed man sitting in the saloon could see into the newly-awakened houses, through windows which were changed into palace casements, seen through the tree-tops' leaves. The slow gold of the sun's hot days and rays had melted through the leaves, it had not been lost, for now the whole world was dancing and shimmering in a haze and net of gold.

Voices sounded like those of birds; they floated through the open windows as from a nest of leaves; people were rising from their beds, dressing, eating their breakfasts, making plans for to-morrow, just as if there was no Death—little people sheltering against the dark. In one room, a young father was playing with his four-year-old son, and the Governor could hear their laughter as the train slowed down; and he, too, smiled, remembering the time when his own first-born child had been four years old. But his smile soon faded, for it seemed to him as if they were running and laughing on the shore of a vast sea, and that soon, in the roar of the oncoming waves, their laughter would be lost. And he felt suddenly cold, his bones seemed as stiff as if they were already claimed by death. He thought of the day to come with weariness and sadness. These people, toiling and resting, warming themselves in the happy sunshine, hated him, seeing his flesh not warmed by the sun and frozen by the wind like their flesh, seeing never that he, too, was a prisoner on the treadmill of the days and nights. To them, he was a tyrant: their poverty, their murdered liberty, the taxes under which they suffered, were the result of his crimes against the light.

He sighed. The expression on his face, his great moustache, above the stiff military collar of his uniform, made a brave pretence of endurance and optimism, but his cheeks were yellow and lined with fatigue and worry, and his dark protruding eyes had the sad loneliness we see in the eyes of a bird; they seemed as if they were looking out on an immeasurable plain. Discipline, discipline, and again discipline. Duty, duty, and again duty. A hand so weary he could scarcely raise it, saluting. Military bands, their sound blaring through a sleepless brain.

His equerry appeared in the saloon. "The train is due to arrive in ten minutes' time, Sir," he said, "and your Excellency has a fine day for the ceremony!"

"Thanks, von Eltheim. But I shall be thankful when it is over; I have had no sleep for nights."

"It will soon be over now, Sir," said the equerry, smiling, "and then you will have plenty of time for rest."

So the day rose, and far away, sunk in the green darkness of a forest, one whose gigantic shadow was already cast upon the world contemplated the greatness of man, seeing him from above, as we see the civilisation of the ant. "How contemptible a thing," he wrote, "was human grandeur, which could be mimicked by such diminutive insects as I: and yet . . . I dare engage these creatures have their titles and distinctions of honour, they contrive little nests and burrows that they call houses and cities; they make a figure in dress and equipage; they love, they fight, they dispute, they betray."

So great was the heat when noon came and the mists were gone, that even the shadows were changed, till those of ordinary men seemed powerful and ravening giants, negro heroes, or were shrunken and shrivelled into the ghost of a flea, or into little fawning dwarfs creeping in a world of dust. The roads seemed eternal and as if they had grown throughout time like the branches of great trees, grown out of the necessities of man as branches grow from a trunk, a proof of man's pride and his strength.

Along these roads came the carriages of the rich, and these, in the great heat, seemed rippling like water; sometimes a parasol like a gold sun was raised, and you could hear clear laughter like a waterfall as the young people passed by. In the woods, where the grass was soft as the bosom of birds, young girls were sitting under leaves so sharp that they seemed tinkling like the sound of a zither—and they were black with shade, but where the light fell through the leaves their hair glittered like jewels.

A peasant woman, standing in the doorway of her cottage, was calling to her little four-year-old son. She was young and gay, and with her black hair cut in a straight fringe over her forehead and piled up on the top of her head, her eyes dancing like the light under the boughs, and her laughter like a bird dashing through leaves, she looked as if she were for ever walking beneath the bright chestnut trees of spring—as if this was all that shadow could ever mean to her.

She had been hanging out the washing under the low apple trees that grew outside her door, when her next-door neighbour called to her: "Frau Orthoven, Frau Orthoven, your little boy has run into the fields, he heard the soldiers go by and went to watch them. Elsa is there too, and I think he'll be quite safe. Still, I thought you'd like to know."

"Thank you, Frau Kossor. I'll call him in a minute, as soon as I've finished what I'm doing."

She finished hanging up the washing and then, going into the field that stretched beyond the cottage, called "Hans! Hans!"

She could see him standing under the low bright shrill-coloured boughs of the apple trees that grew among the corn. He was still very little, and unsteady upon his stout rounded legs, and his cheeks were round and soft like the cheeks of a pussy-cat. In one hand, he held a scarlet toy soldier which he sucked from time to time and then, finding his fingers wet with bright red paint, he would rub them on his pinafore, which, by now, was covered with scarlet stains. He had been watching the soldiers march by on their way to join the procession. So gay they looked, and their uniforms and muskets were so bright that they seemed like sparkles of the heat—you would never think that darkness could overtake them; yet their shadows under the huge gold sun were haggard and ragged, were all bent and broken, and looked as if they were already old—or as if no hope was left in all the world. These foolish mockeries walked side by side with the strong young men, so full of blood, so full of hope, the promise of the future. And the steady trained march raised up a lot of dust—you would think that the whole world was made of dust, the whole of existence, everything that you touched, that you loved, that you knew. And in the great heat the sound of their footsteps seemed intensified, far louder and more hollow, so that you could not believe you were listening to the sound of only two companies marching. You would have thought that six million men were on the march— yes, six million men.

Now they were passing out of the sunlight and into the shade, and soon they would be gone, with the companies of the inevitable and all-conquering dust surging about them like a sea. And as they passed, Hans held out the toy soldier to them, wet and sticky with red paint.

His mother, coming up behind him, took hold of his hand. "You naughty boy," she said, "look at your nice clean pinafore!" She slapped his hand; and he looked at her sadly as if he were going to cry, so she picked him up in her arms, and pressing her cheek against his, kissed him. "Mummy," he said, his face still pressed close to hers, his arms round her neck. "Give Hansie pretty fireworks." "Fireworks! The very idea! What next, indeed? Fireworks are for big boys, not for boys who behave like babies and get their nice clean pinafores dirty." But then, relenting, she said:"Well, if you'll promise to be a good boy now, you can go with Elsa and watch the procession." For Elsa, who lived in the house opposite, was thirteen years old and could be trusted to take care of him. "Run and find Elsa," she said, "and mind you hold her hand all the time."

He walked through the gate that led from the shadowed path, into the happy living sunlight and in a moment was gone— so small that now he seemed only one more little shadow among the others; yet his body, before he left the strong sunlight, cast an ever-lengthening shade upon the dust—one graver and older and quite different from the little happy playing shadow that she had seen running through the flickering light that fell through the branches of the trees.

His mother, who had watched him until she saw him enter the shadow of the trees that surrounded the house where Elsa lived, returned to the kitchen and began to prepare the goose for dinner, happy and at peace, warm in the shelter of her home. She thought "We never know what is in store for us!" Could it really be only six years ago that she heard her husband's name for the first time? Yes, it was in bright flashing summer weather, just like this, that a young foreigner had come to her country in search of work on the new railway they were building, and she had seen him for the first time. It seemed to her as if they had lived, all their lives, side by side, for she could not believe that the time had been when she did not know him, when she had not heard his name or known that he existed. Yet he had been born near Munich, and she, far away, among people who had different customs, spoke a different language from his.

She prepared the goose, singing at her work, while, in the public gardens, Hans and Elsa listened to the military band that, half hidden in a nest of luxurious leaves, was playing gay marches and waltzes as bright as the daylight. Elsa was a lanky child with a flat staring face, a mouth that was always open with wonder, and thin flaxen pigtails. She was very kind, and liked to see other people enjoying themselves, which made her feel as if she must be happy too, if she could only realise it, although she always felt that something was missing—someone, perhaps, to whom she could tell what she felt without their laughing at her gaping expression. She admired everybody, endowing them with a mythical beauty and romance—with wonderful lives and great titles and honours, and now, as she walked with Hans holding tightly on to her hand, look-ing at the crowds that were waiting for the Governor to pass, her mouth was gaping even more widely open than usual.

There seemed to be a great many women dressed in black walking in the brilliant sunshine with their own shadows trailing after them like birds—so feathered they seemed, these shadows that lengthened with time; and there were foreigners who looked ill and unhappy—strange dark-looking people whom Elsa thought must have come from the Indies, or in any case from very far away. They must have known that something important was going to happen, or they would never have been there.

Now the two children wandered into the street again, and stood waiting for the procession to pass. Quite close to them was a very young man, with a limp body that seemed to have been poured into his clothes as if it were sand; Elsa did not believe his body was real. His clothes had once been black, but now were patched and colourless from all the weathers and circumstances he had passed through; his face was dulled like that of a person who is already dead. He was standing under the jagged torn shadow of a tree, and his body appeared like that of a ventriloquist's dummy, it jerked so oddly; he reminded Elsa of one she had seen when she was a small child at a fair at the seaside. She had lain on the sands, kicking her heels in the air, and thinking that perhaps the audience had been blown away by the cold wind, perhaps had never been. Nothing remained but the wheezing wind whirling quick and light cold memories of ragtime songs, round and round, through the gaps between the lodging-houses that stood, surrounded by dark sparse-branched bushes, on the edge of the sand. And those tunes, blowing through the inconsequent mind of the wind, were no longer human and warm, but dead out of tune, and they blew along so quickly that they were out of hearing, out of heart and out of mind, almost before you knew they were there. So the sea-air blew, like lost tunes, in and out of the lodging-houses where nobody is real—neither the landladies scuttling sideways like crabs in their crustacean silk

25

gowns, nor the old generals with mayfly whiskers, nor the ladies laughing in summer with a mummified dusty sound like the trills of the old hurdy-gurdy moon, nor the American child like the small wicked ghost of Metropole Hotels and trans-atlantic steamers, Pullman cars and oyster bars and white-slave traffics lost by time. They would fade in the open air, you would see them outlined against the sea, and then they would begin to fade—first the head, then the shoulders, then the whole body. But the child, whose face was as pastel-flat as the mechanical piano's notes drifting from the oyster bars on the sea front, and whose frock seemed tinged with tentative and half-soiled hints blown by the wind, came now to lie and kick beside Elsa on the sand, and if she turned her head at all, she looked at Elsa as if she did not see her, so that Elsa felt as if it were she who was not real.

Lying and staring at the Fair held on the sand, it seemed to Elsa that some of the sand had drifted aimlessly into a piece of canvas and had been sewn up to form the body of the ven-triloquist's dummy, it was so limp. The dummy was lolling and jerking and shrieking in a high bird-like ghostly voice against a background that was painted to look like a sea; but Elsa knew quite well that the sea was only a pretence, and if you walked up to it, and stretched out your hand to touch it, you would tear it, and there would be nothing beyond it; and she thought, too, that the voice was not the dummy's voice at all, but that of the showman, and that he was not real either. And knowing this, she felt afraid and began to cry.

The sight of this young man inspired in her much the same feeling. His face was long and rather empty, his eyes deep and black like holes, and utterly blank. The faces of most hungry people look as if they were made of grey rock, hollowed out by some still stronger shadow, but this face was of limp grey canvas, blown by every wind; and sometimes it looked as if somebody was whispering to him, and as if, at any moment now, the whisperer's voice might break through his lips, raised to the same ghostly bird-like half-mad chatter as that of the dummy she had heard shrieking. Half hidden in his hand, he held, so the children thought, a ball. But it was a very strange ball, not of the usual shape, and of a dark colour and yet glittering as water glitters at night. Nobody but the children paid any attention to the young man, but from his twitching movements, Hans thought that he would throw the ball very soon, and that then all the gay crowds would begin to run; so, taking his hand out of Elsa's, he moved a little nearer, and looking up in the young man's face, began to laugh, holding out his hand to catch the ball. "Throw the ball for Hansie," he said. "Throw the ball!" But the young man took no notice of him. He was too small and unimportant. And besides, the voices were speaking.

The voices said: "Your moment is at hand. You will be the deliverer of your country, and the tyranny under which it has suffered will be gone for ever. Now the world will know that it has passed over with contempt one of the greatest figures in its whole history, thinking him too poor and insignificant for notice." The voices said: "You will be famous throughout the world, and through the whole of time. Your name will be on the lips of all men." The voices said: "You are about to justify your existence, your physical insignificance, your unheard voice. What will it matter, now, that you lived in an empty hollow, alone with hunger, your only companion?"

The procession drew nearer. And then, for some reason, the Governor turned his head. He looked straight at the ventriloquist's dummy, whose hollow face was now filled with shadow. His arm was a little raised.

.   .   .   .   .

Far away in her kitchen, Hansie's mother thought how much he must be enjoying the procession. And happy and peaceful, she felt that she did not envy the Governor himself, though he was to have a great procession marching in his honour. For to be grand and famous is not everything: simple happiness, a peaceful life of work and of rest, the sight of the summer fields made holy by the light and by the bread of mankind, love and child-bearing and then sleep in a quiet grave, are not all these blessings for which to praise God?

So the moments passed, flying like the shadows in the fields outside. And from time to time she glanced at the clock. . . . An hour. . . . An hour and twenty minutes. . . .

Surely Hans would be coming home soon? And her husband, too. He had said he would be back early from work to-day. She walked to the door and looked out. No, nothing living was in sight, excepting an ant, staggering along beneath the weight of a piece of paper. Nothing was written there—it was meaningless and blank as are many lives; but to the ant, for some reason, it was precious, although he had no idea what he was to do with it. For it could not be used as a lining for the nest, nor was it good to eat—it was large, heavy and cumbersome, and at the same time slippery and inconvenient to hold. He was obliged, owing to the weight and shape and the general difficulty of managing it, to walk in zig-zag sideway patterns as he carried it, but he was determined, now that he had secured the prize, not to let it fall; for he was certain that for some reason or another it would prove to be valuable, and so he did not want another ant to obtain possession of it. Therefore he staggered along beneath it, and Frau Orthoven watched him idly.

Then, suddenly, it seemed as if the whole world was uprooted and tossed into the air by an appalling roar, a sound so vast that it seemed as if the universe must have collapsed into dust.

And silence fell upon the ruins.

Frau Orthoven, raising her face at length from her shaking hands, thought that the whole of life must be over. There would be no more life. There would be no more light. But that silence was followed by the noise of hurrying multitudes, their footsteps making a sound like that of a storm in a desert or millions of leaves being blown along a dry road, rushing towards the centre of the town.

"Hans!" she screamed. "Hans!" But her voice died away,

and she rushed with the crowd, her mouth wide open, trying to shriek.

It was an hour before she found him, under the wreckage made by the bomb. He was lying on his face, very still; he looked as she had often seen him look when he was quite a baby, and asleep on the bed at home. That was all she saw at first, but his pinafore was covered with scarlet as if all the paint from all the soldiers in the world had been rubbed over it, and the fronds of his hair were all dabbled and stiff as if they had lain in some dreadful rain. His body was so broken that, little as he was, his mother could scarcely gather him in her arms. Yet sitting there through many hours, huddled ape-like with her long maternal arms sheltering her ruins, in the broken sunlight, she could feel his small hands squeezing her heart, knocking at it as he had done in the long months of waiting before he was born.

.   .   .   .   .

Rocking him in her arms, she crouched there among the stones and the waste, long after the ruined light had died and the darkness fallen.

And far away in the cities, the newspapers of Europe contained the news of the murder, all the newsboys in the capitals were shouting it along the streets: "Murder of a Governor! Bomb thrown at a procession!"—a sensation, but unimportant and to be discussed idly for a moment and then forgotten. For there were plans to be made for to-morrow and the days to follow, houses and big businesses to be built, credits to be established, schemes to be begun, marriages to be celebrated. But in the darkness under the trees in the great cities, the young girls held the hands of dead men, pressed lips to lips that were already cold. For the two nations that alone inhabit the earth, the rich and the poor, walking to their death in opposed hordes, had found the only force that could bind them together, a cannibalistic greed, hatred, and fear. No longer need they fear each other, for both nations will be swept away.

Thus began the Plague that was to sweep Europe until it reached the silent house in a forest, where a man sat dreaming of a universe peopled by horses of an infinite wisdom, superior to mankind—imagining, in his ferocious hatred, "twenty thousand of them breaking into an European army, confounding the ranks, overturning the carriages, battering the warrior's faces into mummy by terrible yerks from their hinder hooves." His gigantic laughter falling like thunderbolts or black meteoric stones amid the wastes of the thunderous darkness, he contemplated the grandeur of man. Contemptible indeed, with his white skin so soon to be corrupted, his pretence of rearing upward to the sky upon his hind legs, when soon he will topple from this height and fall downward upon the dust. Therefore does the Horse, secure in his knowledge of the benefits Providence has bestowed upon him, complain of the body of Man, seeing that "my nails were of no use either to my fore or hinder feet; as to my forefeet, he could not properly call them by that name, for he never observed me to walk upon them; that they were too soft to be on the ground; and that I generally went with them uncovered, neither was the covering I sometimes wore on them of the same shape, or so strong. as that on my feet behind. That I could not walk with any security; for if either of my hinder feet slipped, I must inevitably fall. He then began to find fault with other parts of my body; the flatness of my face, the prominence of my nose, my eyes placed directly in front, so that I could not look on either side without turning my head; that I was not able to feed myself, without lifting one of my forefeet to my mouth: and therefore Nature had placed two joints to answer that necessity. He knew not what could be the use of those second clefts and divisions in our feet behind; that these were too soft to bear the hardness and sharpness of stones, without a covering made from the skin of some other brute; that my whole body wanted a fence against heat and cold, which I was forced to put on and off every day with tediousness and trouble." So does the Horse, superior in his strength and wisdom complain of the body and the reason of

30

Man. "What you have told me" (said my master) "upon the subject of War, doth indeed discover most admirably the effects of that reason you pretend to: however it is happy that the shame is greater than the *danger*; and that nature hath left you utterly incapable of doing much mischief; for your mouths lying flat with your faces, you can hardly bite each other to any purpose, without consent."

And, in the shadow cast by the giant, pygmy man wrestled with pygmy man under a black sun, their footfalls leaving no trace in the enormous plain of sand, where flows no water, and for shade there is only this aching and hollow waste of rock.

Chapter III

YOU WOULD think, would you not, that the Dead would show us some compassion, who are not yet of their company? They are so many, and we are so few, walking in the gold air of sunset or through the white fields of morning among the sweet dews, looking in each other's eyes, clasping hands and saying farewell, or waiting for a footstep that will never come.

If we, who are living, could learn the dark and solemn speech of the Dead, so that we might commune with them in their own language; if they, those unrevengeful and most loving ghosts, could come back to us and teach us their deep wisdom! But they lie in silence, clasping to their breast the one memory they took to be their grave's long sun, the three words that built a universe, spoken in a youthful voice, a child-like kiss, a day in summer. And we, who have not Death's patience and peace, must go unwarned and untaught. Perhaps they come not to warn us that the being who was our light will cast a long and darkened shade at evening, because their wisdom is greater than ours, and they know that the shadow is cast by the sun. It will pass, but the sun will remain.

The young girl in the house sunk in a world of gardens, walking in the long avenues when the great gold sun of evening burnished the leaves like the armour of the ghost from the Roman Road, was unwarned by any voice of ghost or of bird-philosopher: "You have been here before: this love has returned to you from a long way: it has come back from beyond the grave."

The house was sunk so deep in the green world, so far from mankind that it seemed as if no alien being would ever find it, even by following the flight of a bird through the leaves; no bird-song would ever betray its secret. Such was the silence, so profound that it seemed a form of dream, drifting beyond the great gardens, to haunt the ancient fig trees and the trees whose apples falling on the grass boomed like summer rain.

The girl sitting at the dressing-table by the open window of her room, brushing her long hair, looking out over this world of growth, felt the green airs lifting the muslin of her gown, drifting through and around it and wandering over her face that was in shadow from the long drip of her straight hair and from the great leaves that grew round the sill. The window was so shrouded in leaves that the light that came from them was echoed on the dark drip of her hair and her eyes that were like those of a young lion, as leaves are reflected in dark water. She had a face with a broad forehead and cheekbones, and it was covered with little freckles as if it had been dusted over with gold motes of the light, her mouth and eyes were wide, and as she moved or was still, the light seemed to move or pause with her, as if light and shadow were part of her being, of her mortal dress.

Until the day when the being who was her visible and invisible world, who had been her friend in childhood, had returned after this absence of years—all summer long, while the green century of rains lay on the leaves, she had thought

32

that the shadowed life she had known must last for ever—Time whose sound was but the drip of rain would last for ever. But now as she sat in her room, looking through the open window at the green summer heat, it seemed to her that her body, her face, her long hair could not be the same as those of the girl she had known last year.

She lived now, since her mother's death, with her distant relative Sir Henry Rotherham and his cousin and housekeeper Miss Mintley, listening to the silence of the one, the chatter of the other. All her life, since her childhood, she had been constrained through poverty to live in the houses of others and on the outskirts of other people's lives, in silent houses when the owners were away and the rooms were in dust-sheets—creeping like a young threadbare black shadow up the stairs, looking and listening through the windows at the living dazzling world outside in which she scarcely dared believe, the sudden showers of glittering gold motes, the swinging darkness of the greenery, the laughter splashing like fountains as the young people walked beneath the windows. It seemed as if silence were a person in those empty houses: you heard her open the door and drift towards you, you heard the echo of her voice.

This was before Anna had come to live in her cousin's house; and then, sent there after her mother's death, while she was still a child, she had seen Jonathan for the first time. He had taught her everything she knew of the visible and the invisible world, she could not imagine the world without him—but he had gone again, after a while, and she had returned to her life of a little foreigner in mourning, playing with the other children as if they were shadows.

She had not believed that he would ever return, but now he had come, and with this new life, Anna was no longer a ghost walking beneath the trees, a shadow passing up the stairs and along the lengthy corridors at the summons of the old— her voice an echo of their empty voices. It was she who was the reality now and they were but drifts of dust. Soon, her heart told her, the being who was for her the meaning of life and the answer to all questioning and the end of every quest would be gone again, and with him her life would ebb away; nothing would be left of her heart but the amber dust of a rose, now that the summer is over. Yet if, when she was as old as the world, as blind and deaf as the world, he should return to her and lay his hand upon hers, she would know his touch from that of any other hand in the universe.

It seemed impossible that all around her should be unchanged, the talk, homely and familiar as the tick of Time, ever the same, eternally the same, the daily life, the shadows, the drifting of Time. Now the door of her room, blown by a little air, opened with a dark strawy noise like the wickering voice of a bear, and Anna could hear Sir Henry pacing up and down the long passage at the top of the house, the sound of his footsteps mingling with the drip of rain. This indeed was the only sound to be heard in the house all day—this and the noise of the mowing-machine before the rain began, the sound with which Noon, the old gardener, gnarled as the roots of the apple trees, and whose eyes, in their network of wrinkles, seemed dark and glittering birds caught among the fruit-nets, tried to keep his sorrow at bay, the thought of his only child who was soon to go to the war, and of his boy's entanglement with Susan Daw, the child of a gypsy mother—one of them dark Egyptians, as he called her, and half-mad hymn-singing father. All day long, under the sun and under the moon that makes men mad and draws their blood like the tides, and under the raggle-taggle rain, he thought he heard their voices sounding through the leaves; though as often as not it was only the wind, and his anger and misery were in vain.

So the two old men walked up and down, one avoiding the thought of his sorrow, and the other the thought of his ruined ambition. For Sir Henry Rotherham had not always been a ghost whose only existence, for the outer world, lay in the sound of a footstep. During many years, until his nerveless hands had fallen from the world, too weak to grasp it, he had been a Minister of the Crown and Secretary of State. But in the end, his natural mental supineness, masquerading as philosophy, as a kind of heroism, had led him to a retreat from the world, since he could no longer be troubled to pit his will against those that were stronger and had more staying-power, and now his laziness appeared to him as a kind of stoicism of the intellect, a philosophic disdain of power and of the world. A noble-looking old man of seventy, his black hair bore scarcely a trace of white, and though his face had a strange likeness to the breakwater of a sea that has long since retreated, or to the head of a vast and broken statue staring across a limitless desert, he was exceedingly active physically, and he had adopted his custom of pacing the passages because, he said, by cultivating such a habit one ceased to trouble or even to notice if the days were wet and cold, or torrid and weighted by the heat, if the days were drawing out or drawing in. It was true that an awareness of the weather was useful as a basis for conversation, but Sir Henry did not care for conversation, and, as well, if you paid no attention to the fact, it ceased to exist. Only the sound of footsteps, and the care for his health, these remained, binding him to reality. On the other hand, he did not believe in taking risks, and though an agnostic by profession, he said his prayers every night, on the chance of this proving to be a good invest-ment. When pacing the passages, he walked very slowly, occupy-ing as much time as possible in order that the house should seem even larger than it was—for he liked to feel that it was very large. Occasionally, about once or twice a day, he would pause outside a door, if he could hear voices speaking in the room beyond—not because he wanted to eavesdrop or to spy, since there was nothing he could hear, now, that would interest him, but because he was enabled in this way to touch, for a moment, the world in which others moved, thought, acted, without being obliged to become a part of it, and this made him feel real to himself, real in his isolation, in the separation of his identity from the world that he could yet touch at will. He would, too, spread various objects belonging to himself all over the house, in the many rooms—his hat in one room, his stick in another, his spectacle case in a third, because when he came face to face, once more, in the course of his wanderings, with these records of his own personality, he was reminded of himself, which was pleasant, and because it enabled him to stake his claim on every room in the house as sole inhabitant. Should another person enter one of the rooms in question, Sir Henry would follow him there, and, conveying suddenly the impression of great age, would make it clear by his manner that he had intended to rest there, and had hoped that he would not be disturbed; then, having by this means routed the intruder and put him to flight, he would continue his walk.

When he was not pacing up and down the passage, Sir Henry spent much of his time in walking up and down in front of the house, and when he did this, he would succeed in appearing like a procession of one person—he being the head, the beginning and the end. You were conscious of the State Umbrella. On these occasions he would begin by walking rather fast and briskly, yet with what appeared to be determination; but it was noticeable that his left foot turned inwards toward the right as if seeking for reassurance; and after a while it became apparent that he was going nowhere in particular; he seemed to be walking solely because he wished to feel the earth solid beneath him and because he must find some way to occupy his time till the world came to an end. He rarely spoke to the members of his household and family, or to visitors, seeming, indeed, to be separated from them by an endless plain, a stretch of centuries, perhaps, a continent with all its differences of climate, or the enormous space that divides our earthly nature and characters from those of beings on another planet. Occasionally, however, a gesture or wave of the hand, a smile of great kindliness, would be flashed across the plain, from planet to earth. And he had a habit of talking to himself, if not to others, muttering phrases in an unused voice: "They may *think* I shall, but I shan't!" Or, with his head a little on one side, he would whisper down to his shoulder: "And if *they* do that, then *I* shall take the opposite direction." And having

36

said this, he would, once in a way, give a queer rusty creaking laugh, whose sound was that of a gate that had been shut for so long that it was difficult for it to move upon its hinges, more difficult still for it to open wide. Then, having laughed, he would take out his watch and look at it shamefacedly, although Time meant nothing to him, since there was nothing to do but to think about one's health, about the past, and the philosophies that were dead.

So he walked up and down, with a sound like the beat of Time in the empty house, a sound like the drip of the rain falling from the leaves, echoing through the house, penetrating through the door of the room where a young man sat writing a letter.

But now the sound of the rain and the footsteps ceased, and a gold sound, misty and mysterious, drifted through the branches. Outside in the avenue, the huge gold sun of evening changed the leaves, the hair of the girl now walking beneath them, till they shone like the armour of the ghost from the Roman Road that stared at her through the branches—a ghost looking at a ghost, but for a moment only. Then the glint of his armour, his dimmed face, faded, and with a sound like that of a bird dashing through leaves, he was gone and she was alone, walking where the raindrops falling from the branches sounded like faint bells heard among the leaves. Jonathan Hare, looking up from the letter he was writing, staring at her through the long window of his room, thought that her hair was like the helmet of Fortune or of Fame, seen amongst the glitter of the ilex-grove.

.   .   .   .   .

Of Fortune or of Fame . . . the bright sound of those words, like that of waves breaking upon an unknown shore, with the glitter and the glamour of that helmet of dark hair strewn with gold by the dying sun, shining among the leaves, were gone.

So he would see her always, as Power that had fallen within

his grasp, as Fame with her strange and glittering hair, walking in the avenue, as a being, even, on whose beauty age would cast a grey shadow, but never as one whose bones within her flesh wept to be dissolved, to be fleshless at last, after their long and bloodless vigil wherein she had known and suffered a giant's tenderness. Through the long years, when her beauty was fulfilled, she would seem to him like the figure of Afternoon, sitting with bent head and vast limbs at repose among the sheaves of corn, like the harvest gathered and the light ripened, never as a figure in a plain of dust, with eyes that ran over with stones fallen from the smoky ruins. Tears were the only signs of mortality unseen by him, unheeded.

Sitting with his hand resting on the unfinished letter, he looked into the long years that lay ahead of him, in which he would inhabit the soul, the mind, the will, the whole being of this girl, as the souls of the dead come to inhabit the bodies of the living.

But first there was an empty and unwanted being which must be abolished by the light of the truth that ruled his life—Lucy Linden, who had believed that she possessed his heart. "I live under a black sun," he had said; and beneath the morbid pomp of this sun that rules over Africa and the dark continents and all dark natures, the furrows of the earth which should hold the seed are huge as tombs, under the light that is more terrible, more piercing in its truth, revealing and laying bare the skeleton beneath the skin, all motives and desires, or lack of desire, than that which illumines the world of common men. How could he know or endure a normal love, he who knew the odour of mortality arising from the most beautiful breast, as if it were already corrupted, seeing the rankness of all human nature, the terror of Nature, and her monstrous breasts in whose shadow he must lie as he would lie in some vast plain beneath the shadow of two hills, or on whose peaks he must be exposed to the light until the world died.

Womanhood was to him a symbol of Nature, a monstrous creative force that, in order that it might create, was willing
38

to destroy all previous life and forms of creation—a force more terrible when it was overlaid with civilisation than when it was rank and naked. "They would often," he said of these giantesses of Brobdingnagia, "lay me at full length to their bosoms: wherewith I was much disgusted, because, to say the truth, a very offensive smell came from their skins, which I do not mention or intend to the disadvantage of those excellent ladies, for whom I have all manner of respect: but I conceive, that my sense was more acute in proportion to my littleness; . . . and after all I found their natural smell was much more supportable than when they used perfumes, under which I immediately swooned away." Beside these monstrous symbols of Nature, and her blind creative power, the giant felt himself to be a creature no greater than an ant.

To love, as human beings love, appeared to him as a form of physical decay, was, as he had said, to "ruin oneself out of a maggot." Yet throughout his life, when he felt power slipping from his grasp, when he was poor and out of Fortune's favour, when he was angered or despondent, he would pursue and inhabit the heart of a woman, seeing in the ultimate death of all her natural impulses, only the result and symbol of his mysterious power.

So, years ago, he had pursued Lucy Linden, when he was very poor and Fame and Fortune were so distant that he could not even hear the sound of their names. He had pursued her, and she, in resisting him, had weakened the power of the giant.

Chapter IV

I T SEEMED impossible to him that any remnants of the unreal life through which he had drifted at Lucy Linden's side—a life whose unreality, even, was now dead, should still cling about him. The face of the girl in the forest of white thorn trees and flowering cherry trees, a face that had once meant to him all the terrible poignancy of spring, its hope, its pain, its blossoming—this was a face, now, in an old and forgotten photograph—the photograph of someone whom he had never known, found by chance, in the place where it had been stored away, long ago, by dead hands.

For a year or two after he had left Ireland, his letters had come fairly frequently, and Lucy, hunting in them for signs of any change, could find none. It was true that he made no reference to their future together, but she told herself that this was out of consideration for her, that he was waiting only till he should have a settled position to offer her, for the tone of his letters did not seem to have altered, and there was no hint that he wished to put an end to the understanding between them. Only the future—the future seemed dead, or hidden by an impenetrable mist. He never mentioned the name of another woman, excepting once, when, in a letter written soon after his arrival at Rotherham Park, he told her: "My little pupil, Anna Marton, is here, and very much changed. She is eighteen now, and I should never have known her. But it is strange how the imprint of my teaching has remained with her, for you would even mistake her handwriting for mine." And that was all. Any importance or meaning it might have had soon faded from her mind.

Then, after a while, his letters grew rarer.

She missed them vaguely, during the weeks in which they did not come, but when they did, they gave her little pleasure now—they were too noncommittal, they did not really alter the dullness of her days, which dragged their empty weight along, to-morrow echoing yesterday with but little change. In summer, there were picnics, and before the war came, gymkhanas at the barracks; she would sit in a summer gown, and watch these, and talk to the officers. From time to time a new young man would appear, would haunt the house for a short time, assuaging her vanity, rekindling for a while the dying fires of her youth and the hope that had once been hers. But after a little, noticing the threadbare condition of the carpets and the curtains, the meagreness of the fires and the food, the visits would grow rarer. And then would come the day when, worn out by her efforts to make both ends meet, tired by the pretences and the subterfuges made necessary by her poverty, she would be a little out of temper, and would answer sharply when her mother or sister spoke, or she would appear in an old and unbecoming dress, because the other was being mended. And after this, he would cease coming at all, or if he did come, he would be inattentive if she spoke, and would scarcely look at her, but every quarter of an hour or so, would glance surreptitiously at his watch, jumping to his feet with alacrity when he could with decency make his escape, and pleading any lame excuse when asked when he would come again.

At these times, she was glad that Jonathan's letters still reached her, although with long intervals between. She thought: "He cannot be meaning to let me go entirely, or he would not write to me at all." She could not ignore the fact of his growing fame. It was odd, she thought, how her mother and her younger sister Penelope had laughed when she talked of his pretensions as a writer—but now even they were forced to admit that they had been wrong. And, too, though they hated him, they had always felt a strange fear in his presence. Then, at last, came a letter containing the news that now his future was assured. She could read between the lines and knew, now, from the very names of the men who believed in him that a great career was in store for him. And though he made no reference to sharing it with her, it raised in her a strange feeling, one that she could scarcely analyse.

What did she feel? Her life was so uncertain. She said to herself: "I must have *something* in life, some hope, something in which I can bury my thoughts, something to build." And she thought: "Soon, if this life goes on, I shall no longer even look in the glass."

41

She had persuaded herself by now, that his letters were all she had to lift her out of this dismal life of make-believe, of barely-hidden poverty masquerading as an easy comfort under prying eyes. And pondering over the ever-increasing rarity of those letters, she began to spur herself into jealousy. There must be some other woman, she told herself, there *must*, to account for this change. And she set herself to imagine, with increasing hatred, the face and form of her rival, inventing for herself scenes between this unknown being and Jonathan—scenes in which she, Lucy, was brought face to face with this woman who was taking him from her.

At first, the jealousy was almost pleasurable, because at least the pangs told her that she was not quite dead; but after a while, it changed into an ache like that which is felt by the starved under a cold and pitiless rain. She knew, now, that he meant to escape from her if he could.

It was difficult for her to know what steps to take; she had always been afraid to take any decisive action. But at last, hearing that his uncle was in Dublin, she chose an afternoon when she knew her mother and sister would be out, and wrote asking him to come and see her. It was urgent, she said, for she had to speak to him about a most important and difficult matter. But when the day came, Mrs. Linden and Penelope, having, on one pretext and another, delayed going upstairs to put on their hats, and having made numberless excursions in search of missing gloves and handbags, decided, at last, that it was too late to go out, and took possession of the drawing-room. "They *know* he is coming!" thought Lucy. "They are doing this on purpose"; and she decided to receive him in the dining-room. This added to her embarrassment, for the dining-room was even shabbier than the drawing-room, and the fact that she received him there would make clear to him the fact of the cramped space in which they lived, their lack of privacy—all due, again, to poverty. And this was not a moment at which she wished to appear to him as poor.

It was a very hot afternoon, and though the blinds were

drawn the room seemed glazed by the heat, as if everything, the lives within it, life itself, had been put under shining glass in order to preserve them from reality. But the furniture seemed bear-furred by the little fringes of shadow that they cast, and you could scarcely tell shabbiness from shadow. She was standing by the sideboard when he came into the room, and with her face that looked as if it had been carved by some smooth dark wind from the Pyramids, her black hair looped heavily at the back of her head, and her tightly-modelled lustreless black dress, she seemed like a portrait by some French painter of the eighteen-eighties. But with his entrance, the illusion of intensive life concentrated in stillness vanished, and in the place of life, there was only restlessness.

Taking up, now one object, now another, then putting them down again aimlessly, scarcely knowing how to approach the subject, she said, at last, in a hurried breathless voice: "You know, you must realise, that I have devoted my whole life, the whole of my existence, *all* my thoughts to Jonathan, for years now, oh, yes, for long years." And as she spoke, the knowledge of the truth of her words, the realisation of the nobility of that selfless sacrifice, grew upon her. What might not her life have been, if she had never known Jonathan. Remembering a phrase he had used to her when they were walking in the forest, she added: "My life has been given up to helping him make *his* life." She paused. "Not a day passes but I re-read his letters, read the last present he gave me." And selecting a book at random from the shelves, she opened it. A thin, hardly perceptible spray of dust drifted from the cover and she replaced it again, continuing her monologue without looking at the old man.

Walking round the room, touching the flowers, the ornaments, the books with uncertain fingers, she explained the situation to him—or the situation as she, by now, saw it. For years, during all the time when she had waited for Jonathan, she had buoyed him up with her trust, her unfailing faith in his future, her courage. She had refused several good offers of marriage for his sake, proposals by men so rich that their money alone would have tempted any other woman. She, however, had never given them a thought, she had never for an instant been dazzled by what they had to offer. She had understood the advantages perfectly, but had put them aside resolutely, calmly, for Jonathan's sake. It was true that at one time her health had not been good, and she had been obliged to put off her marriage with Jonathan for a short while, but now that her health had improved there was no longer any reason why they should not be married immediately. For one thing, it would be better for *him*—he needed looking after, he needed a home and a wife who would study his comfort. Yes, it would certainly be better if they were married at once. But as she spoke, her face grew more and more despondent, till at last: "I *cannot* believe," she said, "that now Jonathan is sure of the future he will bring himself to cast off the woman who has stood by him for so many years." And she burst into tears of self-pity.

The old man looked at her from beneath his shaggy eyebrows. The sun by this time had succeeded in penetrating the blinds, and her illusory appearance of being a dark and smooth-faced sphinx-like character in a portrait by Manet had gone. He considered her carefully. She no longer wore dresses that would be fashionable next summer, and the gown that she wore at the moment was very old, though some attempt had been made to freshen it, to make it seem of a newer style. Her face was still beautiful, but there were little lines round the corners of her mouth, and he had noticed, even before her outburst of tears, that she looked tired and dispirited. He understood her perfectly, knowing enough of her past life to realise that although what she was saying was in part a half-truth, in part entirely untrue, she believed utterly in its truth at this moment. He said: "But are you certain that you really wish to marry a man who is still poor—or at any rate very far from being well off?"

"Oh, yes," she answered eagerly. And forgetting for a

44

moment that she now believed that no fear of poverty had ever made her hesitate, she added: "For he will not *always* be poor, will he?"

Mr. Hare, saying: "Then if you are sure that you still want to marry him, I will speak to him on the subject—if you really wish me to do so," looked at his watch, and murmuring something about another appointment, left the house.

On hearing of this conversation, the bitterness in Jonathan's heart increased. She had left him to face all his struggles alone, but now that he was within sight of victory she intended to share the spoils with him—she who had weakened him by her cowardice; and he thought of the many things he had endured in the years that had passed since he had asked her to marry him—the injuries to his pride, exacerbated by her desertion of him—the terrible sense of dependence upon the will of others, the long cold and bitter waiting for a change of Fate—endured alone. His bitterness, his frozen sense of power were awakened to a more painful sense of life by this change in her, this frantic pursuit of him now that she knew that Fortune was within his reach. "Ah, yes, my dear," he thought, "you are not growing any younger, and you know it!" And he remembered the little lines that the sunlight had shown him in the forest of white cherry trees. He thought of her family, whom he hated, of her silly younger sister, laughing at everything he said, when she thought that he could not see her, making covert grimaces at her mother, sly winks and little gestures meant to convey an understanding between them on the subject of this queer, unusual and above all, *poor* young man who—so absurdly and presumptuously—wanted to marry Lucy. He thought of her pretentious, acquisitive mother, always ready to contradict him in the hope that it would make him look ridiculous in Lucy's eyes. If he spoke about a book—and this he did but rarely—Mrs. Linden invariably "happened to know"—a favourite phrase of hers—"from So-and-So, who is an intimate friend of the greatest living authority on that particular subject, that the theory contained in the book had been superseded."

She only listened if he spoke about literature, because he was a writer, and it was pleasant to contradict him on this matter. If he spoke on any other subject, she did not even trouble to pretend she was paying any attention to what he said, unless Penelope, her younger daughter, was sitting opposite to her, and they could signal to each other.

She was ill-bred in other ways as well, and would, in a tone of great significance, carefully averting her gaze from his feet, comment on the shabbiness of other people's boots—in their absence, of course. He left the house, always, with the feeling that greatness of mind, alone, could never hope to win a place in the world, a niche in history. It is the boots that count!

She had lost no opportunity of humiliating him, but now that she, too, knew the future that would be his, she could bring herself to send a sycophantic message by her daughter. She had always, it appeared, been *so* fond of him, regarding him, indeed, almost as her own child; he was *too* dear (a phrase to which she was particularly attached, and which, for all its synthetic sweetness, invariably made Jonathan feel as if some cold sour substance had found its way into a hollow tooth). And it had always been her dearest wish that he and Lucy should marry. Penelope, on her side, sent her darling Jonathan her love.

This was the company that Lucy had preferred to his. She had been intimidated, in the past, by their open sneers at him, and now she was going to be punished.

By now, her letters arrived by every post, and in each one she made further claims upon him—it was evident that she had never understood the import of what he had said to her in the wood. She was, by now, increasingly urgent in her demands, and her reproaches grew day by day more violent in their tone. *Why* did he write so seldom? Why were his letters so changed? Should she come to him, so that they might be married immediately? Oh what *could* have kept him from her for so long? Was it, could it be, that another woman had come into his life, and was drawing him away from the woman who loved him and who had waited so patiently for years?

He was forced, at length, to send a reply. She could marry him if she wished, if she insisted; but no woman was a fit wife for him unless she could face and endure the truth—Truth that is the skeleton within our flesh—Truth that endures when the flesh is gone.

He began the letter by assuring her that he was "extremely concerned" by the account she gave of her health. "God forbid," he continued, "that I should ever be the cause of bringing fresh trouble into your life, as you seem to hint. The letter you wished me to answer I have read several times, and thought I had replied to it fully; however, as you have repeated certain questions I will try to answer them as best I can. You wish to know what has changed the tone of my letters since our last meeting. If there has been any alteration, I have told you the reason over and over again. I have used every argument and inducement, I have begged you, implored you, not once but many times, to leave the place where you are living, your family and the people with whom you are associating at present, both for the sake of your health and your character, which I thought would undoubtedly suffer very much in such air and with such examples before you. All I had from you by way of an answer was a great deal of argument, which was sometimes so imperious and high-handed in tone that I thought it might have been spared me, especially when I looked back on everything and remembered how much you had been in the wrong. The other thing you want to know is whether this change is due to there being another woman in my life. I swear to you that it is not: and that I have never thought of marrying any other woman. I have always felt that fundamentally you were sweet-natured and sweet-tempered, and whenever you behaved in such a way that it seemed to point to exactly the opposite, I put it down to you wanting to impress a man who was in love with you; but I have noticed since then in very many of your letters such signs of an absolute indifference, that I began to think it was hardly possible for one of my few good qualities to please you. I never knew anyone so difficult to influence, even in matters where it would have been to your interest to listen to advice; at first when we were merely acquaintances, that did not matter; but since then, there is no way of accounting for this unyielding attitude in you, than by imputing it to a lack of the slightest friendship for me, or respect for my opinions. When I asked the amount of your income, I had no such ulterior motives as you pretend to imagine. I have told you many times that in England any young man with ordinary common sense can marry a woman with more money than you ever laid claim to. I asked, only in order to think over whether it would be enough, when added to mine, to keep a woman like yourself in comfort, if we married. According to you, it comes to almost a hundred pounds a year, and I cannot believe that any other young woman in the world, having even so small an income as that, would dwindle away her health and life in such a sink and among the sort of conversation that your family indulges in. Your letters have never once been able to persuade me that you value me in the least, because you have paid so little attention to what I have said so often on the subject. The dismal account you say I have given you of my living I can assure you is a true one; and since it is a dismal one even in your opinion, you had better draw your own conclusions. The place where Dr. Bolton lived is in a living which he keeps with the deanery, but I have been ordered to live at a place that is within a mile of a town called Trim, and the only thing to do is either to lease a house or to build one on the spot; it is hardly possible to do the first, and I am too poor to do the other at present. . . . I cannot find either the time or the money to visit you at present, for my work keeps me here; but in a few months I may be able to afford the time and money for a short journey. But by that time I hope other friends of yours, who have more influence over you than I have, will have persuaded you to leave the place where you are living at present. Please

48

remember me to your mother, in return for her message, but as for having anything else to do with her, I must ask you to excuse me; and I think I have more cause to resent your wishing me to have any dealings with her, than you have to be angry at my refusing. If you like such company and conduct, much good may it do you. My education and bringing-up has been very different.

"My Uncle Adam asked me one day in confidence—I imagine according to your directions, what were my intentions with regard to you, saying it would do you harm and injure your prospects if I did not make up my mind soon, one way or the other. The answer I gave him, which I suppose he has passed on to you, was to this effect: that I hoped I was not standing in your way, because the reasons you had given why we could not marry were your poor state of health (which has not changed) and that you think, that my income is not sufficient. I said, too, that if your health and my income were what they ought to be, I would rather marry you than any other woman; but in the present state of both, I thought it was against your own wish that we should marry, and that it would only lead to your being unhappy; that if you had any other offers which your friends or yourself thought more to your advantage, I should think it extremely wrong of me to stand in your way. Now for what concerns the money side of the question, you have answered it. I shall be glad, therefore, if you will let me know if the state of your health has changed since the doctors advised you not to marry. Have you, or they, altered this opinion. Are you prepared, and fitted, to run a household on an income of less, perhaps, than three hundred a year? Do you love me enough, and have you enough respect for my wishes and tastes, to fall in with my way of living, and try to make us both as happy as you can? Are you willing to follow the plans I will draw up for improving your mind, so that we can be good company for each other, and not dull, when we are alone, and neither visiting nor being visited? Will you be willing to bend your inclinations according to mine—

like the people whom I like, love those whom I love, and be indifferent to those to whom I am indifferent? Do you love me enough to change from a bad temper to a good one, the moment I come into the room? Is your temper sufficiently good for you to try to smooth me down when something has gone wrong and I am irritable in consequence? Will you be content and happy to live in the place to which I am sent, preferring it, because your husband is there, to courts and cities without him? I am a man with a wide knowledge of the world, and all these qualities are absolutely necessary to me in a wife. To a woman who has these qualities I shall be proud to give everything in return that is in my power, so as to make her happy. These are the questions I have always meant to ask the woman with whom I intend to pass my life; and when you can answer them satisfactorily, I shall be happy to have you in my arms, without considering in the slightest whether you are either beautiful or rich. All I ask is cleanliness of person, and a small —but sufficient—income. It is true that I envy rich people, but I would far rather that the money was mine, though I could bear it if my wife was able to reproach me that it was hers.

"I have said all I can possibly say in answer to any part of your letter, and have told you, frankly, how matters stand between us. I singled you out at first from all other women; and I expect not to be treated as an ordinary lover."

And so the letter ended.

In her small bedroom, far away in Ireland, now that all the household noises had ceased and the prying eyes were shut in sleep, Miss Linden, who had passed the last fifteen years of her life in pulling strenuously at frayed ends, without any hope of reconciling them, behind hermetically sealed doors, whilst showing in public a languorous and admired coquetry, with the coquetry increasing as the admiration diminished, finished re-reading the letter. She had read it, not once, but three times, so that she might be certain that nothing had escaped her, and now, putting it away hurriedly and secretively, she sat down again, looking round the familiar room. Once, her eyes caught those of her own reflection in the glass, and she looked at it curiously, as if she were seeing the face of an acquaintance whom she had known in past years, expecting to see traces in it of a long illness and of many adventures of which she was ignorant. It was strange; even a month ago, when she looked in her mirror, it had seemed to her smooth and beautiful—her face and her whole body had looked as if it were carved by some calm and dark wind from the Pyramids. But now—and perhaps it was only because the insufficient light of the one candle, stuttering like an idiot's tongue, told one nothing, the darkness of her face seemed changed; it was no longer smooth, but full of abysses as if she were already very old and her life was over. There were depths of hollow darkness about her, behind the vast black blaring shadow of her eyes, tunnelled harsh and animal as the braying of an ass, in her wide nostrils that opened upon darkness, in the large beast-furred mole near her lips, that belied the tip-toeing life that she had led for so many years. Her body, her face, seemed blackened, charred, and twisted, as if some enormous fire had devoured her life and had then died in the daylight, leaving only this ruin, this empty hulk slumbering behind lidless and wide-open eyes.

This, the stuttering idiot tongue of the candle told, but she understood nothing. She only sat there, looking at the reflection of a woman whom she thought she had known, from behind those lidless eyes. It was very late, but Miss Linden returned to her life of making both ends meet. Lighting the stumps of three more candles, she took the feather of a dead bird from a box and contemplated it. With this, and half a yard of new ribbon, her winter hat of three seasons ago could be made to do service through the hail, the snow, the rains of the coming cold.

For many days, and in many weathers, Jonathan waited for her reply, even, at last, with some degree of interest. But none came, and after some weeks of an uneasy expectancy, chilled and surprised by this new example of the irresponsibility and changeableness of womanhood, he realised that none would ever come.

Chapter V

HE WAS free at last. There would be no more importunities, no more dangers of her sudden appearance at Rotherham, no further reminder of the life that was gone; it was dead and he could forget it as if it had never been. And he felt gay and as if a new life had sprung from his destruction of the old, as he drove along the country roads in the dogcart, on his way to fetch Anna who was returning in the early train from London.

He had such a strange sensation in his heart as he saw the train steaming in; but he told himself that it was only because laughter would sound again in the woods and the fields and far from the echo of the old men's footsteps in the house and gardens. There she was, walking along the platform of the small country station, waving to him. She was wearing her tight dress that was the colour of winter shrubs, pine and dark laurel, daphne and magnolia leaves when shadowed by the winter, and laurestina. You imagined that her face might suddenly become a bouquet of the pale stars that shine from that green darkness . . . (oh, where had he heard that phrase before, a long time ago and in woods that were far away?) . . . But her face that, when he knew her first, had been little, transparent and pale as the flowers of the Christmas rose—had been a winter flower, white and shadowed with green in the darkness of the woods, seemed now as if it were caught in a net of gold—the happy gold freckles of the light danced upon it. Or were they real freckles? Anna must have been sitting under the light of the great gold sun, far from any shade.

The country roads looked as if they were made of thick gold, it seemed as if they must stretch to the end of the world, and as if he and she would drive along them till the end of time, side by side, in a summer that would never fade, under the sun whose great flames seemed stretched across the firmament. In the heat you could almost see the gold and hidden planets spangling the bucolic air and all the countryside as they circled round the sun in their goat-leaping planetary dance.

But now they had left the country roads and were driving through the forest, a place of dark vast trees with huge leaves and of darker caverns and rocks from which leapt goat-footed waterfalls, and here the light lay like drifts of snow, silver and quivering, upon the paths and the dark rocks, upon the hairy trunks and the huge leaves, or fell like cascades among the trees, so that it looked as if it must be cool to the touch; yet, at moments, even here, the heat of the sun was so great that it brought out the primeval forest-smells of the pine trees, till thick drops of their perfumed gums oozed through the trunks and the branches. And Anna in her green dress seemed part of the forest.

"Anna," he said, "you are freckled; you have been sitting under the hot sun, and all his little golden feathers are dancing over your face. But now you must come with me into this darkness."

"If you had been with me, Jonathan, dark as you are, I think you would have changed into a blackamoor. I have never seen such a great hot sun."

He said, "Shall we stop for a moment? It is so cool here, and it will be very hot again when we come out on the main road." And reining in the horse, they sat for a few minutes in silence, enjoying the shadow of the trees.

She had taken off her hat, so that she might feel the cool of the forest and the snows of the light, falling between the branches, upon her forehead and her hair. Looking at her, he said: "Where did you get that wild and glittering fleece of yours, Anna? No bright birds have such rich feathers. I should like to be the sun and pour down upon them all these ripening gems, the drops left over from the night." And he shook a great branch thick with dew, until the drops fell sparkling and dark upon her hair.

Then, as they drove on again through the forest, his mood changed. She had hoped for one moment, that he was going to say—she hardly knew what, but something that she had waited, all her life, to hear, but now that moment had passed and he said: "I am glad that you have come home again, Anna."

Burying her disappointment, she thought: "At least he is pleased that I have come back," and she said: "Oh, Jonathan, did you miss me—did you really? Are you pleased to see me again?"

"Quite. I really believe I did miss you. For every evening I used to think something had been wrong with the day, because you weren't there. . . . But why are you alone? I knew from the telegram you sent that our good Mintley wasn't coming; but why has she stopped in London? Is it caprice, or has somebody killed her in the middle of one of those anecdotes of hers?"

"Good Mintley comes to-morrow," said Anna. "She was in such a fuss wondering whether she ought to wait for the arrival of all the thousands of parcels she had ordered at the last minute, and leave me to travel alone, or whether she ought to desert them, cast them to the winds of heaven, and chaperon me. She was torn between the two duties. She assured me that I should be murdered in the train, and seemed distressed at the thought, but on the other hand, as she explained to me, there were a thousand dusters and two thousand new glasses, her own spectacles that were being mended, a new dress, and a hat with feathers that will make Loory turn pale with envy—and all these were due to arrive. 'You may think these are little things, Anna, but life is made up of little things, not big.' So she decided to wait. I doubt if we shall discover her when she does arrive, she will be so obscured by her luggage. We shall see, approaching us, what appears at first sight to be a perambulatory Tower of Babel, every parcel quarrelling with every other parcel; the Tower will stop, breaking in pieces at our feet in all directions, and from under it will emerge Mintley, like a snail appearing from its house."

"She is rather like a snail, in some ways, with that slow silver pace, and that milky silky face of hers. But only when she is walking along the country roads. At other times, the noise, rustle, and flurry attendant upon every movement turns her into a Poltergeist."

She laughed, and said: "Yes, she is a Poltergeist—but so kind, so warm-hearted. And that is not generally true of a Poltergeist, is it?" And she added: "I shall have so much to tell you, Jonathan. Did you get my letters?"

"I did indeed. And it was most kind of you, Anna, to remember to write to me, a great condescension on your part to remember me in the midst of all your grandeur. I suppose that now we shall hear nothing from you for at least five months, but talk about 'we courtiers.' And we shall see you dressed more splendidly than Loory in all his glory."

"And how is sweet Loory? How is that most virtuous and highly-respected bird? Are his feathers shining, and is he well?"

"Loory is well, and he presents his humble duty to my Lady and love to his fellow-servant; (I see that Tray has stopped in London to look after Miss Mintley, so I can't deliver the message). But he was the most miserable creature in the world while you were away, always sounding a melancholy note, in spite of everything I could do to try and please him. And if so much as his finger ached, I was in such a fright you would wonder at it. Here are three letters for you, Anna, that Molly would not send on to you, because she says you told her not to. And, Anna, did you remember to give Mr. Mose's and my love to the King? Don't forget you have promised to tell us what he said to you. I had such a fright whilst you were away, because Robert told me the Czar was in London and had fallen in love with you and was intending to carry you off to Russia. Mind, Anna, if he does, you must buy plenty of muffs and sable tippets to take with you. But I must tell you: in a way I almost wished you would stop in London longer than you did, for I lived in great state whilst you were away, and Mrs. Midwinter came in every morning to ask what I would like for dinner. I would ask very solemnly what was in the house, and then give orders for a pigeon pie."

"A pigeon pie in war time? What would the King say if he knew? If you had written that piece of news to me while I was in London, I should have told him; but now it is too late. Aren't you afraid that when Becky Mintley returns from London she will have your pigeon pie taken away from you?"

"Oh, Becky will have had so many new Frenchified receipts given her by the women at Court, that, rations or no rations, we shall never have any of the good old-fashioned English food now."

The forest was left behind them, and now they were driving once more along the country roads. Sometimes, in a cluster of dark trees whose thick quilted leaves were mosaic'd with gold, there would be a white cottage that seemed nodding, nodding down in its sleep, in the great heat. The roads were as thick with walled gardens as a child's picture of heaven, and from time to time an old woman looking, in her bunched wild-columbine-coloured gown, like a housekeeping old hen in a useful feather bustle, curtseyed and squawked a greeting, or a farmer, driving to market, his planet-round face fringed with a dark and leafy growth, would call out "good day." Mr. Mose the steward, in his square hat and tightly-buttoned coat, an old man who seemed made of the same brown leather as his own saddles, an old man who always seemed as if he were riding or driving under a jovial red-faced bucolic sun, with

56

his face as round as the sun, raised his hat to them from behind the autumn-coloured horse of his dogcart. And presently they met a young man walking along the road. He was a tall young man who gave the impression that he was standing on the edge of a cold and incalculable sea. Perhaps it was his fear of poverty that gave him that appearance. When stationary, he had a strangely rooted appearance, as if nothing could ever move him; but when he was walking, he seemed to put down his feet unwillingly, and, chilled, to withdraw them as suddenly again. When he turned a corner, he did so with such rapidity that you felt that a hundred dogs were yapping at his heels, or else that this cold and onrushing sea was surging forward to engulf him, and that if he did not turn the corner in a great hurry he would be overwhelmed and lost. He had rather prominent goggling eyes, which gave him a perpetually startled look, and he was exceedingly plain, but his smile had a touching sweetness, and his permanently ruffled hair gave him a childlike appearance. He flushed slightly as he saw the dog-cart approaching.

"Oh," said Jonathan, "William Ayrton. Good fellow, William—a thoroughly good fellow, a little dull perhaps." And fixing his eyes upon Anna's face, he asked: "Do you see much of him, Anna? I suppose he runs in now and then to see you, doesn't he? I have so much to see to, now, with all this work for Sir Henry, and my own work as well, that I can't keep pace with all your visitors."

"No," she said, "I can't say I see much of him; more now, perhaps, than in the past. But he comes to see Becky, I fancy, more than me."

"Well, if I were you, I wouldn't overdo it. A thoroughly good fellow, William—but I shouldn't see too much of him. One can have enough of a good thing, you know."

"Jonathan, what an odd thing to say! What do you mean? I think it is very unkind of you to speak like that of William, who is so good and kind, and who is so devoted to you."

"Oh, I see! Then he *is* a friend of yours. I thought so! Poor Anna, I suppose you are very dull at times, now I am kept so hard at work, and we can see so little of each other."

"Jonathan," she said, turning and looking at him, "are you by any chance trying to quarrel with me?"

"You know perfectly well," he replied, "that I never quarrel with anyone."

"I am glad to hear it. Well, as you have asked: of course William is a friend of mine, but it is more like being friends with a tree than with a man. He is so countrified, I expect his fingers to sprout into leaves. Every morning when I wake up, I expect to hear that he has turned into a tree—a cherry tree, probably, with very young leaves. For William would never cast a shadow."

"How absurd you are, Anna! But it is true, every human being in this part of the country seems rooted in the earth, life here seems

Annihilating all that's made
To a green thought in a green shade."

They drove on in silence for a while, then Anna said: "I came back by this early train to see Jim Noon—poor boy, oh, poor boy! It is the last day of his leave before he goes to the front. I can't bear to think of it. Jonathan, why had they got to take that boy of nineteen—oh, yes, I know he is the same age as me. But he seems so much younger. What does he know about anything? He has never seen any other place but this, he has never even been up to London, he doesn't even know that there is a country outside England excepting by hearsay, and from having to learn the names of foreign places on the map at school—why have they got to take a boy who never hated anyone in his life, and teach him to hate, teach him to be afraid?"

And a pang shot through her heart. She said to herself: "It might not have been poor Jim, it might have been Jonathan to whom I must say good-bye to-day. If it were not for his deafness. God, how long will this evil last?"

And she thought of the long line of recruits she had seen torn from this countryside—poor country lads, marching along in their clumsy boots, herded like cattle, their eyes full of a bewildered misery, and the forelocks over their foreheads giving them an even greater resemblance to helpless creatures being driven to an enormous slaughter-house, over the earth they had trusted, under the trees they knew and would see no more.

Chapter VI

IT WAS late in the afternoon, nearly six o'clock, when Anna set off for the gardener's cottage, in the great walled garden, to see Mrs. Noon, whose only child must go to the war to-morrow, and to say good-bye to Jim, whose nineteen years had been spent in that garden.

The slow heat of the lion-strong sun seemed to have melted into the earth. "Lions hoard not góld," she said to herself; but this strong lion, hoarding the honeycombs, hoarding his thick gold, had let it sink deep into the earth, to lie there till it ran like sap in the veins of the trees and penetrated through the thickest leaves, melting into the golden apples hiding among those leaves, the pears and sun-round apricots and peaches of next summer.

The whole garden seemed walled in by great leaves, mosaic'd with dark gold, like temples in a forest. It was a place of slow and peaceful growth, a place for slow and imperishable love, thought Anna, where

> *My vegetable love shall grow*
> *Vaster than empires and more slow.*

She walked past the potting-shed where Noon, so Jonathan declared, potted out the long-leaved stars for the flower-show —for, he said, they must be stars, they were far too large and too bright to be ordinary flowers and fruit, those huge strawberries shining like fire and freckled with bright gold, under their thick quilted dark leaves, those calceolarias as fat and red as the strawberries and powdered too with gold, growing in great leaves that were green as water in a forest, the candy tufts like thin greenish snow on a garden path, zinnias, bright and glittering as their name, jangling like water, and coarse-frilled bumble-bee-coloured African marigolds. She passed by the glass frames with their creeping melons, yellow dogskin flowers, and fruit dark green as forest caves and full of waves of honey; and, knocking at the door of the cottage, she opened it and called "Mrs. Noon! Mrs. Noon!"

"Come in, Miss, do. I'm in the kitchen, doing a bit of ironing."

The house, which was large and square, and made of sun-soaked red brick, had been built in the eighteenth century, and was thatched with dark straw, thick as a bear's fur. The windows had diamonded panes, and when it was very hot, these had patterns of water on them like the strawberry flowers and strange Icelandic mosses and maps of far-off lands and seas that Jack Frost drew upon the window-panes. Crossing the passage to the kitchen, Anna walked in.

Mrs. Noon was an old woman with a wide brow and a face with broad planes. The sun always seemed to be shining on it, and you could not imagine her in the dark, even if it were cast by the great leaves that enclosed her world; you felt that the sun would still flicker between them, send little freckles of light to dance upon her. The broad bosom and the wide flat planes of her face that seemed to have been carved by a dark-fingered bucolic wind from the forest and the gardens—these gave her an ancient and primeval look, so that you could imagine her giving Noah and his wife advice about the first plantations of trees, and the first fruit and vegetables they had sown and planted after the Flood. But Anna thought of her, always, as Eve—an old woman in a broad-brimmed straw hat, with the freckles of the light falling through it, standing in the shrill green grass of an orchard, pressing one finger to her lips, as a warning to be very quiet (for fear lest Noon should hear and discover the theft), and then reaching up to a branch, feeling among the flickering green leaves, and giving a little girl a forbidden parrot-bright apple. For that was her first memory of Mrs. Noon.

Now she stood in her kitchen overlooking the great field of corn that bordered the walled garden, bending over the table and ironing out her black silk dress. Jim used to say it was so rich and thick it looked just like plumcake, and that it was so stiff he was quite sure it would stand alone even if she were not inside it. It would be quite safe, he said, for her to leave it standing in the cornfield, it was so heavy that the wind would never be able to blow it away. How proud she had been in the spring-time long ago when, on Sundays, he and she had walked together, she in that dress and he in his first Sunday suit, in the lanes and under the flowering trees splashing down like water. Even the hedges seemed turned to country wreaths, when Jim and she walked down the shady lanes that ran between them, in spring-time when the sun was warm.

But that was long ago, and Jim did not go for walks with her on Sundays now. He walked with Susan Daw, and his mother rarely knew what he was doing. And she was ironing her dark silk dress because she was going to put it away, folded in tissue paper, in the cupboard that stood outside the bedroom on the landing upstairs. What was the sense of keeping it out where the moths might get at it? She would not be wearing it again till Jim came home from the war. (Oh, Jim, Jim, how cold it will be out there. You'll miss the kitchen fire then. You'll wish you'd sat by it more often. Why *don't* you come in—the evenings are growing cold even though the days are so burning hot—why don't you come in and warm yourself? There's such a little time left. Yes, that is what

61

he had said to her two days ago, when she had got such a nice tea ready for him, and he hadn't come in because he was out with that girl. "I have such a little time left, Mother." . . . Jim! He was going to the war to-morrow.)

She greeted Anna silently, with a smile that did not show in her eyes, but hung only upon her lips. Her eyes were dark with pain. Anna, kissing her, said: "I only came back from London this morning, my dear. I came back early on purpose to see Jim. Where is he?"

"He is not here, Miss."

"Not here? What do you mean? Surely he hasn't . . ."

"I don't know where he is, Miss. I never know nowadays. Out in the fields somewhere, I suppose, with that girl. I *did* think that to-day, his last day, he would come in for tea— and him going to-morrow. But no." She paused. "That girl's cast a spell on him. She's drawn the soul out of him and given him hers instead. Sometimes when I look at him I think he isn't my own son at all, but a changeling, for it isn't his own soul that's in his body. Out under the sun and the moon they go. He's hardly ever at home now."

Anna looked at her sadly, but Mrs. Noon did not return her glance. Getting up and taking an iron from the fire, she bent once more over her dress, pressing out the creases. Anna thought "But she too, this old woman with her wrinkled hands given over to household tasks, she too has been driven mad by the sun and the moon in her blood, she too has let her soul go wandering into another's body." And she said: "Don't you think everyone in the world is like that when they're in love? And they have known each other all their lives. Oh, no, it isn't that she has cast a spell over him, they have grown to-gether like two trees—grown together till they are one person —that is what falling in love has meant to them." And she remembered, a child herself, seeing them walking hand in hand from school, under trees whose leaves were so round and flaxen they seemed like country clouds of clotted cream, and whose flowers were soft as a dove's breast. There they were, walking along together—Jim carrying the school-books, as sunburnt as hay he was, and his eyes were blue and fiery; he wore a suit whose trousers and sleeves were a little too short for him: he was a little taller than Susan Daw, and her curls that were the colour of the creamy chestnut flowers on the trees, or buds of the wild lilies of the valley, did not quite reach as high as his hay-coloured thatch of straight hair. Her neck and hands had been tanned by the sun to the colour of coral— just like the coral feet of a small sad bird, her hands were. Jim could not have been more than nine then, which was Anna's age, too, and Susan was seven. Not a day passed but she met them running in the fields together, chasing the butterflies as if the lovely shining or rich and dusky creatures were the happy fleeting moments that would fly away and be gone for ever.

Anna said: "They *had* to fall in love," and added under her breath, "poor Jim!"

Mrs. Noon did not answer, but presently rising to her feet, she took her ironed dress from the table, and putting it carefully over the back of a chair, she said: "And Dad is that furious! I'm frightened sometimes! Miss, he said a terrible thing this morning—a wicked dreadful thing. Whatever *do* you think he said? He said: 'I'm glad my boy is going to the war, if it'll get him away from that girl and the wickedness she'll lead him into.'"

Anna thought: "He'd rather his boy went through that hell, than find heaven with that girl." And she turned scarlet with anger. "I think that is one of the wickedest, most cruel things I have ever heard in all my life! And then he pretends to love that boy."

"He *does* love him, Miss, oh yes, he certainly loves him." And Mrs. Noon sighed. "But love is sometimes precious near to hate. You'll excuse me getting on with my work, Miss, but I've a good bit of darning to do." And reaching across to the horse-hair sofa by the window, she took up a basket full of wool that was standing on it. Putting a sock over her hand,

63

she held it up to the light. "Full of holes these things are," she said. "Jim's that heavy on his feet. Ah, well, there'll be many a long day now when I can sit idle and wish I'd a bit of that boy's mending to do."

Anna, her chin resting on her hands, sat watching her for a moment, then she said: "Mrs. Noon, why does Noon hate poor Susan? What has she done to make him hate her so? You both used to be so kind to her when she was a child, and now I should have thought any human being would have been sorry for her, poor creature—half-starved and worked as if she were some wretched worn-out old cab-horse. Think what her life at home is like! Terrible—you know that as well as I do. If they could prevent it, she'd never be allowed out of the house, and I am sure that when she *does* meet Jim, she must have had to run away from that father of hers, and face a beating when she goes home again. If one sees her out of doors, she is always creeping along as if she thought somebody was going to hit her. And her eyes look terrified. I can't think how Noon can have the heart not to pity her."

Mrs. Noon re-threaded her needle; she sighed. "He does pity her, Miss," she said. "And that's half the trouble. If you only knew how obstinate he is—obstinate about big things, obstinate about little! There's no moving him. And he is just *angry* at being sorry for her, because he knows he is in the wrong, and that puts him all the more against her."

"Yes," said Anna, "but what *has* he against her? I can't see that there is anything wrong with her. She is a good little creature, in spite of that awful mother of hers; and as for her keeping Jim out in the fields with her, if only Noon would let him bring her here, I don't believe there would be any more trouble. After all, you can scarcely blame him, can you, for going out so much, when he isn't allowed to bring her to his home. And why shouldn't she come, anyhow! What *is* wrong with her?"

Mrs. Noon hesitated for a moment; her face was slightly flushed and she looked as if something had caused her shame.

Avoiding Anna's gaze she replied: "I've got nothing against the poor girl, Miss. But as for what's wrong with her—well, you as good as said a minute ago. It's nothing to do with her, it's no fault you can find in her. It's all the fault of that dreadful family of hers. It isn't what I should say to a young girl, but the whole countryside knows what Mrs. Daw is. Do you think there's a soul in the place that doesn't know how she gets those silks and feathers of hers—looking like an Egyptian out of a caravan—and those gold earrings? Only yesterday I catch sight of her walking along the hot dusty roads under the trees, with her silks trailing in the dust—and she black and glossy as the daw she's named after, in her dark silks and with her hair as black and bright as feathers, and a gold chain round her neck. Walking as proud as a queen she was, and when she sees me she tosses her head. For you know the upset there was here, a while ago? Oh, yes, Miss, there's a knock at the door, and when Noon goes to open it, there's my lady, if you please, with her great hat and the feather covering it, and she with her cheeks painted as glossy and bright as any apple in the garden, and those dark silks of hers flying and rustling like the leaves before a storm. Noon was for shutting the door in her face, but the Madam makes a stand, she puts her foot in the door so's he can't close it, and she starts to rage and to storm. Her girl wasn't good enough for our boy, wasn't she? What had we got against her, she'd like to know. Her girl was good enough for anyone in the land! Like a thunderstorm all over the garden it were—you'd have thought all the fruit trees would be ruined. She was going to have the law on us for slander; *we'd* see if we could miscall decent people. She was going to make us pay for what we'd said; she was going straight to Sir Henry, and see what *he'd* have to say about decent people having their names called! And fair's fair all the world over, and what not! And that finished it with Noon."

She shook her head. "She's bad enough, in all conscience. But as for that hymn-singing rascal of a husband of hers, with his fox-coloured hair and his eyes always looking up to heaven so as not to catch your eye—and his whining harmonium voice and his chapel-going, and his way of slinking round a corner like a fox that's out to steal a chicken—(proper like a fox he is, and foxes and Egyptians understand each other, I'm thinking! Out for thieving all they can get!)—d'you suppose *he* doesn't know of her goings-on? Else where does he think the money comes from—and him not doing a stroke of work since he gave up being gamekeeper to Sir Henry—not a stroke, unless he's dragged to it! *Of course* he knows, and that's why he turns his eyes up to heaven the way he does, so's not to be forced to see what she's doing, so as he can hold out his hand all unconscious-like and take what she's holding in hers."

"Yes," said Anna, "and it isn't only that. The way they knock that girl about is a disgrace. I don't know why it is allowed. The father beats her because he says she takes after her mother—oh, yes, I can imagine what is waiting for her every time she has run away and gone out with Jim—and the mother beats her because she takes after the father, is sanctimonious and a prig. What has she got in all her life, excepting Jim? . . . and now . . ." She did not finish her sentence.

"I know, the wretches!" said Mrs. Noon, and fell into silence.

Anna looked round the kitchen. A great clock hung in the corner; no glass covered its face that was wrinkled and quince-brown like that of a winter moon; on the mantelpiece, between two vases full of dried grasses, was a plush-framed photograph of Jim at the age of seven, in a velvet suit and with his face so faded by the light that it seemed as if, soon, it must fade away altogether, and no memory of it remain. Throwing the mended socks into the basket, and putting it back on the sofa, she said, suddenly: "It's Dad being old makes him this way, I'm thinking. It isn't he forgets what being young is like, so much as that he wants to live his youth all over again in that boy—to live Jim's life instead of *his* living it. He wants to own him, heart and soul. It wouldn't matter who the girl was, he'd want to chase her away. He's like one of them swans on the lake, come to that, hissing and spreading their wings out and chasing away anyone who comes near their young. It's terrible." She sighed.

Anna thought: "They are thieves, Daw and his wife—wild thieves of the hedgerows, fire-bright fox and dark-bright jackdaw, thieving and sly. One would steal the cock from the farmer, the other'd steal anything glittering left on the window-sill. They can't help it; it's their nature. But Noon is worse, because he is *against* his own nature. He is a thief, too, creeping along under the leaves. He wants to steal his boy's youth, and says it is because he loves him."

Shaking her head, Mrs. Noon said: "He's that obstinate, Dad is! You can't do a thing with him—not a thing! He'd rather be in misery all his life than give way. But I think what makes him worse than ever about Jim is because he was born when we weren't young any more. Oh, yes, I was well past forty when Jim came." She paused. There was no sound at all excepting the loud ticking of the clock, the gentle voice of a wood-dove floating down from the high trees outside the kitchen garden, and that of a bee upon the window-pane, singing some old country song. Anna thought: "Their lives would have been made up of gentle things like this—had it not been for the Flood that has come to sweep them away." Mrs. Noon, her hands lying idly in her lap, sighed again. "There was another, you know, Miss, born after we'd been married two years. But she died. Died when she was three years old, she did." Looking straight in front of her, she said, after a moment: "I can see her now, poor little thing—lying there. . . . It's dreadful to go through what one does, all those long months, all the pain—just for nothing. Nothing at all."

There was another long silence, and then Mrs. Noon, looking at the clock, rose to her feet heavily, and going over to the fire, took the hissing kettle from it, putting it into the grate. "No use to keep the kettle boiling any more, I'm thinking Jim won't be coming in for his tea now." And she sat down again, smoothing down her apron, then folding her patient old hands in her lap. Still looking straight in front of her, at the fields of waving corn that could be seen through the window, she said: "Oh, Miss, if *only* he'd come home! It's past six now, and him going away to-morrow morning—going to the war. If only things were like what they used to be! Ah well, I suppose there'll be many a day now when I'm thinking, 'If only things were like what they used to be! If only Jim would come home!' "

Chapter VII

THE CALM countryside lay under the fire of the great moon—fields of corn growing to the edge of the owl-dark sleepy woods. Here and there, growing among the corn, an apple tree, with smooth leaves and glittering fruit lying as thick on the branches as the stars in the sky, threw out a sharp scent. There was no sound in the fields and the woods, excepting the occasional drowsy note of a bird, nor was there any light but that of the moon and the stars, excepting where, in the house in the walled garden, one candle threw a thick gold thread through the dark and quilted leaves.

In the long stretches of the dew-wet fields, where the star-light fell like sparkling waterfalls among the trees, through the fields of the long corn and beneath the great dark trees where the warmth of the moon lay on the leaves, the boy and girl walked, their arms round each other's necks, their cheeks pressed closely together.

"It will soon be midnight," he said, "and then—oh, Susan—it will be to-morrow!"

"Jim, Jim, it will never be to-morrow. There is no to-morrow for us. Time will stop to-night when the clock strikes twelve."

"Don't leave me. Oh, don't leave me. Not for a little while. We have so little time left in which to be together."

"How can you say that? How can you? You know I'd never leave you. I'd hide somewhere, if everyone walking upon the earth was hunting me to find me and take me from you—even if it meant my hiding outside the world till, for them, I was dead and free to come to you again. And if they found me and chained me under the sea, the waves couldn't keep me down. If they buried me under the earth I'd break from it. Not all the roots of the trees binding themselves round my heart, not all the villages and towns and the churches with their steeples full of bells ringing out despair, piled upon me, could keep me down. I should break loose and come to you. But I could not hide you. Why should I have a heart, and my heart be filled with you and greater than the earth—and I not be able to hide you in it? Oh, Jim, they'll tear you from me, but I'll follow you—you'll see! I'll come to you, Jim, wherever you go."

"You can't come—where *I* am going."

"I will. I will."

"Oh, Susan, love me for ever. Love me when I am old and grey."

"Your hair . . . your eyes . . . your lips. . . . You will never grow old."

"Did you love me from the first moment you saw me, when we were both babes?"

"I loved you before I was born. Oh, before I was born I had to take *some* way to break into the light, for to break into the light meant to find you."

A little chill starlit wind blew through the darkness of the trees, lifting the muslin of her dress, cooling their lips, lifting his hair.

He said: "It always seemed to be spring when we were together. And now, it will soon be winter. How cold I shall be out there without the warmth of your kiss; it will be cold even when the spring comes again. Do you know, Susan, I

69

think sometimes that I shall be cold now till the end of the world."

"It won't be the spring without you. I shan't see the young leaves growing, with you out there. I shan't feel the warmth of the sun. Only I shall think of the time—even if it is at the end of the world, when we shall be together again, never to part any more."

They lay side by side among the long grasses, not knowing the coolness of the dew or the fire and warmth of the moon upon the leaves, his young head pillowed against her neck, his hair brushing her cheek.

"Oh, Susan, my own love, my Susan, my pretty one, I ought not to keep you out like this. You ought to have been home long ago."

"Home! I have none excepting you, you are my home, and always have been since we were little children. Home? Even the hedgerows have roots, but I've none. I'm just like one of those flowering weeds blown by the wind. I don't even know if I'm *his* child. Often he says I'm not. Perhaps that's why your Dad hates me so bitter."

"And yours hates me. Susan, why *does* he hate me so?"

"He says you want to do me wrong. He says you want to make me like *her*."

"Oh, he is black as hell to say such a thing—black and burning as hell, to blacken our bright love. How *can* I go out there, knowing I'm leaving you to such a one! How can I let you go back to him? Stay with me, Susan, stay with me. We have such a little time left. Don't leave me. Oh, don't leave me."

So he had cried, many a time to his mother, when he was a little child and afraid of the darkness.

They lay side by side in the light of the moon, among the long grasses, his head pillowed upon her breast as if that childish bosom was the consoling maternal earth in which his young body was so soon to find rest.

Chapter VIII

ALL NIGHT long there had been a shivering sound among the leaves, a rustling like that of far-off seas; but now the sound had died away again and there was a long silence in the moon-haunted woods and the dew-wet fields. Then, after the great corn-coloured moon had set and the warmth of its light upon the leaves had died, the little smooth wind that comes before the dawn blew aside the round leaves of the apple tree that grew outside Anna's window; a few stars still shone with a faint radiance upon the smooth leaves wet with dew and the apples that glittered upon the boughs, and upon the long wet corn amidst which the tree had grown. The tree was so large that it seemed a wood of trees, and the fields of ripe corn stretched far into the distance.

It was still too dark for the young man standing in the wood of apples, almost knee-deep in the corn, to see the face of Anna as she leaned out through the wet leaves, but soon the fields would be dusky with dawn and the air would seem like the brown owl's soft feathers.

"Rapunzel, Rapunzel, let down your golden hair," he called to her. "Only I am not trying to keep you in a prison, or to cast a wicked spell over you; and *your* hair is dark, Anna. But for some reason, sunlight, moonlight, the light of the stars, all hide in it as if it were a forest, and when the sun and the moon and the stars are gone, they leave their light upon it as they leave their light on the leaves and on dark water. Perhaps it is a net they have woven. And for what great bird are they fowling in that net, Anna? Can it be me, and are you in league with them?"

"How was it you came so quietly?" Her voice floated down to him through the branches. "I did not hear a single footstep;

and when I saw you standing there, I swear I thought you were a ghost. You are not a ghost, are you, Jonathan?"

"No, no, I am a bird, caught in the net. But a great bird, Anna, a bird of the everlasting night, a strange and sinister bird with a dark and terrible voice. Do not loosen the net, Anna; and keep the sunlight, moonlight, starlight haunting the net of leaves—for if I should break away . . ."

"You were so silent, standing there beneath the tree. What were you thinking about? And what on earth are you doing, roaming about at this time?"

"I couldn't sleep, and I am a native of night. . . . What was I thinking of? I was thinking about the darkness."

"How strange, so was I. Wait, I am coming down. I am going into the fields to pick mushrooms. Will you come with me?"

It was still dark when they set out, and the fox-coloured jangling sun of dawn found them walking over the white and gauzy fields, ankle deep in the white mists of the cobwebs and the sparkling dews left over from the night; and as Anna and the young man at her side walked in the silence, they might have been two shades, and the fields the long meadows beyond the river of Lethe. Those fields seemed to stretch for ever, beneath the jangling reynard-hued sun, that fox with a Golden Fleece that had been brought over bright, soundless and unknown seas.

"This is the field where the mushrooms grow," said Anna at last, her voice floating in the silence with a strange sound like that of woodwind heard over the fields.

The mushrooms, sprung in a night from the darkness and the dew, were dusky as if they had grown near the wells of Lethe and had been watered by these; they, too, seemed shades and as if they might melt at the touch. "We have met before," said Jonathan in a dark and sleep-haunted voice. "Before I came to your cousin's house—long before your childhood. And we have walked in these fields before, under just such a sun of dawn. But it was very long ago."

72

"Yes," she said. "We have met long ago. But where? I remember, and yet I have not a full memory."

The dark being at her side fell back again into silence.

So they walked, quiet as the fields that stretched for ever, walking onwards until at last the light was high. Anna said: "How sad that it cannot always be dawn. One sees everything far too clearly in the full light."

A fox ran through the field of corn, his red-gold fleece wet with gold spangles of the dew, his wild dank and rank ragged-robin smell haunting the corn after he had passed. And Anna said: "He is so happy, running home to his vixen and his cubs. But they will hunt him, I suppose, and kill him soon, and be proud because they have done it. And his lovely red-gold fleece will be spoilt. Yet all he has done is to steal chickens because he must eat. And how is he to know that they are not his to take?" They walked along in silence, then, as they reached the door of a walled orchard, Jonathan stopped and said to her: "Anna, I want you to come in here for a moment, and walk under the trees, where we shall be sure of not being disturbed." He looked at the basket she was carrying and said, laughing: "Oh, you needn't be afraid of being late with the mushrooms. It is only seven o'clock now, and Mrs. Midwinter will have them in plenty of time for breakfast. And I *must* talk to you—one can't talk, stumbling along in the fields. There is something very important I have to say to you, now that we have a moment to ourselves."

They opened the door of the orchard, and walked together over the long bright grass, where the apples boomed down from among their warm wet leaves, and Anna thought: "this is where I used to try to gather the snow, because I thought I could knit little coats from it for my birds to wear. How bright it would look against their dark sleek heads!" and she saw a picture of a little girl with straight black hair and a fringe cut low over her forehead, in a dress the colour of bright green apples, picking up the snow under the sweet-smelling apple trees, when winter first began to change into spring. But there

73

were no coats for her birds to wear after all, for the snow would
never stay with her, the brightness faded and died at her touch.
Now, as they walked under the trees, Jonathan said to her:
"I haven't told you, Anna, that I am going away—leaving
Rotherham Park. In two months' time I shall be gone."

She could not speak, for the noise of her heart, the rush
of its blood, overwhelmed her. She had not known that the
beat of a heart could be so loud that it could overcome a
world.

Looking at her eyes that had grown desperate with misery,
he added: "At this time I shall not come back again. I didn't
tell you until now, because nothing was settled definitely. But
now it is. I have been offered a living in Ireland, and I have
accepted it, because I shall be freer, there, to do my own
work."

She did not stop walking, but in the blindness that had come
upon her, she could not see the branches, the bright apples,
the warm green light falling through the boughs, so that a small
branch hit her sharply across the mouth. He said: "You have
known me since you were a small child, Anna. Will you miss
me when I am gone?"

The tears were in her eyes. She said: "A branch has cut me.
It will be over in a moment. Pay no attention. . . . Oh . . .
Jonathan . . . I can't . . ."

He stopped walking and put his arm round her shoulders as
if she had been a child, saying: "Listen, Anna, I have been
thinking most seriously about what is to become of you, and, as
I see it, you *can't* go on living here, dwindling your life away.
Why it isn't life! Sir Henry is kindness and goodness itself,
we all know that. But he *is* . . . remote, shall we say? And now
that his sister is a widow and is going to live with him, I don't
imagine that it will be possible for Becky to live here either.
Can you see our good dear Becky, allowing anyone but herself
to give orders in the house, to arrange 'the little things that
are so much more important than the big'? If you can, I can't!
Well, you both have a little money of your own—not much,
74

I admit, but just enough to live upon in a fair amount of comfort if you share a house. Why don't you both come to Ireland, where you can live far more cheaply than here, and settle in a house quite close to where I am going to live? Is there anything to be said against it? There could be no gossip, for really Becky is a chaperon who would satisfy any jury on earth, I should imagine. And in any case we will take care not to do anything that could set people talking. Yes, Anna, you must come to Ireland. Do, oh *do* come! I want you to, so much."

Was it possible that anyone in the world could be so happy?

And yet only a few moments ago . . . Then she remembered Becky, and said in a trembling voice: "Oh, Jonathan! What shall I do about Becky? How shall I ever be able to persuade her to come? You know—I can't think she likes you very much. I am afraid she doesn't!"

"Oh, Becky!" and he laughed. "That will be all right—you'll see. I have never wanted her to like me until now. But you know, people usually *do* like me—if I want them to. It will take a little time, of course. But once we get her to Ireland —or even before—you'll find she will get to like me. I give her three months in which to be converted. Oh, Anna, you *must* come to Ireland. How can you even hesitate? Show me that you are brave, Anna, show me that there is nothing on earth of which you are afraid—except of losing me. For if you decide not to come, I doubt—I think it is very improbable—if you will ever see me again. But if you are brave, if you break away from this useless frittering life, we shall see each other every day, talk and work together, as we have worked ever since you were a small child. And you will help me. For I need your help more than you know. I *must* have someone who believes in me, who has the faith in me that I have never found in anyone in the whole world excepting you."

He paused, then said: "There was another woman in my life, Anna."

"Another woman?" It was scarcely possible to hear the dying sound of her voice; she would not have known it for

75

her own. All the happiness of the future into which she had looked, was dark and buried beneath that phrase.

"Was that—long ago?"

"No," he said, thinking 'Here at last is a woman who can bear the light of the truth!' "Only a little while ago. But she failed me miserably, just when I most needed her."

He added: "She was a coward."

"Oh, Jonathan—and did you love her terribly? Jonathan . . . do you love her still?"

He did not answer, and she stumbled along beside him, her face averted, her hands stretched out in front of her to keep the branches from her blinded face.

He said at last: "Anna, I am asking a great deal—a terrible and grave sacrifice of you. I am asking you to give up your life to me, your thoughts, your heart. Anna, make *me* your life itself." But he did not touch her hand.

"You, Jonathan! Oh, you *are* my heart, you *are* my life. What other thoughts have I ever had excepting of you— thoughts given by you? You have been my life since I was a small child—I have only grown out of you. When you went away before, I thought I should die. And then I thought I *was* dead. Oh, that long, long blank. There was no colour, there was no sound. You taught me everything I know. You brought me to life. If it had not been for you, I should have been only a little mound of dust. It is true, Jonathan, it is true!"

He smiled for a moment, but, then his face darkened and he said: "The life I am asking you to lead, will be hard for you. It might be too hard for any woman—for women are more material than men—they cannot live for the mind alone, as men can." He paused and added, slowly: "For if you come, there are certain things for which most women hope—things which mean everything in life to nearly every woman, that you must give up for ever, for they will never be yours—hopes, wishes, which belong to one side of your nature. I don't know what is in your heart—but this I *do* know. If those dreams and hopes *are* in your heart, they will wither and die. There is no

76

help for it. And there are moments when I tell myself it is nothing but wickedness and blind selfishness on my part to ask you to make such a sacrifice for my sake. For it *is* a sacrifice. Make no mistake about that."

Then, stopping in his walk, he said in a low voice: "But I will give you everything I have it in my nature to give. You will be the only woman in all my life, whom I will call my friend."

Chapter IX

THE WHITE house, nodding, nodding down among the quilted dark green leaves in the haze of noonday heat— it was one of the houses that Anna and Jonathan had passed yesterday in the dog-cart—was so quiet that it seemed deserted. You would think, almost, that nobody had ever lived there; but then, everything died this morning, so you could not be surprised at that. Susan, creeping along the small path to the door, stopped under the shadow of a tree and listened. Yes, the house was nodding in its sleep, and there was nothing to be afraid of—yet her eyes were black with terror, and so distended that the white showed all the way round them and the irises seemed like islands floating in a sea; and there was a loud drumming sound in her ears. No, there was no other sound but the loud ticking of the kitchen clock, heard through the open window. She opened the door and, narrowly escaping tripping over the rag rug that lay on the floor like a dilapidated hen with dirty brown feathers, stole on tiptoe past the kitchen door and upstairs to her bedroom. "You can't keep the dead fast," she thought. "You can't hold them down." Yet, though she felt so bodiless in her misery that she thought even the all-seeing hatred of her parents would not be able to find her out, she would not have dared come back, so strong was the terror

77

of the past, of the time when she had been living, and warm, and could still feel pain, when she had braved all, in order to steal a few moments, half an hour, an hour with Jim—she would not have dared to come back only she must take what belonged to her—her money, in order to escape from them for ever. Now time could never mean anything any more, time was dead, too. And they would not be able to spoil time, any more than they would be able to hurt her. All she knew was that she would not let them touch her—never again; the last touch she ever meant to feel, in all the world, was Jim's kiss, his arms round her when he said good-bye. She had only come back to get the few pounds she had hidden, and, if possible, her other dress—the pink one that Jim said made her look like a piece of honeysuckle, all full of honey—and her scanty linen, and then she would creep out again, and blow through the fields of the world like the weed to which they had likened her—float far, far away. "I'm glad I'm not his child," she thought. "I'm glad I've no roots. Roots hold one down."

She went over to the corner of the room that was furthest from the window; she moved her bed. There, hidden in a hole in the floor, under a board, was the money. Just eighteen pounds she had, yes, just eighteen pounds, because every year since she was five years old, Sir Henry had put aside a pound for her on her birthday, and good kind Miss Mintley had put aside ten shillings, because they were sorry for her; and they had kept it for her till she was old enough to look after it for herself, for fear her father and mother should take it away from her. How good and kind they had always been to her—it wasn't only whilst Dad was Sir Henry's gamekeeper, but all the time. Often Miss Mintley would say she must come up to tea in the housekeeper's room, and then there would be boiled eggs with shells as brown as the nuts in the woods, and shining glossy buns, and butter as yellow as cowslips, and cream as thick as the chestnut flowers on the trees—and all because Miss Mintley was so sorry for her, and thought she did not get enough to eat. It was dreadful. Perhaps she would never see

78

Miss Mintley again, or Sir Henry, and they would be told wicked lies—they would be told that all through Jim, she was like *Her* (she never called her mother by any other name). But shadows do not weep, they have no tears to relieve them; a shadow is a flat thing, drifting across the floor and gone in a moment. So no tears came to Susan's eyes.

She looked round the room, thinking, "This is the last time I shall ever see this place." And she remembered how frightened she had been, often, when she was a child, lying in her bed and thinking that the noise the darkness made in the passage and on the stairs outside her room, was the rustling of witches' dresses. But then she had thought of Jim, and had not been frightened any more. She had fallen asleep comforted by the thought of him. . . . ("Jim, Jim! He is far away.") And she remembered, too—climbing down through the branches of the tree that grew outside her window, when she was ten years old and Jim twelve, slipping down through the dark leaves in the afternoon, while her father was asleep, and her mother out on business, and running with him into the woods to pick wild lilies of the valley, or, later, wild strawberries. They used to get so sunburnt that Miss Mintley said she looked like a little negress, under her curls that were exactly the same colour as the wild lilies. That was only a few years ago, and even then Jim and she were like two trees whose branches are intertwined. . . . ("Oh, Jim, Jim, why have you gone and left me? What ever will happen to me now?")

She took her second dress, and her linen, she laid them on the bed and was just about to make them into a bundle, when she heard a slow and stealthy sound, coming nearer and nearer. Somebody was creeping upstairs. Thrusting her belongings under the bedclothes, she stood by the window, waiting. "If he touches me," she said to herself, "I'll jump out. What have I to lose, anyway?" But though she knew that she was dead, the noise of her blood, the beating of her heart, was like a tidal wave.

The footsteps stopped outside the door. Susan thought:

"He is listening for something. What can he be expecting to hear?" But the pause was only for a moment, and then the door opened, very slowly, and Mr. Daw came in, creeping forward with his body crouched, almost as if he were going to sink upon all fours; on his lips was a wide smile and his eyes were so upturned that they looked as if they were blind. In his hand he held a strap. "Well, my lady," he said, "so you've come back, have you? Back to your decent home." And he crept a little nearer. Susan stood with her back against the window, her hand clasping the framework, her body so taut that it looked as if it might break. Then, as he stretched out his hand to seize her, she gave a shrill scream like that of a dying hare. "Don't touch me! Don't! If you do, I'll throw myself out of the window." And she began to climb out. But he caught her by her hair. "Queans like you," he said in a thick whisper, "Queans like you. I'll not be having this whoring in my house." She screamed again, flinging one arm across her face to try and protect it, as seizing her arm with one hand, his face white and crumpled as if it were a candle that had guttered down, he raised the strap.

Then a sudden thought struck him. She was absolutely at their mercy now, there was no outlet for her, nothing to look forward to, nothing for which to hope. As like as not, she'd never see that boy again—the boy by whose side she had lain in the fields all through the night. And if she did—if she did . . . well, by that time *he* wouldn't want to look at *her*. For by that time her mother would have taught her a little sense. Yes, she would no longer be the girl he had known.

A girl's best friend is her mother, and now, in her disgrace, was the time when that mother's influence must make itself felt. "Susan," he said, still in the same thick whisper, but with a whining note piercing through it, his smile widening, his face becoming still more blind, as if it had been swept by a wind. "Why don't you listen to your mother? Susan, if only you'd do what she tells you, what a much happier girl you'd be. And there's your duty to your dad! About time you showed

80

it, ain't it? After all I've done for you. Where's your gratitude? I'd—been—going—to—give—you—the—beating—of—your—life——! The disgrace is like to *kill* your mother when she knows it. But now I'm thinking different. I'm thinking, maybe it's all to the good, for it may put a bit of sense in your 'ead. You do your duty, Susan, and we'll not say another word about what's 'appened. I'll not give you the beating that you ought to 'ave—if you'll be a good girl now and listen to reason."

Her eyes shut like the eyes of a dying bird, she murmured something.

Still clutching hold of her arm, he shook her; then, with his face thrust into hers, said: "Oh, you'll run away, will you, *my lady?* . . . Where'll you run to? Who'll take you in? Yes, my fine madam, who's going to take you in—*after what you've done?* D'you suppose there's a soul in the village what doesn't know by this time, *what you are?* . . . And you a bastard, too!"

But he released her arm. Better not to beat her now, for the marks would show, and he was hoping to get some money out of Sir Henry—money to keep that young Noon out of court. For by this time Mr. Daw, labouring under a sense of his injuries, was fully convinced that he could "have the law" on his enemies. And if he went to Sir Henry and put the matter before him, as like as not that interfering old cat Miss Mintley would insist on seeing the girl. Yes, better not to beat her—yet awhile, at any rate. Giving her daughter a push which threw her on the bed, he said: "You stop there, my lady—and don't you dare to move. You stop there till I come back." And shutting the door behind him, he locked it.

Crouching there, too frightened to cry out, too frightened, at first, to move or even to think, at last the thought came to her: "It only means waiting—for quite a little while. Then, when he's gone to the pub, I'll—why, I'd forgotten. There's the tree outside the window!"

Creeping along through the fields and lanes, kicking savagely from time to time at the silly useless flowers, with his heavy

81

boots, Mr. Daw meditated on his position. There was something sly and deprecating even in his walk, something vulpine, as if he destroyed only because he could not steal. He had started life as a poacher, ascribing this activity to his political convictions and to his determination that "Britons never never never shall be slaves," but when the fire of his youth was waning, he began to find this toil insufficiently remunerative, and having noticed, with envy, the rewards conferred upon the virtuous, he became converted to religion, with many outward signs of repentance for his past sins—groanings, mouthings, and eyes upturned till they looked like plovers' eggs; he became, in short, a pillar of the chapel, and the show piece of the congregation. At first, there had been certain difficulties attendant upon this conversion; it had been almost impossible, for instance, for him to induce in the pastor, a somewhat slow-witted man, the notion that Mr. Daw's constant attendance in the public house was due to missionary fervour—his longing to bring his former companions into the paths of virtue; so, realising that this arduous attendance was ascribed to other causes, he set about evolving a new reason. After a short practice, he was able to produce a very creditable imitation of a fit—a form of seizure which increased in frequency and which, by some chance, occurred invariably when he was within a few yards of the Rose and Crown. Sympathisers seeing this performance for the first time would then bear him to that shelter to await recovery, and would, as often as not, shocked by the duration and severity of the malady, pay for restoratives out of their own pockets. And this was almost a necessity to Mr. Daw, since his old companions no longer showed any pleasure in his company— indeed they avoided him, and showed a callous indifference to his sufferings, never so much as offering him a pint of beer; so that unless a sympathetic stranger was at hand, he was obliged to pay for restoratives out of his own hard-earned money. For by this time, Mr. Daw had entered the ranks of wage-earners; his conversion had been only a step on the upward path, and after a while, under the spell of the belief that it takes a thief to

82

catch a thief, Sir Henry had appointed him to be gamekeeper. Mr. Daw was genuinely attached to pheasants and partridges, with their shining ruddy-gold and dusky feathers, and at first, too, he found it distinctly pleasant to arrest his former companions and mouth texts at them, deliver homilies on virtue, point out the difference between their precarious state of livelihood and his own, whilst he was conveying them to the police station. But after a while, even this failed to satisfy his ambition. Rheumatism attacks the virtuous as well as the wicked, when it comes to spending a night lying on the wet grass in a wood, or among the corn; his new profession, too, involved a certain amount of toil—and Mr. Daw was averse to toil. He had a conscience, and he remembered his political convictions. He resigned, therefore, from the post of gamekeeper, on the score of ill health, and with many lamentations at the way in which he had been maltreated by fortune; and from then onwards relied entirely upon the talents and energy of his wife to provide him with the comforts necessary to a man of his worth. "Ah," he thought, as he walked through the wood, "if only Susan had taken after her mother, in the way of common sense!" She seemed to have no gratitude—none—and after all he'd done for her. Why she wasn't even his child! Or so he said sometimes. She alternately was and wasn't, according to whether he wished to force her to perform a duty, or, when this failed, wheedle her into doing something from a sense of gratitude. Like many people, he wanted to have things both ways at once, and, whilst lamenting this lack in her of her mother's common sense (for, of course, he had no idea of the form this took in that lady's case, and, although he accepted the resultant benefits, preferred to ascribe these to an act of Providence), he beat Susan often and hard, on the score of her gad-about ways, which, he declared, could only lead to wickedness.

Now, walking along the avenue which led to the house, his meditations were disturbed by a voice. "Good morning, Daw. Who do you want to see?"

Turning with a start, he saw Lady Arlingford, Sir Henry's

sister, a tall, thin, shrewd-looking old woman with a kind of frost-bitten beauty like that of smooth cold blue moonlight. Mr. Daw, his thick white crumpled face looking like that of a country clown, under his mop of fox-coloured hair, considered her. What bad luck that she should have seen him! Sir Henry would have been far easier to manage. Well, perhaps there was still a chance of getting at him. Standing in a very humble attitude and twisting his cap in his hands, he said in an unctuous voice: "I've come to see Sir Henry, please, m'lady. It's something very important."

"Well, you can't see Sir Henry," said Lady Arlingford, sharply. "What are you doing here? You have been told, often enough, not to come up to the house. What is it you want?"

Mr. Daw turned his eyes up till the whole of his face was one blind expanse of white, like a wall to which there is no door. In his whining harmonium voice he said: "It isn't fit talk for your Ladyship to hear, what I'll be having to say. Please, m'lady, you'd far better let me see Sir Henry."

"I imagine," said Lady Arlingford, pushing back her hat impatiently and arranging a wisp of hair, "that nothing you could say would be an overwhelming shock to me, and I've told you already that you can't see Sir Henry. Say what you have to say to me or go away."

"My lady," said Mr. Daw, in a breaking voice, "my girl, my girl I'd 'ave died for—my girl I've brought up in the fear of God, she's been seduced by a rascal, a domned black-souled rascal—(domned in the Biblical sense, my lady) . . . All night out in the fields they were. She's ruined, my lady, ruined. But there's a law in England that punishes the likes of 'im—ah! and I'll 'ave the law on 'im *and* on 'is godless father. I'll make 'em pay for what 'es done."

"Ah," said Lady Arlingford, "I thought it would come down to a question of money. Well, first of all, Daw, I don't believe one word of what you're saying, and secondly, what has all this to do with Sir Henry?"

84

"I thought p'raps, my lady," standing in a crouched attitude as if he were too humble to take up more of the air by standing upright, "that seeing as that domned rascal's father is Sir Henry's head gardener, and seeing as *I* was 'is gamekeeper till my 'ealth . . ."

"You *were* his gamekeeper," said Lady Arlingford, beginning to walk slowly in the direction of the house, accompanied by Mr. Daw sidling along like an obsequious shadow, "but you are not now. And as for your health, Daw, there is not much the matter with that, excepting that you don't take enough exercise. You should try doing a little work. There is nothing like that for supplying the deficiency. But I understand you perfectly—better, perhaps, that you would wish. You are hoping that, for Noon's sake, and for the sake of that unhappy girl of yours, Sir Henry will buy you off. Well, you will be disappointed, for not one penny will you get from him. First of all, even if young Noon has done what you say—which I don't believe for a moment—the law doesn't come into it, and secondly, I should advise you to think things over before you try to extract money from anyone on account of this cock-and-bull story of yours. Do you know the name the police would give to your behaviour? You don't? Well, I'll tell you. They would call it blackmail, and people who commit that sometimes get as much as ten years' penal servitude."

Two pinpoints of reddish darkness now showed in the white blind expanse of wall that was Mr. Daw's face.

"It's for my girl's sake I'm doing it, m'lady—only for my girl, my poor innocent deluded girl, so as to see her righted. Ah, it'll break 'er mother's 'eart when she knows what that girl's done. She don't know yet; I'll 'ave to break it to 'er. Out all night, our girl were, and never come back to 'er good 'ome. What 'er mother'll do I *don't* know—and a good mother she is, trying to train 'er in the way she should go."

"Yes," said Lady Arlingford, reflectively, "I heard that Mrs. Daw was trying to train Susan to follow in her footsteps. It would have been profitable for you, would it not?—and no doubt you are disappointed that the plan failed. Still, I wouldn't encourage it, if I were you. It might get you into trouble. And may I ask *why* Mrs. Daw doesn't know yet of this disaster that you pretend has happened?"

"She was away, m'lady—away. She'd just gone over to the town to do a bit of business, and to see 'er Cousin Fred, that's been so good to 'er. Ah, a good wife she's been to me—and what she'll do when she finds out what's 'appened to that girl, I *don't* know. Worships the very ground she walks on, does Mrs. Daw. Ah, I don't know *what* she'll do."

"Well, I should advise you, for your own sake, to see that she doesn't beat her." By this time they had almost reached the house, and Lady Arlingford stopped. "And now, Daw, I've had quite enough of this, and you can go. But let me warn you that if I hear of you ill-treating that girl of yours, or if you try to extort money, either from Noon, or from anyone here again, the police will be told, and you will get into very serious trouble. Now go. And don't come back."

Chapter X

IN THE world of sunny greenery, where no sounds were to be heard but the dark or the shining songs of birds floating through the trees, and where, for companions, she had only the little shadows running across the grass, Anna was re-arranging the books on the shelves in the library. Miss Mintley was far away in her bedroom, separating the hordes of opposed parcels by which she had been accompanied on her return from London, Sir Henry was resting on his bed, under a snow-drift of documents and notes that seemed to have floated down from the ceiling like snowflakes to lie on the bed, floor, tables, and chairs, Jonathan was at work in his room, and would not appear at tea, and Lady Arlingford had driven over to call on some neighbours who lived in a house surrounded by great walled gardens. Anna, as a child, had believed that the people who lived there must be members of a fairy aristocracy, but she had never seen them. Sometimes, when she was driving past the gates, she would hear their laughter floating through the trees, or see a white dress like a trail of heat-mist or of snow, and that was all. But once, when she was eight years old, she had been allowed to walk in the gardens, and ever afterwards, remembering the peach trees with eighteenth-century names that grew there, she had believed they must belong to the tall and magnificent fairies in Madame d'Aulnoy's tale—the fairies who had fruit for which a queen longed in vain.

A small child with black straight hair that dripped like water over her shoulders, she had walked under the great gold sun of late afternoon, staring at the tall peach trees that grew against the walls, and reading out their names from the tags attached to the stems. The glittering wind-thin flushed flowers had died, and the fruits hung on the boughs like a constellation of suns among leaves that were cool, smooth, and dark as water, and that rustled like water. Here grew the White Nutmeg, grafted upon an apricot stock, (lest it should be too weak), and to be gathered in the heat of July—the Red Nutmeg, or L'Avant Pêche de Troyes, ripening under the August sun, and the Yellow Alberge, whose leaves are even darker and more water-smooth than those of the other peach trees, and the flesh of whose fruits, also ripening in August, is yellow and dry as gold. Then came the Mignonette, or Double de Troyes, with fruit that is very red on the side that is next the laughing sun, and full of rich and vinous juice—the White Magdalen, ripening early in the heat of August, the Early Purple of the middle of that month, La Belle Chevreuse, and the Red Magdalen; and from among their smooth leaves the perfume came like a cloud of gold. Growing next to these, like a whole system of suns, were the Bellegarde, or Gallande, whose

87

fruit is of a deep purple colour as if it had been woven by the heat, whose kernel seems made of clustered amethysts, and La Petite Violette Hative, with small leaves and modest flowers, whose fruit is of a violet colour where it is turned towards the sun, and whose flesh, ripening in the hot mists of the September days, is of a pale yellow, deepening to red near the stone, and melting to the taste. Then last of all, came the Bourdine, ripening at the beginning of September, the Rosanna, with cool amber flesh deepening to purple, the deep red Persique, and the Monstrous Pavy of Pomponne, that ripens at the end of October in the warm autumn days. Looking at them, Anna thought that they would surely shine all night through their leaves, like suns, and she wished she could see the fairy aristocracy to whom they belonged.

She was reminded of these tall peach trees now, when, arranging the books in the library, she found an eighteenth-century book on gardening. The pages were dark and stained as if the book had lain in long dew-wet grass through a summer night, but it was still possible to decipher the old, pointed print, and there, glittering on those darkened pages, were the very names, the ghosts of the flowers and fruit that grew on those trees.

She thought: "I shall never see them again. All my past life, all this dream-like existence I have known, will soon have faded like the nets of dew in which the fruit was hung, and the light on their leaves."

Now, for the first time since this morning, Anna found herself alone, and she said to herself: "How strange it is that only a few hours ago Jonathan and I were walking together in the orchard, only this morning our new lives began together" —the glory that she would know through Jonathan, a glory that she could never touch with her hands, that would be as remote to her as the wonder that waits for us beyond the grave. Not until night fell would she think of the hopes that she must let die of starvation, of her renunciation of her own life, and of all the warmth that we know in living. She knew only that she would spend her life in sustaining him with all the powers of her nature and of her belief in him—soothing him when he was angry, reviving his pride and his belief in himself and his own destiny—and that she must cherish no hope, suffer no grief or anger apart from his; that she must be content to have her part in his life, almost her very existence, kept secret from the whole world, because he wished no soul on earth, excepting Rebecca Mintley, to have any suspicion of the meaning and the extent of their companionship. She must destroy all his letters to her, and every record of their friendship, stifle her pride, schooling herself to hear him spoken of by other lips as if his innermost thoughts were not hers; she must endure to be treated by the outside world as if she had no particular meaning for him, as if she were only one amongst a hundred who shared just that particular degree of friendship. And in return, she would be given—what? Did she ask for a return, she who, when the time came for her to die, would take into the grave the words, "You are the only woman in all my life whom I will call my friend."

Yes, this new life had begun this morning, but the outer world was unchanged. At luncheon, for instance, the talk had been even duller than usual: you would never guess that anything had ever happened, in the whole of the world. Once, after a long silence, Anna, addressing Sir Henry, had said "Cousin Henry, Jim Noon is going to France to-day." Sir Henry put down his spoon; an expression of extreme distaste overspread his features. At that moment he had been engaged in trying to remember the exact date in the early eighteenth century when the Dutch gave up wearing their hats in church. Shutting his eyes, giving a slight click with his tongue, and moving his head downwards, with an impatient gesture towards his confidential shoulder, he said, in a rusty, wilfully ancient voice: "Who—*is* Jim Noon?" Pause. "Jim Noon, Cousin Henry, your gardener's son."

"Oh!" (still more impatiently) *"Jim Noon!* Why couldn't you say so?"

For the war had disturbed Sir Henry, who in his cultivated philosophical way, had decided not to notice it more than was necessary . . . (if you pay no attention to a thing, it ceases to be there. . . .)

"Dear, dear, young Noon! Really!" And Sir Henry decided he would send him thirty shillings. He would probably need it out there. He felt a distinct crick in his neck. . . . He hoped it was not another attack of the old trouble beginning. Better rest, he thought, till dinner-time. One could not be too careful.

Now, looking at the clock, Anna sighed. It was half-past four, and in a moment tea would be brought, and good kind Miss Mintley would descend upon her, and she would be enveloped once again in ordinary life—or an existence that is not life, but only a tired stranger's conversations with life, that sleepy old housewife that is for ever warring with the dust. Even now, outside the door, she was conscious of the Poltergeist-like commotion and turmoil, enveloped in, and then escaping from, the density of bosom, mind, hair, and personality that were the phenomena attending Miss Mintley's slightest movement. These, and the sound of her voice, flat and high, floating down the long corridors as aimlessly as the wind, blowing little drifts of dust and of feathery comfort up and down the wide stairs and under the doors, night and day, had a strange effect upon animate and inanimate nature. Should, for instance, she visit the kitchens or the farmyard on a tour of inspection, in a moment all the servants would be quarrelling, all the bells ringing, doors banging, hens squawking (with their feathers flying as if a high wind were blowing). All the cockscombs in the fire would be flaring, weathercocks turning, water boiling over, milk in the pans hissing and burning, dogs barking and chasing cats—maddened into activity by the sound of her complaining voice, the meaningless hiss and whisper of her skirts.

Since her return from London, that very morning, Miss Mintley had been aware that some change had taken place in Anna. It was an emotional change—of that Miss Mintley was certain—(probably something to do with Mr. Hare, and of *that* young man Miss Mintley did *not* approve)—but she still could not guess the exact nature of the emotion, if it were happiness or unhappiness. But she intended to find out, for, as she told herself, she did not believe in secrecy or nonsense of *that* kind. Of one thing she was certain: she ought to leave Anna alone as little as possible; company, and especially Miss Mintley's company, was what she needed, for now was the time to show her a little kindness.

Miss Mintley's life was, indeed, taken up with doing small kindnesses, and it was a source of bewilderment to her that these were so seldom appreciated. Genuinely warm-hearted, she was in the habit of making such remarks as, "I think one should always be kind to the poor . . . after all, they have just as much right to live as we have." Nor was her kindness confined to these unfortunates, for it was extended freely, also, to persons of her own station in life. Should, for instance, a person just returned from a long walk sink into an armchair for a moment's rest, Miss Mintley would not be satisfied until he had been induced to rise and to move into another part of the room in which he would be more comfortable; and no sooner had this migration taken place than she would notice that the light was in his eyes and would insist upon another instant removal. So it went on. Wherever you were, Miss Mintley was determined, for your own sake, that you should move to some far-distant spot, and whatever you were doing, Miss Mintley suggested either that you should stop doing it and do something else, or that you should do it in a completely different way. For she longed to help, to count for something in the lives of those around her—she who had never known her own life. Then, too, she could not bear that anyone should feel neglected, and to read a book was a proof that this was so. She would, therefore, immediately sit down beside the reader and immerse him in conversation, being confirmed in this habit by the fact that she herself did not care very greatly to read.

Her thought for others was unceasing. If, for instance, a fellow-being was, for some reason, in a state of acute distress of mind, and was giving utterance to this, Miss Mintley would, with a masterly stroke, cut off the conversation in the middle of a sentence by interpolating some remark about the weather, or the ducks in the pond, or the fact that the lime trees in the avenue were about to blossom, some reminder that the sufferer had dropped his handkerchief or that his bootlaces had come untied, a request that the window might be opened if it were shut, or shut if it were open, that the curtain might be drawn to let in the light, or the blind pulled down to exclude it; that the door might be opened and the dog admitted, or the door shut and the dog banished. By this means she would divert attention from the sorrow and prevent the sufferer from dwelling upon it, proving to him, also (by the fact that it was obvious that she had not listened to a word he was saying), that it was but an unimportant matter.

These methods were now concentrated upon Anna, to whom Miss Mintley clung without intermission, excepting for the time which she devoted to sorting out her parcels.

It was with evident regret that, at last, she retired to her room for this purpose.

This room, which was very large, had an enormously high ceiling and tall windows looking out over the gardens. It was a room in which it was difficult to tell which was the shadow, which the reality, and where everything looked very grave. Pyramids of shadow lay on the floor, cast by the four-poster bed whose canopy, so high that it almost touched the ceiling, bore a tall stiff bunch of feathers. And with these shadows, these pyres and pyramids of shade, were others, that had a strange half-animal character; they were like the ape-philosophers, the satyrs from India, Animaut and Perimal the Magnificent, of whom Mr. Hare's friend Mr. Arbuthnot had written, and who have now fallen into silence. The shadow of Becky, as she stood at her dressing-table, lay across the floor like some dark grave nun, a Tabitha or a Dorcas, asleep.

Cutting the string and rustling the paper of her parcels, sorting the contents and smoothing them down or shaking them out, Miss Mintley pondered over the situation. Yes, she was certain now that Mr. Hare was at the bottom of the whole thing. "Poor Anna! Poor girl!" And Miss Mintley shook her head. Ah, the day would come when she would *know* the kind of man with whom she had to deal! And she sighed. What a pity it was that the girl would *never* listen to the advice of older, wiser people. What, she wondered, would Anna do if she knew that until quite recently Mr. Hare had been receiving almost daily letters from another woman! Miss Mintley knew the handwriting quite well. It was not exactly that one *looked*— (one does not read other people's letters)—but, after all, one can't *help seeing*—can one? And once, not looking, but having the sight forced upon her, she had been unable to avoid seeing the signature on one of the letters. Lucy Linden— that was the name. Unfortunately, however, she had not been able to see the address also, since Mr. Hare had returned unexpectedly to the breakfast room before this had obtruded itself upon her notice, so that she was still rather in the dark. Yet the fact of the letters remained (although, by now, they seemed to have ceased altogether), and the day would come when Anna would *have* to be told about the mysterious shadow that was haunting her. And of course, as was invariably the case when an unpleasant duty had to be performed, it would fall to Miss Mintley's lot to tell her. She would go to her and say: "Poor Anna, poor child, you don't know what men are! You can never trust them. In the end they will break your heart. All men are alike." And Miss Mintley's face crumpled up as if she were going to cry. . . . Ah, well! . . . And then, too, why did not Mr. Hare join the army? It was true that he had said he had been called up before a Medical Board and rejected on account of his increasing deafness. But surely he could have found *some way*? He would say, sometimes, "William Ayrton and I are a pair of old crocks. William can't go to the war because of his eyesight, and I can't go because of my deafness.

For which I'm heartily thankful." Miss Mintley said to herself that William's case was quite different from that of Mr. Hare. She liked William.

And then there was Mr. Hare's attitude towards the little things of life. Sir Henry had said he had a great mind, and a great career ahead of him; but surely if he were *really* clever he would not be above *little* things! Only, to-day, at lunch, when he had been talking to Anna, and Miss Mintley had interrupted him in order to tell them something most interesting about a new kind of runner bean, he had looked at her—well, almost as if he hated her!

Then, as she considered the situation, her mood changed. Those who make their beds must lie on them—but, although Anna had been behaving most wrongly, had been inattentive and had taken no interest in details—(it is the *details* that count)—something would have to be done to prevent Mr. Hare from spoiling her whole life; and if that foolish girl would do nothing to protect herself, then she, Becky, must do it for her.

Chapter XI

MISS MINTLEY poured out the tea with dignity, carefully avoiding looking at Anna, or giving any hint (excepting that of handing her a cup) that she was aware of her presence. It was noticeable that she was flushed a dull red, as if she were suffering from indigestion, and her face, and especially her mouth, bore a wry expression, as if she had just tasted a sour hard-textured unripe plum, whose filaments had clung about her teeth and set up a slight ache. She ate a good deal, but in doing so preserved, throughout, the appearance of one who was performing a public duty, quietly and resolutely, but against her will. When tea was over, she picked up her embroidery and worked at this, never raising her eyes from it, and preserving a complete silence unless she was spoken to, when, totally ignoring the speaker, she would raise her eyes to the window and, addressing the birds who were feeding outside, would say "Cheep—cheep—Tweet—tweet . . . you pretty things . . . *I* see you, you saucy boys!" She would then resume her work. The only other sound was a rhythmical tattoo upon the ground, made by the tapping of one foot. At last, however, she was unable to bear this repression of her natural instincts any longer, and, laying down her work with some appearance of ceremony, but keeping her eyes still fixed upon her lap, she addressed Anna for the first time.

"Anna," she said, in a voice charged with dignity, "for some time now I have had it in my mind to speak to you *most seriously*; and now, dear, matters have come to such a pitch that I consider it——" She paused, and then making a movement with her head and throat like that of a duck swallowing weed, added—"a *duty*."

"Why," Anna wondered, "do people take on a duty as if it were some kind of an official search-warrant, a permit which allows them to pry into the souls of other people, and make them uncomfortable?"

"You are making a great mistake, dear," the good Mintley continued, "in your treatment of Mr. Hare. And I am not the only person who has noticed it, believe me, Anna. We *both* feel——"

"Both?" said Anna, who had risen from her seat and was now standing looking out of the window. "May I ask, who is the other person?" But she knew. She said to herself: "Mr. Debingham has been making mischief again, I suppose. He always succeeds in putting Becky into this sort of mood."

"I am not at liberty to say, Anna," replied Miss Mintley, with increased dignity, "and I am surprised that you should ask. How can it possibly concern *you*? And don't try to distract my mind from the subject I was going to speak about. You are making a great mistake, dear, a great mistake, believe me, in your treatment of Mr. Hare. You allow him to feel far

95

too much at home with you—you show a far too obvious pleasure in his company. It never pays, dear, *it never pays*. No man has any respect for a woman who always agrees with him, who is obviously pleased to see him, and who is always punctual, always there when he wants her. *It does not do, dear.* All men are alike, and that is *not* the way to preserve one's pride, or to win their respect. One should always keep men waiting, and one should never show that one is glad to see them. Take my case, Anna. Never in my life until now, when" (her face softened) *"a very great friendship* has come into my life, have I ever shown any man that I was pleased to see him. You have often heard me speak of Mr. Wapster, Anna, the young vicar of Marshover, though you never knew him. It was before your time. Well, as I think I told you, he was a constant visitor at our house at one time—in fact he was always there, and his mother confided to your dear Aunt Lucy that he was greatly attracted . . . that he, well, came to the house principally for *my* sake. But I never showed him that I was pleased to see him. I was far too proud, I had too much dignity. Men like dignity in a girl, dear. I made a point of contradicting him as often as possible, I kept him waiting, I was not *always* at his beck and call. I remember once, when I had promised to lunch with him. We had arranged to meet under the clock at Charing Cross Station. It was a terrible day, raining in torrents, and I kept him waiting for nearly an hour. It is these little things which gain a man's respect, dear, which show you in your true colours, believe me. And look what happened! After four or five months' constant attendance at our house—suddenly—he stopped coming altogether! Think, Anna, what would have happened if I had behaved like you!"

"Well," said Anna, "I suppose you would have married him. And as for myself, I don't particularly want to drive Jonathan away and never see him again."

"That is a most indelicate statement, Anna. You will forgive me, dear, but I am always frank. *It is my way*. I think it is a great pity that you do not listen to the judgment of people who are older than yourself, and who know more of the world. Believe me, running after a man never pays. And this, well, *friendship* of yours with Mr. Hare is doing your character no good. No good at all. You are a changed being, Anna. Inattentive to the little things of life—and it is the little things that count, dear, and the *little people*. It takes all kinds to make a world, and we cannot have great people all the time. It is the little people who do the work of the world. Think of all the mute inglorious Miltons! In their hearts, Anna, they have far greater poetry than Milton ever sang."

"He didn't sing. He wrote. And what is the use of being mute and inglorious? And in any case, how on earth can you know that they have greater poetry in their hearts than Milton's if they are mute?"

Miss Mintley, taking no notice of the interruption, continued: "And sometimes, dear, you are almost rude in your inattention when one is speaking. If one is telling you a most interesting thing, you snap one up before one has finished, simply because you cannot bear to pay attention to details. You seem to have no patience. And patience is one of the most wonderful qualities in the world. Where would *you* be, Anna, if I paid no attention to details?"

"Where I am now, I suppose," said Anna, whose face by now bore a sullen expression. Leaving the window, she resumed her seat again. "Do you imagine I should dissolve into thin air?"

"That remark is really unworthy of you, Anna. I do not know what you are coming to. It is so unlike what you used to be, dear. And believe me, I am not the only person who has noticed it, by any means. Only a few days ago, while we were in London, a very distinguished man indeed—*quite*" (with an indignant shiver) "as distinguished as Mr. Hare—a man who takes a real interest in you for *my* sake, knowing how deeply devoted to you *I* am—was lamenting this change in you."

Anna thought: "Then I *am* right. It *is* Mr. Debingham again!" And she said: "I wish Mr. Debingham would mind his own business."

Miss Mintley closed her mouth with a snap. She rose with dignity, folded up her work with great deliberation, and prepared to leave the room. As she reached the door she paused, and, opening it, "You make it impossible to speak to you, Anna," she said. "I shall say nothing more."

For Mr. Debingham was her oracle and her god.

Chapter XII

STILL PRESERVING her dignity, Miss Mintley reached her room, but, once there, she sank into her armchair, and her face crumpled up once more as if she were going to cry. This was what always happened when you tried to do good in the world—to help other people. You were ignored as if you did not exist, simply because you were trying to perform an unpleasant duty. People who avoided duties of this kind at all costs—who never sought out another person in order to tell them the unpleasant things that had been said about them, who never enquired how they were going to pay their debts, or reminded them that they must soon undergo an operation— *these* persons, shirking duties of the kind because they were painful, avoiding them out of sheer laziness—these were appreciated, whereas . . . Oh, if one could *only* be ill—*really* ill, so that people thought one was going to die. *Then* they would realise the worth of what they were about to lose. Or, better still, if one could have an accident as the result of performing some brave action! Then they would all cluster round her bed and listen avidly to the recital of the events that led up to the disaster and her behaviour. She had often thought how surprised they would be if she stopped a pair of runaway horses (yes, frail as she was! For it is the *courage* that counts!) —or rescued a child from drowning, although she was unable to swim . . . "The pain is nothing," she would say to the anxious crowd clustered around her bedside . . . (and perhaps it would not be very bad) . . . "I only did my duty."

Or better still, why could she not make some great discovery, invent something, a medicine which would cure every disease simultaneously, banish the pains of childbirth, ward off old age, prolong life. . . . "Miss Mintley, your name will be remembered for ever. What can I and my grateful people do to show our gratitude?" "Sir, I need no reward. *My* reward is here"—pointing to the crowd of healed sufferers. There would be an explosion, of course, whilst she was perfecting the discovery and she would be blown up and for the rest of her life—(since, through a tragic coincidence, the discovery could not cure her although it could cure all others)—she would be a nice comfortable invalid, lying back in her armchair or on a sofa and being waited on assiduously by everyone around her. And how happy the world would be to devote the whole of its time to ministering to her wants. It would be very good for Anna—would make her less self-centred, and she would not have so much time to go gallivanting about with Mr. Hare. . . . Oh, *why*. . .

But now, interrupting her meditations, she became conscious of a slight sound at the other end of the long passage, and, opening the door, she listened, much as an owl listens—her head bent sideways. Yes, it *was* Mr. Hare's door being opened, and in a minute he would come down the passage and she would have him at her mercy.

For some time Mr. Hare had been under the impression that Miss Mintley wished to speak to him about some momentous matter. Continually, if he found himself alone with her for a few minutes, she would open her mouth, and then, with a snap, a sound like that of a reticule being closed, she would shut it again. Now, opening the door cautiously, he listened for a moment, his deafness increasing his fear. Yes, she was standing at the door, waiting for him, with her eyes fixed upon the spot where he was about to stand, as if he were a ghost whom she alone was enabled to see.

As Hare approached her, feigning an increased deafness and abstraction, and, at the same time, heightening his speed, and making as if to pass her, Miss Mintley became suddenly galvanised into life, an extraordinary mechanism of movement. Darting forward with a curious circular motion, made necessary by the long and meaningless train of her skirt, thrusting forward her long thin neck like that of a swan about to strike, she began to speak, her voice creaking through the silence with a complaining sound like that of a door being blown to and fro by an uneasy wind, or a rickety wicker chair that has just been deserted by the sitter.

"Mr. Hare," she said: "I have been meaning to speak to you for a long time, but have not had the opportunity. But now . . . if you would be good enough to spare me a moment. It is rather a delicate subject, but I am sure that you will realise that I *only* approach it because Anna's whole happiness depends upon whether matters are *changed*. They can *not* continue as they are at present. I am sure that you yourself must realise that. I think it is most inconsiderate. . . ."

Making an impatient gesture, with a face indicative of still increased deafness, he was about to pass her, when he changed his mind. A smile overspread his face, and, advancing towards her, he said: "Oh, yes—dear Anna! We *must* have a talk about her—but not to-day, not on the day of your return. I am so glad, I am really thankful you have come home, and that the house will be properly run again. It has gone rather to pieces whilst you were away, you know. But I am afraid I am glad for a selfish reason, too. Has Anna told you that I have been given a living in Ireland and shall be moving there in about two months' time? I should have told you myself, but the news only came while you were in London. And now, I have a very great favour to ask of you, but you must promise me to tell me if it is too much trouble. You see, it is like this: I shall have to buy everything for my new house—furniture, carpets, curtains, utensils for the kitchen, everything! And you know how completely helpless men are, when it comes to doing anything of *that* sort. I have no sisters—no one else whom I can ask who knows anything whatsoever about household matters; and I am so much in need of the help of a really practical experienced woman. Can you see me knowing how to furnish a house—or to run it when it is furnished?"

Miss Mintley's face changed. She had never liked Mr. Hare—never. Still—it *is* nice to know that one is appreciated—is it not? It was odd! She had always thought that Mr. Hare would have been the last man to realise *the way* in which she ran the house. But, there is good in everybody, is there not, if only one can find it? And for some reason, there was something in her which seemed to bring out the best in everybody. Perhaps it was *sunniness*! Mr. Debingham had said only three days ago that there was something sunny about her.

She softened:—really, in a way this was quite a nice sensible young man. She said: "Well, Mr. Hare, if there is anything I *can* do to help, of course——"

"Oh, there is, there is indeed. There are all the curtains, the carpets, the crockery. And how can I be expected to know what are the most practical things to buy!" He looked at her. "You have known me for a good many years now, haven't you? But yet you still call me Mr. Hare. I have often wondered why —and have sometimes felt even a little hurt."

"Well, then—Jonathan!" She smiled. "I was just going for a walk. If you cared to come with me, we might talk over the things you will need. Oh, you will see! I shan't let you be extravagant." She paused and then said: "I am sorry you are going. Anna and I will miss you—yes, we shall certainly miss you. The house will be dull without you."

They walked along in the gold and misty sunset, through the long avenue, until they came to the world of cornfields.

Then Miss Mintley, stopping suddenly, pointed: "Why, what in the world! Look—look!—why, I believe that is Susan Daw. Surely, isn't it? What in the world is she running like that for?"

Like a bright flowering weed blown by the cool wind of evening across the fields and the hedges, there, running across the fields, was Susan Daw. And as she ran, she cried in a high strange voice—the voice of a little ghost that has no home: "I'm free—I'm free—I'm free. . . ."

Chapter XIII

WINTER IS the time for comfort, for good food and warmth, for the touch of a friendly hand and for a talk beside the fire: it is the time for home. It is no season in which to wander the world as if one were the wind, blowing aimlessly along the streets without a place in which to rest, without food and without time meaning anything to one, just as time means nothing to the wind. All that means anything to the wind is beginning and ending. And coldness. But here, in the city's circles of Hell, sunk deep beneath the world-height of the enormous houses, twenty thousand persons creep who have neither friend nor shelter.

All through the day, under the Bedlam's daylights' murderous roar, changing to the enormous Tartarean darkness of a fog, through these deepest circles of Hell all forms of misery loomed and faded, monstrous shapes, their sightless faces turned to the unheeding sky, tapping upon the ground with a hollow noise that seemed to echo down millions of fathoms to the very centre of the ball of the earth. For in this city of universal night, only the blind can see.

Then the fog changed; it was no longer a muffling deadening

thickness, a world-wide chaos, it was another form of night that had suddenly descended upon the city, black, appallingly clear, and cold as the blackness of Hell's day. And in this darkness the palaces appeared even more world-high; the enormous city seemed of black marble and basalt, and even the trees were changed to this.

Sometimes an elegant figure would shine through this night, circling swiftly as if it were a swallow, or floating, a black swan, on the wide water-black marble pavements, and a faint perfume would fall like the first faint flakes of snow. But these beings came from another world, from a universe where there are waterfalls of satin and of velvet, where there are fires like the Midnight Sun. Their faces Chinese from the cold, high cheek-boned, ancient and mysterious, these beings passed by, circling like swallows, floating like black swans, or alighted from motors and stepped into the shops.

Then the universe of beggars rushed towards them, a sea of rags fluttered about them; as the carriages stopped beside the shops, so brightly lighted in the blackness that the windows seemed fountains of jewels, the beggars, their shapes made monstrous by the changing darkness, huge and menacing, appeared from all sides. "These," wrote the man under the black sun, "watching their opportunity, crowded to the sides of the coach, and gave one the most horrible spectacles that ever an European eye beheld."

One woman had a disease, into the wounds of which, into whose unutterable misery "I could easily have crept and covered my whole body." There, in that lulling maternity, whose disease is the symbol of the horror into which we have deformed Nature, one could seek a refuge, even as we creep into the wounds, the diseases of civilisation, and lie at ease there. In the gigantic fog, the shapes of all men were changed, misery loomed larger. "There was a fellow with a wen on his neck, larger than five wool packs, and another with a couple of wooden legs, each about twenty foot high. But the most hateful sight of all was the lice crawling on their clothes; I could see

distinctly the limbs of these vermin with my naked eye. . . .
And their snouts with which they rooted like swine."

In the centre of the city, near the enormous lumbering
palaces of commerce, little smooth people were running to and
fro from the Exchange, running or walking slowly.

But it was in the fashionable quarters, along the wide pavements that were long and hard as Hell's huge polar street,
cold as the universal blackness of Hell's day, that the fluttering
towers of rags and bones were swept—each a universe of
misery, a world of hunger and polar wastes, shut off from all
others. Some were young, and these had nothing between their
one outer covering of rags and their skin, so that it seemed they
had early been made ready for the grave. With those who
were older, it was as if all the nations of the dead with their
million-year-old rags about them, had risen to denounce us.
They had no identity, their faces were extinct. They would
have been sexless, as the dead, were it not that from time to
time we could see that one of these holds a child pressed down
among the fluttering banners of its misery.

Watching the beggars and their despair, in this civilisation
that was made safe by war, the giant from the continent of
darkness wrote: "A child, just dropt from its dam, may be
supported by her milk for a solar year with little other nour-
ishment . . . which the mother may get . . . or the value
in scraps, by her lawful occupation of begging. . . . A young
healthy child well nursed is at a year old a most delicious,
nourishing, and wholesome food. . . . I do therefore humbly
offer it to the public consideration, that of the hundred and
twenty thousand children" (of beggars) "twenty thousand may
be reserved for breed, whereof only one fourth part to be males,
which is more than we allow to sheep, black cattle or swine. . . .
That the remaining hundred thousand may at a year old be
offered in sale to the persons of quality and fortune, through
the kingdom, always advising the mother to let them suck
plentifully in the last month, so as to render them plump and
fit for a good table. . . . I have already computed the charge of

nursing a Beggar's child . . . to be about ten shillings per annum, rags included, and I believe no gentleman would refuse to give ten shillings for a good fat child."

Rag castle after rag castle, the world of beggars was swept along, and night fell upon the two nations who alone inhabit the earth, the rich and the poor.

How far are they divided, those two nations! They speak a different language—that of their opposed necessities; their civilisation, their love, their instincts, even their very smell is unlike; for the thin sour smell that haunts the very poor is no longer like that of the living: it is the smell of a lesser death. So reduced and abased are these two nations by the war and the division between them, so opposed are they, that to the one, love has sunk into a barrennness that contains and seeks no future, that is, indeed, only another form of hatred and the search for possessions, whilst to the other it is a pitiful bulwark against Fear, a provision of future fighters who will be used as a shield against Hunger. Now, as the two nations lie in the night, so small and helpless in the enormous and universal darkness that they seem like the unborn child in its innocent sleep, you would think that the darkness would pity them, seeing them so divided in their weakness. But even the darkness is changed, is no longer maternal and consoling. Only the endless pursuit of nothingness has ceased for a while, the cannibal market is deserted.

.   .   .   .   .

In the night the black houses seemed of such a vast height they must tear the sky, and stretched across them, now that the fog had vanished like a ghost, was a monstrous black bat's wing of evil cloud, sagging like a tarpaulin that is blown by the wind, and ready to drop its weight of darkness upon the world.

At the foot of these black rocking houses hiding emptiness, an aching blackness, were a few benches, and on these sat some of those unrecorded beings who wander the world without one hand they could touch in friendship, who have a name, but there is none to utter it.

It was so late, that only one living being approached them—a young girl who, appearing out of nowhere sat down on one of the benches, timidly and humbly, in the neighbourhood of an old woman who looked like a heap of cobwebs, an oldish man, a youth aged about seventeen, and an undersized boy of fourteen. She looked at them deprecatingly. "Perhaps they'll drive me away, like everyone else," she thought. But they paid no attention to her. Each was his own world—a world of endless hunger and of polar night—and outside it there lay no other. So she took her place among them, and when, the rain began, they huddled up to her, as if she had been something inanimate. At first, the wind drove the black armies of the rain onwards with a tornado's speed, with a hard black clatter like that of armies racing across a plain; sometimes they splashed into the gutters in a ragged company, in tatters like those of the beggars sprawled upon the benches. But now those armies had conquered; it was a universe of rain.

"I can't stand this much longer," said the seventeen-year-old boy. "I'll go and sink myself in the river. After all, that's where I'll be in the long run, and I won't know much difference between that and this. You'd think the rain was a *century* of rain. Christ! It's enough to melt the last flesh from one's bones. It used to be warm once. There was a sun. But never now. God knows what's coming to the world."

His appearance inspired pity and tenderness. His childish face, illuminated by a pair of fiery blue eyes, was young even for his seventeen years, and he had the clumsiness of a growing boy; his hands were enormous and red, and his wrists, for which his sleeves were too short, were very thin and lanky. Those hands were covered with chilblains, and would be for the rest of the short time that remained to him. This was the least mark left upon him by the icy nights he had spent under the railway arches, "stretched out amongst unknown men without age, without feeling," with the ice and snow cutting

106

the heart that had once held the world and the hope of all adventure. He looked as if he must once have had a home, and somebody to speak his name and to care whether he lived or died, but perhaps they were dead now, or had forgotten him. During the lovely summer and the early autumn he had seemed undismayed by fate, though his suit was threadbare, being worn away in places into holes through which the absence of any other clothing might be perceived. And now that the warm September weather was over he had at least, unlike the other wreckage upon the benches, an overcoat, though it was, by now, so "ideal" that it had scarcely any reality left. In his whole appearance he resembled another derelict, also seventeen years old, who, years ago, in just such circumstances, had written:

> *Je m'en allais, les poings dans mes poches crevées;*
> *Mon paletot aussi devenu idéal;*
> *J'allais sous le ciel, Muse, et j'étais ton féal,*
> *O là là, que d'amours splendides j'ai rêvé.*

But now all was changed. Winter had withered hope, and love, and only the cold was left.

The wind tore at the beggars' rags, and the older man uttered a faint sound—echoing it, defying it—who knows? Then a moan broke from him. "O-o-oh! What have we done? What have we done? What have we done? That we should have been thrown down into Hell? Night after night! Week after week, month after month, year after year. . . . How many moments go to an hour, how many hours go to a night, how many nights go to a year, how many years go to a life? And every night an eternity of cold."

"Why don't they bury us?" the boy said. "Oh, why don't they bury us? It'd be warmer there."

"Hell. Eternal cold."

"What's Hell?" asked the undersized child beside him. Raising his face, white as a fish's belly, he dragged his clothes

107

that had the colour, consistency, and shapelessness of mud, closer round him. They seemed, indeed, a part of the slimy mud of the river, as if it had already engulfed him. "Jee-e-eze!" he said. "If only the war is still on, when I am eighteen, or a bit bigger, I'll join the army, quick as a knife, and go out to fight. Plenty to eat out there! They feed you prime—else you couldn't do the fighting. I'm too small, that's what 'inders me. They won't so much as look at you when yer my size and can't *show* yer eighteen. And much chance you get to grow in a life like this."

The old woman from under the ancient tomb-dust of her bonnet and hair chuckled. For many years now she had blown along the windy empty streets like a black and filthy cobweb waving in the draught of some dusty window. There were summer days, though, when this aged cobweb enjoyed the open air, warm days when she was suspended gratefully on a bench under the dark trees. In an untidy parcel by her side, lay huddled a few useless memories. No piece of fluff or dusty nothingness that had ever come into her possession had been allowed to leave it again, unless she had been able to sell it. Two photographs, taken in summer against a background of a bright sea, a piece of stale bread, a bit of moth-eaten fur that would fit no particular niche, either neck or wrist, and that seemed as if it could never have been part of any particular animal, these were her treasures. And in the lovely summer days when her bones felt warm, sitting alone on a bench under a tree, she would open the parcel and count her riches to be sure they had not escaped her, touching her possessions and looking long and searchingly at the fading meaningless faces in the two photographs, pondering over them.

Now, hearing the boy's voice, she chuckled. "Hah!" she said. "Go on, you silly. What, go out *there*? They give you plenty to eat, do they, feed you prime? What would be the use of that to *you*? You can't eat if you haven't got a mouth to eat with, can you? My boy, 'e came back from France three years ago; 'e'd got a name, and 'e'd got a number, but 'e 'adn't
108

got a face, an' 'is girl left 'im. What's the good of a name that don't mean anyfing, and a number that don't mean anyfing? It's yer face you kiss with: and they lose their faces out there! . . . No, lad! Better give yer bones to the rats. You'd be feeding something, any'ow. It's life of a sort."

"Well, there is plenty of that life out there," said the older boy. "And if it goes on much longer, it will be the only life left."

"I've often wondered," said the thin man, who had obviously once known a very different life from this, "what the universe would be like if it were ruled over by rats. After all, they don't betray each other (excepting when they are driven by starvation, and then brother will destroy brother, just as if they were men, destroy in order to grow fat), they have the instinct for preserving their species, and they foretell danger and fly from it, unlike mankind."

"It's an idea, anyhow," said the older boy.

"Chaw!" said the old woman. "What's the good of *ideas*? That's what's brought the world to *this*. Wind in the stomach, instead of food—that's what ideas are."

"My fingers ache," said the child suddenly, "the cold it is. Making them ache through the bone. I think I'll be *losing* me 'ands. The cold'll 'ave them."

"What'd they give us hands for?" asked another tattered creature who had joined the group. "They're no use now, there's nothing to make, and no food to lift to our mouths. Animals don't need fingers. One pretence at a thumb and a block is enough. D'you know what I think the world wants? It wants us to eat without hands—when there's no work for us to do with 'em, no more ammunition to make—sink our mouths on to the earth and crop what grows there—like the beasts!"

"No wonder," said the elder boy, "they say we're like wolves."

"We ought to 'ave been given fur, like them, all over our bodies, to keep us warm. And we ought to 'ave been put down

109

on all fours, so as to be nearer to the earth, so as to sink into it easier. Christ, the way is long, with a skeleton made like ours!"

Two sluggish tears crept down the child's face. "What's the good of it all? What's the good of anything?"

There was a pause. Then: "Where are you going to?" the older man asked him.

"How should I know! Coming from nowhere, and going nowhere. Like everybody and everything else. Christ! I wish that the world would end."

"Perhaps it *has* ended," said the man.

Chapter XIV

IN THE empty sky, the sun in its dirty brown and white bird-skin dress of cloud, hung like a skull with a dull yellow face of clay moulded upon its bones, to hide where the real face rotted away; and on that unreal face, one red plague spot brayed.

Under the phantom sun, the immense city seemed as silent and as deserted as if it had been laid waste by the Plague. Vast ribs of shade lay across the waste, like the ribs of some gigantic derelict skeleton. There was no life, there was no sound. But presently the dead will come once more to fill the streets, and when these reach the cannibal market for the daily sale and barter of souls and hearts and hands and tongues, a mask will be worn across the bones, so that none may see the marks of the Plague from which they died—the belief in an unhearing heaven or in mankind, the rage for life, devouring the bone with a tigerish fire, the grief that has shrunken the heart to dust, the shapeless worm-soft unshaping sin.

The city seemed an enormous plain, deserted excepting by

hordes of black and wolfish creatures, eaten to the bone by the cold, who roamed from place to place, seeking for a crust, for shelter. All these great lumbering palaces, these warehouses and marts, and not one place where they might shelter, not one!

At four o'clock, Susan, with the sleeping beggars, had been turned off the bench on which they sat huddled together, and for the rest of the night she had walked aimlessly about the streets, with the cold invading her bones, her blood. But now she sat down once more, on a wide parapet. Behind her, the river crept darkly onwards to the wide sea; and beyond the seas were horizons where the suns rise over strange lands, and there all adventure and all hope may lie. But that is far beyond sight, and beyond sound. Susan said to herself, as she rose to her feet again: "There is no wind to help me along. Dependent upon myself. That's what *I* am."

Carts were rumbling along the streets, doors were opening. Soon the cannibal market would be astir.

She wondered why she had this strange feeling of limpness, as if her body were not made of flesh and blood and bones at all, but of rags. "I'm like one of them rag dolls one sees," she thought. And she suddenly had a vision of herself turning into one of those terrible girls she had seen, with their rag faces painted like Hell's fires and their empty poll parrot voices, standing at the top of the easy steps of a slum, lolling down—down—down.

Could it really be only six months since she had run away from her mother's cottage and come to London? How many lives, she wondered, can one live through in six months? Yes, it had been August then, and now it was February. . . . At first she had found a little work to do, here and there, doorsteps to clean, papers to deliver, and so she had managed to exist. But now there was no work; there had been none for some time. She had gone into a munition factory, but there had been an explosion, and now that was shut down. And she had had to spend all the money Sir Henry and Miss Mintley

111

had given her on her birthdays. All—excepting twopence. "I can't write and ask Miss Mintley for help," she thought. "I can't!" But she was completely destitute; nothing was left but her misery and Jim's few letters. "Do not forget me," he said. "Do not forget me." Over and over again. Just that—nothing more; and it was as if her memory of him was all that could show him he was still living. "It is so cold here—so cold. Oh, Susan, if only I had your kiss to warm me!" He seemed to be walled up and imprisoned in the ice of the polar night. Even his words had no warmth now, and Susan thought: "If I could go to him and give him my kiss—he would not feel it. It would not warm him." Week by week, his letters came to the post office where they had arranged he should send them, but they were all the same. She did not feel he was really there. Nothing was left now but want, like a cruel rat eating down to the heart. Soon the heart, too, would be gone; but even then, want would not desert her; it would remain, gnawing there, till no flesh was left on the bones, till there was neither hope, nor memory, nor, at last, even the will to die.

All day long she crept from place to place, in the slums, between the swollen thick houses, or the bellying houses like fouled nightgowns blown this way and that by nothingness that seemed a wind. She wandered beneath the huge lumbering palaces of commerce, and the streets lined with small shops, and at the doors of these shops she asked, in a timid voice, if there was any work to be done. "I'd do it," she said, "just for my food." But hardly anyone seemed to hear her voice. Or if they answered, they did not look at her. "Perhaps," she said to herself, "they can't even see me now!" She was beginning, had she but known it, to have the faceless appearance that dead misery wears, a look as if no record is left of the soul within. She was so desperate that, in a lonely street, meeting a lady walking alone, she had stolen up to her and spoken. . . . "I'm terrible hungry," she said. The lady had a kind face, she thought, but when Susan spoke to her she paid no attention.

112

Then Susan looked at her again, and realised that she was stone deaf. "She thinks I'm asking the way to somewhere," she said to herself; "all the city seems like that. Deaf, that's what the city is."

She seemed to have walked for miles. . . . Why was she walking like this? She'd got nowhere to go. Still, you never know your luck, do you? . . . Perhaps.

And then at one eating-house into which she had gone, there had been an old man with an enormous face like the figurehead of a ship, and white hair like the crest of a wave. He had given her a cup of coffee and a doughnut, and had said to her: "You meet me here to-night at ten o'clock, Missy, and I'll let you into the yard where I work. There are two taxis there, and you can kip down in one and get a bit of a sleep. The Boss is a good-natured sort of chap—he won't mind. He knows a pore soul with paralysis sleeps in one of them taxis every night, so's to save him from the streets, but 'e turns a blind eye, pretends 'e's not noticing anything. I'll just come along with you, so's to make sure you get in the right one. You don't want poor old Gentleman George giving you a start when 'e comes 'ome. *H*ome," he added, aspirating the h with violence. "That's what he calls the taxi. But if you *should* see 'im, 'e won't do you no 'arm. It's only 'e's a bit startling to look at."

Now, as the clock struck a quarter to ten, she walked along the Embankment, towards the street near the Strand, towards the eating-house where she was to meet her new friend. "Only two streets more," she said to herself.

Then, as she walked along, a monstrous and grotesque figure appeared before her, like an embodiment of Death. Through the night, whose blackness seemed to have a noise like thunder or the rolling of a million drums, this effigy, this sinister marionette, was making his way to his nightly home, the taxi in which he was allowed to sleep—he who had once lived in one of those lumbering palaces of darkness that loomed above him. Now nothing remained to remind him of those

113

past days of riches, excepting a battered and ancient top-hat, perched jauntily on the side of his shaking, eternally grinning skull, to which a few strands of rope-like, rotting black hair still clung; his drum-taut skin was stretched tightly across his face and this, too, twitched as the bunches of capering, prancing nerves urged him onward in his endless dance. His frame shook as if it were in the grasp of some huge machine, his legs, like those of a gigantic marionette skeleton, jerked out from under him in his violent yet slippery dance; sometimes, indeed, they flew wide apart as if he did not know which part of the earth or which roaring and gibbering pleasure must draw him. Yet his balance seemed controlled by some infernal force that would not let him sink into the abyss too easily.

So, through the immensity of the night and the city, he passed with a gait which seemed to drag his nights and days after it. And his body looked as if it had been shattered and dispersed in the thousand whispering alcoves where, companioned through the thick night and murky days by an endless procession of ventriloquists' dolls—(rag faces, fathomless black holes for eyes and mouths, nothing living about them excepting their ceaseless dance, their smile like a gap into Hell)—he had begun that perpetual movement, growing ever faster and faster, until in the end, with this, the epitome of their lives, they had sealed him their own, had made him their ghost.

Ghosts have no money. They have no home. The real ghost has lost even the place of its haunting.

And the beggars on the Embankment watched him go by in silence.

. . . . .

She had always known that Jim would be waiting for her at the end of the lane, where they had met ever since they were small children. They had met there when they were going to school together, and when they had a holiday and were going out to pick wild flowers, and when she had had to climb down through the branches of the tree that grew outside her window, in order to escape from her father.

And now he was waiting for her there in the blue dusk where the honeysuckle grew in the hedges, gathering up all the sweetness of the dusk and holding it in its long fingers. She would see him soon, with the sun of evening shining upon him; and then the sun would sink and the skies would be all golden with flowers and dew, like the buttercup fields in which they had walked together when they were children. He had come all the way from over the sea to meet her and take her to the country fair. And now there was nothing to keep them from each other. Her father and mother had gone away without leaving a word, so that she did not know where they had gone, she only knew that they had gone for ever, and that Jim and she would walk together along the wide gold roads of evening in the blue dusk; they would be together now till the end of the world.

Yes, there he was, standing at the cross roads, smiling. It was just as if they had never been parted. He stretched out his arms to her. "Jim, Jim," she cried. "My Jim! My heart that is in your breast has brought you home to me. You could never be lost to me, Jim—never—never! My heart would come to me like a homing bird. It would bring you home."

But the being at the cross-roads did not answer. He only looked at her.

Then . . . Oh, God! It wasn't Jim. It wasn't Jim. It was Death—the effigy and ghost of Death.

With a clattering as if a million bones had been upheaved from the tombs of the dead, and swept together by the wind that heralds an earthquake—with a rattling and quaking as if those bones from a thousand different ages had been bound together by the growing hurricane, and were trying to escape, one from another—this world's confession, this figurehead before the procession of all the sins crashed from the sky, crushing her beneath it.

And scream after scream broke from her lips.

But still the effigy lay. Gentleman George, finding his way home for the last time, held her fast in his last and most cold embrace.

Chapter XV

THE SNOW, fading on the boughs that grew outside the windows, seemed now a faint perfume, now a dying sound, as if a rose had changed into a ghost, a ghost turned to a perfume on the leaves. But under the pine trees, where the dying strawberry leaves had a dim perfume, the snow seemed dark green as these, and it was piled into shapes like haycocks. It was here that, while the daylight lasted, Anna fed the birds that floated under the branches like clouds—a rosy cloud of bullfinches, tiny blue-tits like the mist in a winter forest, wood-doves like the first cloud in spring, and dark clouds of thrushes, and blackbirds. But when night came, and the full moon of February spilled its sparkles—rubies and sapphires—on the window-sill, they would flock round the windows and Anna, looking out through the leaves in a dress that was the colour of violet-blue cinerarias, would feed them there.

Now she was walking with Jonathan in the dark green snow and the strawberry leaves under the pine boughs, where the cold air seemed to have died. And, as they walked, a rosy cloud of bullfinches descended on the strawberry leaves. "Look, Jonathan," she said, "are not their feathers just the colour of the firelight shining on the snow round the eaves?"

It was the first time she had seen Jonathan since his return from London, where he had made a stay of a fortnight. "I am glad to be at home again," he said. "You are still feeding the birds, I see, Anna. Oh, by the way, Patrick is bringing you, or rather Becky, a new one, but for the house, not the pine wood. Last night I went to put some coals on the fire after he had gone to bed, and there I found a poor linnet he has brought back for her; it cost him sixpence, and is as tame as a dormouse. I believe he does not know he is a bird; where you put him, there he stands, and seems to have neither hope nor fear; I suppose in a week he will die of melancholy."

"Oh, we will see that he doesn't do that," she answered. "We'll feed him and cosset him and talk to him and cheer his spirits. He'll soon feel he is among friends—you'll see! And when spring comes, he'll be happier. This morning, I found the first red bud on the japonica that grows against the house. It will soon be spring." And she added: "I could never have believed that we have been here for a month already. Could you, Jonathan? I never thought for a moment that we should really come. I felt sure that Becky would find every sort of reason why we shouldn't, and would have made objection after objection. But no! There was scarcely one. A few forebodings perhaps, and an owl-like prognostication or two, but nothing serious. How *did* you manage it? You must have bewitched her!"

He laughed. "Oh, it was quite easy. For one thing, she knows that I really like her, and value her, although she finds me inattentive to the details of her conversation. And she seems perfectly happy here, arranging this house and mine. She feels she is really necessary to someone, for the first time in her life. And she has a warm heart, you know. That fireless existence of hers on the outskirts of other people's lives must have been very hard to bear—and you, Anna—are you happy, too? Confess, now, that you are, in spite of your sulkiness, when you arrived."

Anna thought of the evening when, after a long journey, a seemingly endless drive through the winter landscape, she had seen, for the first time, the house in which she would spend the rest of her life. "Look, Becky," she had said, "doesn't it seem like a great bird from here, a tall bird like a heron; it looks as

117

if it had grey feathers!" But her heart was beating so wildly that the words seemed muffled, even to her own ears.

The days before she had left the house in the forest had passed so quickly that there was scarcely time for all the things that must be done. There were the people whom she had known all her life and to whom she must say good-bye—Mrs. Noon, for instance, and all the cottagers on the estate. There had been many memories, small things that bound her to her childhood, to which she must say farewell—books that she had had as a child—and there was the schoolroom where she had first seen Jonathan. A part of her life was gone, as if it had never existed. And in the evening before she left, sitting in the library, she had felt, suddenly, as if she were an old, old woman. She thought, "I am only nineteen. But my youth is gone for ever."

But the next morning, driving with Becky by the ermine bells of the foam, the soft winter flower-bells of the seas, this feeling vanished, and a new life filled her. The whole of her past existence, everything she had known and cared for—all excepting Becky, who was her friend, and Jonathan, who was her whole world, had been left behind. But what was the rest worth? And to-day, this very day, after several months of separation, she would see Jonathan. She would know what it meant to him that she had come.

Now, as the door was opened and she walked into the hall, almost she stretched out her hands. She had known from the moment their journey started, that Jonathan would be waiting for her. He would be there, looking out of the window, waiting to hear the sound of the wheels. But nobody stepped to meet her from the shadows, no voice spoke her name. Only the coldness of the empty house enwrapped her. She had had to sit down on the large chest in the hall for a moment, to recover herself, for the sound of the beating of her heart was so loud she felt as if she were drowning. Then she asked, in a quiet voice, "Are there any letters?"

He was not there, and something must have kept him. But

of course there would be a letter—there could not be a doubt about that. Yet in a moment the maid came back, saying, "No, there is nothing for you, Miss." There was not a sign, not a hint that he had remembered that this was the day when she would arrive. "Perhaps," she thought, "he has been too busy, and will ride over later, or at least will send some word." But night fell, and there was still no sign from him. And her heart sank. He had forgotten. It meant nothing to him— nothing at all, that she had come. And all that night she scarcely slept.

Then next day, just as Becky and she had finished luncheon, he appeared. There he was, standing in the doorway, smiling, just as if nothing had happened—as if he had seen her only yesterday. He said: "Did you have a nice home-coming, Anna? And will you and Becky admit I am not so unpractical after all, in spite of everything you have said? Just see how much trouble I have taken to find you a house." Then looking at her: "Why, Anna!" he exclaimed. *"You sulky!* It is the first time since I have known you that I have seen you like this!"

"Oh, Jonathan," she said. "Everything would have been perfect. Only—I *did* think—all day long I had been hoping that if you really couldn't come—(and oh, how I longed to find you here)—that there would at least have been a letter from you, even if it had been only a few words, telling me that you were glad I had come. It would have meant so much to me!"

He laughed and pressed her arm. "My dear child," he said, "you make too much of little things. That is not the way I want my Anna to think. You must be above small things like that. They don't matter!"

Then, seeing her face still unchanged, he added: "As a matter of fact, Anna, I did not come for that very reason. You attach far too much importance to things that don't count— that are of no moment—like this, for instance. And I want to cure that in you—I *must*, if we are to live side by side. And that is why I did not come."

Her face, which was lowered, was very pale. Looking at her, he thought: "You mistake me, Anna. You want me to be subject to the same impulses, perform the same weak, small and tender actions as all men. You mistake us—beings like myself. We are not men. We are some kind of monstrous creation, giants upheaved out of a rough, difficult and terrible earth. Have you ever dreamed of the lives we have lived, enclosed in our experience? Of the life before birth—the change from the worm's shape, the necessities of the worm to those of the fish, then to the likeness of the embryonic ape, dog, horse? Yes, the worm, the ape, the dog, the horse—we are all brothers before our birth. But only we, of all men born, remember that time. We have undergone the experience of all forms and strata of life—only made gigantic, and pullulating under a huge sun. Where should tenderness lie—on such an earth, under such a sun? And in me, who am condemned by the fate that lies ahead of me, to bury it in my heart through all the days of my life?" He shrugged his shoulders. "Little tendernesses!" he said to her. "Small marks of consideration! They are for small men, Anna. But that is what women want; that is all they care for. They know nothing of the vastness of life, and they care nothing; they are incapable of a great conception." His voice died away wearily. Then, "Yes," he said, "small tendernesses are what you want. And I think that you, Anna, yes, even you, would rather have the love, the little blind and perishable tenderness of a small man than the cold undying truth of a giant."

This was a month ago, and now, walking with him in the dark green snow under the pine trees, she said: "I am so happy that you have come. I have been waiting for this all those cold winter days while you were in London. And now we shall have the whole evening together—the long winter evening."

They had left the shadow of the pines and were walking in the open; snow was in the air and the clouds hung down their dull blunt ropes into windless space, but only a few unripe flakes of snow were falling. Their faces flat and Chinese in the
120

ancient cold, they were walking now, where, on the tall trees, the slanting buds were marked like the legs of a stork—one could imagine the delicate plumage that would soon break from them. Anna paused for a moment and listened. "Someone is riding along the lane," she said. "That will be William." Jonathan answered: "He said he might be coming over to-day. Anna, be a good girl and run into the house and tell Carson to show him straight out here. I want to have a few words with him alone, and I'll bring him into the house as soon as we have finished."

Presently, William Ayrton appeared, walking in his usual hurried, flurried way; but when he saw who was waiting for him, the half-timid, half-eager smile on his face changed. His plain face now bore a hurt and bewildered look, rather like that of a child who has suddenly been repulsed by an elder whom he had trusted.

Jonathan, ignoring the look, hailed him with obvious pleasure, putting out a hand to pat the young man's shoulder; but William withdrew his arm, and once again that wounded, puzzled look appeared on his face. Quite unembarrassed, and looking at him frankly, Jonathan said in a voice that was half joking, half affectionate: "Well, William, I received your letter, but only yesterday, because, as you know, I was away, and the fools forgot to forward it. I must say, old man, that I was a little surprised by the tone of it—it is the last letter in the world I should have expected to receive from you. I had thought we were friends."

"We *were* friends," said William, in a low voice, and without looking at him.

By now, they were walking once more under the pine trees, and Jonathan, stopping for a moment, rubbed his feet, which were covered with snow, in a little heap of pine-needles. "*Were!*" he said. "Still are, as far as I am concerned—though you call me unfriendly, unkind, and unaccountable. Frankly, William, there is more unaccountability in your letter's little finger than there is in my whole body. You are full of mysterious

121

hints"—in a still more joking voice—"about something to which I have no clue whatever—excepting that they point to the fact that you think I have some hidden design and that you have found it out: you say that my letter had the effect on you that you imagine I wish it to have, and you are amazed when you think about the cause. . . ." And he laughed.

Now William looked at him, and his plain, rather naïve face, that could never disguise one thought or one feeling, said: "That *you*, of all men in the world, should have done what you have done—that it should be *you* who have so deceived me." But he did not speak. Jonathan went on: "Well, I might, with reason, if I chose, pretend not to have an idea of what you are hinting at, but that would be so foolish that I shall do nothing of the sort." Then stopping for a moment in his walk, that he might give more emphasis to what he was saying, he continued: "No, really your letter was very strange. I don't pretend to understand it. Of course, everyone knows that Anna and I have been friends for years—great and dear friends, I have no greater. She is certainly by far the most delightful woman I know—sensitive, intelligent, with a real mind, although she is so young. I've never met anyone who was a better talker or who had more common sense and was a better judge of people and things. But honestly, William, I was astonished to find that for *one instant* you could have thought that I should wish to stand in your way! I can't conceive what has put it into your head—either that I should wish to, or that my friendship with her could be any barrier between you.

"I am not so selfish," he went on, "as to want to stand in the way of her making a happy marriage if it comes to that—no matter how much I should miss her companionship." And he thought of her with tenderness. Poor Anna, poor little child, condemned to the desert. His heart contracted with pity. Then, once again, he remembered the fate that was in store for him. There had been little warning signs—that was all. But it was enough. And he saw once more the bulk upon the chair, the old madman his uncle, as he had last seen him, after the tempest of madness had died down, leaving nothing but a block of flesh —motionless, speechless. He saw the hurricane of furious madness that had preceded that fearful calm. Yes, he knew what lay before him—what he would be! And how could he sacrifice his Anna, the only being for whom, in all his life, he had felt tenderness, from whom he had known real love, to that? Better, he said to himself, that she should die in the desert, or die of cold. Yet he could not, he would not, let her go from him. That, he told himself, could not be necessary. Why was the only being who could hold a cup of water to his lips in that burning waste, to be taken from him? He knew her well. If he were blind, she would be his eyes. If the beat of the giant's heart stopped, she would take hers from her breast to beat in his, till the giant's work was accomplished. It was her hand alone that could withhold him from the brink of the waiting, watching world of madness that lay silent below him, till the moment came when it would rise to engulf him. She was, to him, his humanity, the drop of human blood among the lion's blood in his veins. And now William, with his love that was that of the world of men, would take her from him!

But it would be better to hide his suffering, and not, by revealing it, enhance the value of the prize.

Walking up and down under the pine trees, where the dying strawberry leaves sent up their sweet dim smell, like that of violets, he saw, now, that William was about to speak, and taking the words out of his mouth, he said sharply: "No! Let me go on! I can only imagine that you must have misunderstood the nature of the feeling I have for her—and, no doubt, the whole situation between us—her coming to Ireland, for instance. Well, I daresay that in a way it is only natural. You are in love with her yourself, and so you think that every other man in the world must be in love with her too. So I had better tell you what my exact feelings are. As I think I have told you before, if I had wanted to marry, and *if* I had been well enough off to do so, I would certainly rather have married Anna than anyone else in the world, because, for one thing, I

123

enjoy talking to her more than I do to anyone else. But that is as far as I have ever gone. And to return to what I said before, I am unable to conceive how you can have got it into your head that this could interfere with you in any way. I must confess—(it is getting colder, William, you had better walk a little more briskly)—that at one time I *did* think that for your own sake it would be inadvisable if you married her; (marriage *is* a drag on a man, it is certainly easier to get on in the world if one is single than if one has a wife); nor did I think you were sufficiently well off to live in comfort if you were married; but those objections are done away with now that you have come into this money."

Here he paused, and walked along in silence. He was thinking: "Small tenderness. Yes, she will weigh my light against his love, and choose—as all women choose." He smiled at William and said: "And it is true, too, that I thought it would be better if you did not speak to Anna herself, until I had sounded her—or sounded Becky on the subject."

"And have you?" asked William in a low voice, looking at him again.

"My dear old man," with a laugh, "of course I have."

Again that confused, half ashamed, half hurt look overspread William's face. "You only have to see any of my letters to Anna," Jonathan continued, "and you will see the kind of friend I have been to you. Naturally I have been careful not to take too much on myself, in the way of actually *urging* her to marry you, because I didn't want to be blamed if anything went wrong. But I did go so far as to say to Becky that people were beginning to talk, and that I thought it would do Anna no good if, now that the matter has gone so far, it went no further."

Patting William's shoulder again, he said: "And now, William, if you are really serious about this, you will certainly need to find out what is her exact income. One must be practical, after all, even if one *is* in love. So I'll find out, and let you know." He sighed. "I envy you, William—I do indeed. You have the kind of nature that can bear peace and quietness and

124

domestic life. You will settle down and be perfectly happy. Now, mine is exactly the reverse, and it has been the curse of my life. I can settle nowhere—all I have in my life are the good wishes and empty promises of a government that is falling to pieces. And as far as I can see, their lives and mine will be over before they have carried out a single promise, or done anything whatsoever to help me. And then Anna complains that I am bad-tempered. Can you wonder?" And he laughed again; but his eyebrows were level and sullen.

He looked up at the house; the curtains were not yet drawn, and he could see the drowsy glow of the fire in one of the rooms, shining on the snow, making it rosy-soft as the feathers of the clouds of bullfinches that Anna had been feeding on the strawberry beds.

Then, after a moment's silence, he looked at his watch. He said: "If you are going into the house, William, tell them to bring my horse round to the garden gate, there's a good chap. I won't disturb Anna by coming in to say good-bye."

Chapter XVI

SUSAN had never thought it would be possible to love any lady so much as she loved Mrs. Sinding. But then, no lady had ever before been so kind and so beautiful at the same time. So she thought as in the green night that seemed like a dark wood with the peaceful airs—with the full moon shining into the room and on her white dress, she ran backwards and forwards from her room to her lady's, letting fall drifts and soundless flakes of snow, her lady's linen that had been mended and must be put away in the cupboard.

She had been with Mrs. Sinding for four, nearly five months, and it seemed to her that she had never known any other life, excepting her life with Jim. Those terrible nights in London —the most fearful night of all—how far away they seemed! She could remember very little, only screams sounding from frozen lips, and then a noise of shouting and of heavy footsteps. The police had come—that she remembered. One had called out, "Hold hard, missie." Then they had tried to lift the dead man from where he had fallen. After that, the next thing she remembered was a middle-aged woman rubbing her feet, and someone giving her coffee. She was shaking and trembling, and they said to her, "Now, my dear, you must try to get to sleep." And they covered her with a blanket. But she couldn't sleep because she was so frightened. The dead man was coming back, she could see him dragging his days and nights after him in his appalling dance, just as she had seen him when he was making his way home. And then, too, she was frightened because they had told her she was at the police-station, and Mr. Daw had instilled in her a wholesome distrust of the police, who, he said, had been put on this earth for the purpose of persecuting sensible self-supporting people, and preventing them from getting a comfortable living. Still, they had been kind to her. They had said to her: "No need to be frightened. The poor creature didn't mean to hurt you. Didn't even know you were there, come to that."

"What—what happened? Oh, where is he?"

The policemen looked at each other. "Well, miss," said one, hesitating slightly, "as a matter of fact he's dead. He was dead before he touched you—fell on to you. But there was nothing to be frightened of. He was a poor harmless sort of chap." He added: "It's as well he's dead. It was a dreadful way of living."

Next morning, they gave her a good breakfast, and then a lady with a brisk, practical, red-brick semi-detached appearance and manner, walked into the room where Susan was sitting, and asked what her name was.

"Susan, ma'am."

"Yes, but Susan what?"

"Susan Daw."

"Where do you come from?"

No answer.

"But, Susan, you *must* tell me. I've been sent here to find out."

Still no answer. Susan's body was rigid, and the pupils of her eyes were black and dilated.

"You can't sleep out as you have been doing, you know, my child," said the lady, after a moment's pause. "Simply anything might happen to you. Surely you *have* a home? Why don't you want to tell me where you come from, so that I can let your mother know? Then she could come and fetch you as soon as the inquest is over. You'll have to answer a few questions at that, of course."

Susan's body grew still more rigid. She said in a whisper: "If she *does* come to fetch me away, I'll—I'll kill myself. I won't go back to that. I *won't*. . . . Beatings . . . all the day long."

"I see," said the lady, thoughtfully. "You ran away. Ill-treated you, did they?"

Susan nodded, her lips pressed together.

"I ain't doing no harm to no one," she said, at last, her hands pressed tightly to her sides, her shoulders arched, her back against the wall. "All I want is to get over *there*. That's what I'm here for. Just waiting me chance," and she added: "I'll be no trouble. No trouble to anyone at all."

"Over there! Do you mean to France?"

"Yes, 'm. To my Jim. He's all I've got, and I'm all he's got —'cepting his mother. His dad's turned on him—along of me. Known him since I was five years old, I have. And him seven. Born side by side we were. Oh, when I think of him out there, I nearly go mad. Oh, I nearly go mad. I'm so frightened. He didn't *want* to go, mum. He's only a country boy—growing things is all he cares for. He can't make out what it's 'all about —none of them can, come to that. There was one young German they took prisoner. Wounded he was. He could speak a few

127

words of English and Jim a few words of German he'd learnt from the prisoners. And Jim asks him what the war's about. 'I don't know,' says the German. 'Because the English wanted to go and take Germany, I suppose.' 'No,' says Jim, 'that's what the Germans wanted to do to England.' Wounded, he was, and used to cry sometimes like a little child: Jim says it were dreadful to hear him. And then he died. Died—and him not knowing what any of it was about. He was a carpenter, he told Jim, and carpentering was all he cared for outside his mother and his girl. He did want to go back to his carpentering. Made such beautiful things, he did."

The lady was very kind; she sat by Susan's side when she had to answer questions at the inquest; and when it was all over, she wrote to Miss Mintley, and Miss Mintley and she, together, succeeded in getting a place for Susan as maid to Mrs. Sinding, who was a first cousin of Mr. Hare, whom Susan used to see when she still lived at home.

Susan had hardly been able to believe what had happened to her. She was not happy, of course: how could she be, with Jim out there, always cold, and her terror making her even colder than him. How could you be happy when your heart is not in your breast, but in the breast of another—and he far away?

Every time there was a knock at the door, she felt as if she were going to die, and into her eyes came that look of blackness that had been there when her father and mother approached. Her hand would fly to her throat. But Mrs. Sinding soothed her. She said the war would be over soon—must be!

It was the first time in all her life that she had slept in a comfortable bed, with smooth linen; it was like lying on a drift of snowdrops. And excepting when she had gone up to tea in the housekeeper's room, or with Mrs. Noon, before Jim's dad had begun to hate her, she had never had proper food before. But here, there was delicious food, and you were allowed plenty of time in which to eat it. Nobody shouted at you in a rough voice: "Now, Susan, eating again! Hurry up and get on with your work."

There was a good deal to do, though, and she was glad of this, because, though she could never forget her terror, her work kept her steady, prevented her hands from shaking the whole time. Now, putting away the drifts of muslin and curd-soft silk, she thought that one seemed just like a waterfall; she almost expected to hear it splash as she folded it; and there was a checked muslin that looked as if lines of summer rain were crossing the cool and darkened air. Miss Burnet, the old dressmaker who was sometimes employed by Mrs. Sinding, had come to help Susan make them up, for Susan was clever with her needle. Poor Miss Burnet! She had sat among the shades in Susan's room looking just like a bear in a forest, with her cross brown face and little curranty eyes and her thick dull hair growing so low on her forehead. She had too, a grumbling voice like a bear, and a thick padded way of walking, due to the fact that her feet were always wadded in bedroom slippers. She suffered from her feet, she informed Susan. But then she suffered from everything—nothing made her cheerful excepting the cups of tea to which she resorted every hour or so, and the occasional mention of another elderly dressmaker to whom she always referred as "my friend," as though one could only have one friend. She had known her friend for nearly fifty years, and there was no one else, now, in her life, to whom she could talk easily, for her friend was the only person who could disentangle the mixed threads of her grumblings. Everyone else belonging to her was dead, and her "boy" (she still thought of him as this) had left her forty years ago, taking with him all her and her mother's savings.

Miss Burnet stayed in the house for about three weeks helping Susan to make up the dresses; and she made a lot of extra work; but it was obviously such a treat to her to be waited on, to have a cup of tea brought her in the morning before she got up, and to have a second person to grumble to, that Susan did not mind the extra trouble a bit.

So her days passed, in sewing and mending, and listening to Miss Burnet, and shopping for her lady, and she knew that she

Es   129 must really love Mrs. Sinding, because, when she looked into the shop windows and saw the silks and the dresses, she never thought: "*I* would like to have that!" She thought: "How I would love for Mrs. Sinding to have that. Wouldn't she look just beautiful in it."

Mrs. Sinding was a young widow, and had nobody to consider but herself; and Susan thought she could not have been very happy, for she never mentioned her husband; there were no photographs of him to be seen, and she felt she would not have been able to bear Mr. Sinding if she had known him. Her lady told her that when the war was over, and Jim came home, she would take him as gardener, and Susan could still be her maid. And when Jim came home on leave—he was due for leave in a little over a week—he must come and stay at her house in London on his way through to see his mother.

Susan could scarcely believe that in only a little over a week she would be seeing him. And she felt sure the war must end then, so that they would never be parted again. For, as she said to herself, "We must have been meant to be together for always; that's why we were born side by side—so we'll not go wandering over the earth all our lives seeking each other and not knowing what we are seeking, and not feeling the heat of the sun or the light of the moon and the stars, because we are not together."

Chapter XVII

IT HAD been a very hot day. The huge gold sun, drinking up the white heat-mist of early morning, drinking up the mist left over from the night dew on the bright sheened fruit, drinking up all the water from the broad flat leaves that enclosed the kitchen garden, had the whole earth beneath its sway. Great roads of gold stretched to the end of the world; you felt that at any moment the being you most longed to see and had dreamed that you would never see again, would come walking along those roads towards you, just as he used to do.

Noon had gone over to a flower-show at Strawby, ten miles away. He was showing spoils from all his green world: melons with gold waves of honey dancing in them like a bright sea, late peas like great emeralds in their green hiding-place, early figs like Fortunatus's purse of gold, vegetable marrows in their green baize leaves. Presently—nearer seven than six it would be—he would come running into the kitchen like a wind—(he always ran, if he could, instead of walking)—and would want his late tea. But until then, Mrs. Noon had the house to herself.

She had declined to go with him to the show, on the score of having too much to do about the house. She wanted, she said, to give the kitchen a thorough turning-out, for there would not be much time to do that when Jim came home on leave. And then there was the boy's bedroom to be cleaned, too. There was a lot to be done, and heat or no heat, she would have to do it. But as she scrubbed the kitchen floor and polished the range, she thought of the days when she would have given up anything in the world to go to a flower-show with Noon—those days long ago when she had loved him. How could everything have changed so much? When she looked at him now, she did not really see him. He was just—well, just a person like everybody else, a private world enclosed in himself, a separate planet, millions of miles apart from her in space.

It was only a year ago, on the dreadful day when Jim went to the war, and his dad fell into that terrible rage with him because he had stopped out all night with that girl, it was only then that she realised the reason for all this. She no longer loved him.

But he would never know that. He would never have the least inkling of the truth. He would never guess that lying by his side, every night, was a stranger, that a stranger sat down beside him at his meals, prepared them, mended his clothes. Even if she should say to him: "Noon, I no longer

131

love you. . . . Your selfishness, even in what you believe is your love, selfishness and self-will, they have killed my love at last. I never thought that you *could* kill it, but you have!" He would not believe her. He would not even be astonished, he would be so convinced it was not true. He would only look at her with that unsurprised obstinate look of his and tell her not to talk nonsense. The man does not live who can believe a woman who has once loved him has ceased to do so.

And she *had* loved him. Once, oh, many years past now, no sun would have been too hot for her to walk under its rays with him, no night would have been too dark. Once they had been the same world, enclosed in each other, knowing and caring nothing for whether darkness or light lay outside, the whole of space or a narrow prison. But that was years ago.

Yet she felt pity for him, guessing dimly at the obscure suffering in that enclosed world of his, a suffering scarcely understood even by himself. He had changed terribly since Jim had gone.

"Ah," she said to herself, "it's been a hard day's work, and in this heat, too." But it was done at last, and now she would make herself a nice pot of tea—the kettle was simmering with a sound like that made by a swarm of bees—and try some of that bread she baked yesterday.

Now she sat in her kitchen, resting after the day's work, her hands in her lap, looking out of the window. She would often sit like this in the days to come, in the long evenings when the ships return, bringing the wanderer home and the dead child, the child unborn and not to be conceived, home to the mother's breast.

Mrs. Noon, enjoying the stillness, looking through the open window of her kitchen at the fields hallowed by the light and by the seed, thought: "If only the war would end we would have quietness for ever." If only Jim were at home again, helping his dad with the beans and the peas, with the world of growing things! He would be due for leave in a little

132

over a week from now, she would see him standing in the doorway on just such an evening as this, with the dying light shining on his face, all covered with earth he would be, as if he had been working in the fields and the gardens and had had a fall. She would feel him solid in her arms, holding him close to her as she had done when he was a little child and had fallen and hurt himself; and the five days he would spend with her would last for ever. Perhaps the war would end before those five days were over, and they would return to their life of country peacefulness, to the life of growth and of harvesting, to the rhythm of the ripening or waning seasons, forgetting the scarring and the desecration of the earth.

Mrs. Noon thought of Bob Armstrong, the son of the farmer up at Harlands. Poor Bob, he had always been so gay and full of life; he was tall and rather stout, the blue eyes in his red face looked sad and lonely, but he was always cheery. He wore his cap on one side and whistled at his work. And Mrs. Noon remembered what his mother had cried when the news was brought to her that Bob had been killed. "Bob, Bob, what have they done to you—what have they done to you? Oh, Bob, unchanged to me, unchanged to me!" All night long she had cried, clutching at her breast as if her heart would burst out of her body in a cataract of blood. Moaning in a voice that had changed to that of some animal caught in a trap, she had rocked from side to side, clutching at the cataract that was about to break from her bosom.

That had happened to Mrs. Armstrong, but it would not, could not, happen to her. These things do not happen to oneself.

Then as she sat there, looking through the open window at the holiness of the summer fields, the life-giving bread of mankind ripening in stillness, there was a knock upon the door. That knock was hollow and long, as if, since the beginning of time, it had been the sole living inhabitant of the Tomb, floating down all the enormous spaces between the galleries of those Cities of the Dead, in that otherwise limitless silence. So it came to her, more awful now, since, with one

133

last effort, it had burst through the mouth of the Tomb into the unheeding sunlight and, breaking through this, had called her to that eternal companionship.

Rising, she opened the door and saw what awaited her. A woman was standing outlined against the animal-purring summer greenery, so living and uncaring, and in her hand she held a telegram.

Mrs. Noon took it, in silence.

Time was no longer a living thing, but through the limitless space into which Time had been transformed, from the silence that was now her universe, Mrs. Noon could see the lips of the woman standing in that distant world of the living move as she stepped towards her. But standing upright in the grave-clothes of her flesh, she was as remote from those encircling helping hands, as if they came from another century yet unborn.

For a space she bore the agony, the fruition, of the living, the silence and solitude of the dead. Then moving heavily, slowly, as if her body were once again weighted by the life of her child, Mrs. Noon turned and, walking to her chair, sank down upon it.

Her soul cradled in the night of her body like a small child in its little coffin, Mrs. Noon sat among the green branch-like shadows of her kitchen. How ancient was that little child who had never known life. The drops remaining from the far-off Flood had inundated the immense primeval clay in which the coffin was embedded; from the darkness it had heard the Priests of Baal crying to an unhearing God for rain. How heavenly was now the peace of that grave, even though the little child, her soul, had never known life and its restlessness; now there was neither fear nor hope nor pain—nothing but darkness and dew.

As she sat motionless, her old hands clasped in her lap, her upward-turned face had something of the humble grandeur of the primeval clay that had known and suffered the Flood and the dryness of the uncaring heaven.

For long she sat there, until as the light died over the fields her heart underwent slowly the anguish, the long tearing of the flesh, that her body had known when Jim was born. But these birth-pangs were to bring forth no new life. She had borne a dead child, dead before his birth, doomed by the blindness, the fear, and the greed of mankind.

PART II

Chapter I

EIGHT YEARS had passed since the maelstrom died, and now, when the sun rises over the desecrated earth, no cry is raised by the race that lies beneath it. Under the dawn the betrayed lie patient. We need not fear to hear their voices. They will not rise to denounce or to pity us till the last day. Only sometimes, when in the noon the streets are deserted because of the too great light, and we walk alone, we shall see a shadow in our path, like a ghost from the solemn and revengeful dead, from the loving and pitying dead, arisen to ask us, what have we made from all the oceans of blood that have spilt for us, from all the worlds that have been laid down for us. What are we now? What have we come to be?

Only a shadow—there is nothing to fear. The dead are beneath the earth and the women who clasped them to their hearts lie in the dawn alone, or—for over the dead the Pygmean empire must be built—grown cold as they, hold to their hearts an alien child grown in their blood but foreign to it, a stranger to their souls.

.　　　.　　　.　　　.　　　.

The sun rose, freshened from deep seas, over the cities, and with the rising of the sun, the noise of hammering was heard, the sound of destruction, of the building of small hopes, small fears. They are building in the Potter's Field, in the Field of Blood.

Under the enormous sun, the feet of the few people who were already abroad and walking in the streets made a sound like that of hooves splashing in deep water. The giant from the

137

dark continent, as he looked down on them from the top of the lumbering palace of commerce in which he lodged, saw them as a race of pygmies; seen from above, their bodies, distorted by the light, seemed shrunken to nothing, their heads almost touched their feet. But their shadows were of such a vast length that they stretched from one end of the street to the other; they seemed dragging the pygmies by whom they had been thrown, into an unknown future.

Standing there, watching the race of atomies throwing their giant shadows across the world, he reflected on the contemptible stature of man seen by the light of truth, the hatred felt by the pygmy towards the giant. Men see others as beautiful only when they are of their own size, and the Pygmean empire comforts itself for the power of the race of giants by blaming the enormity of the blemishes to be found in their skin—in even the smoothest—the great holes like craters, the stumps of the giant's beard that are "ten times stronger than the bristles of a boar." This is the revenge taken by the pygmy if the giant raises him to his level. He will see those blemishes as less, only if he be left to stare at them from below.

In the muttering heat, the race of pygmies runs, worms' spawn beginning in the worm's shape, ending with the worm, pullulating, multiplying, and festering, conglomerating their littleness, spreading and aggrandising it under the huge sun, joining together in a love that is the joining of the cloven maggot, engendering little hopes, little fears, throwing up small sprays of dust, spray by spray, till they have made a universe of dust.

And with them, urging them on, run the philosophers and the scientists who are about to better life for mankind, regenerate the world by the propagation of new ideas.

Here come those architects who have considered the superior wisdom and prudence of the spider, and have "contrived a new method of building houses by beginning at the roof and working downwards to the foundation," and those who will draw out all the sunbeams that have been concentrated in

138

cucumbers and will bottle them in hermetically-sealed vials, so that when the sun is dead we may have them to warm the world. And here run the men who are at work on "condensing the air into a dry tangible substance," and "softening marble for pillows and pin-cushions," together with one who designs to "sow land with chaff, wherein he affirmed the true animal virtue to be contained." Here they run, crossing each other, running like spiders, and weaving their webs. And here comes he who has seen the vision of employing the spider instead of the silkworm to produce silk, since the spider knows how to "weave as well as to spin," and because, owing to the beautiful hues of the flies on which the spiders are fed, all cost of the dyeing of the silks will be spared.

It is a world for the spider, for dark webs woven in darkness.

We can forget the dead. For here is a new hope for mankind.

Now in the Potter's Field, the Field of Blood, the sound of the dawn has died; in the Field the markets are astir. And from Rotten Alley and Gin Lane and Booble Street the beggars stream. On they come, past the monstrous swaying towering palaces of commerce, and the Transatlantic Hotels where the shade is the Writing on the Wall, buildings from which issue prodigious persons, thunderous hulks of emptiness, swaying their mammoth bellies, elephantine torsos, puffy and amphitudinous with nothingness in the centre of which is a small mouse—death. Here they come, with a Colossus of Greek days, that had once looked out over a calm and youthful sea, one of a race of smiling statues, but that now is eyeless in a land whence the sea has retreated for ever. And with them is a monstrosity of darkness, talking of enormities eaten and of Gold Coasts far away.

Not only the night but the noon has its Zero Hour. And past these bulks swarm the beggars, unseen by them. On they come, huge trunks, lumps, hulks and hulls, and their tatters flutter like seas. Or, with rags agglomerating and agglutinating, with wounds coalescing and decomposing under the enormous sun, they sway together on the benches.

The procession sweeps past the Transatlantic Hotel that has never known the sea; and under that huge shadow old Anatomy, old hole-into-nothingness, in her dress like the slime of Lethe's river, is raking for each scantling, scrap, shred or tag, each rag, tatter, cantle, mite, bit, morsel, crumb, scrag and fritter from the bins: remnants, relics, dregs, wrecks, skeletons of birds, and small black ruins like the ruins of time. "Hi, hi! Is that you, old Pharaoh? Does the sun blister after so many centuries of death? Into the light, Alexander, quick worm-seed! Come then, mutton-bone, and you, young starry! All food for my hollow yawning jaw, the black gulf. Come and touch the continent of dryness in the mummy's blood. Rainless, arid, rainless!"

Through the streets of the city, down the river, go all ways of transit, of passage and of gestation, porterage, shipment and plantation—tumbrel, hurdle, velocipede, stretcher, hermaphrodite brig, and ferry—infections from the world's fever, Babel-towers of tongues and of chaos, a rolling Hell of noise, hurrying and rocking, or drifting to nowhere, over the alluvium and detritus left from the Flood.

They, and the crowds, sweep onwards, the mountaineers and the nomads from lands that have never been, the beachcombers from a shore where the sea comes never, the pilgrims to a shrine where lies a God who never lived, an unborn and a bloodless thing, that cannot wake, that cannot sleep, that hears all, bears all, and cannot move, that has no tears for his dryness. Here they come, with the somnambulists and sleepwalkers, the argonauts, aviators, and pilots, the navigators and the fugitives from dream and from reality, the emigrants and mourners. The giant looking down from his high window, saw the procession of them winding past the slums and the wharves, past the lumbering palaces of commerce where the rich man Cain hides from the light, and where the windows seem but the sightless eyeholes of Day.

And with them, gaps into darkness, go the gunmen, the molochs, the matadors and man-eaters. They need only wait, for these are the dog-days, the days canicular, the season for the pyromaniacs, each hiding in his isolation—that will soon become infectious—of fear, of hatred, of greed.

Soon the whole world will be afire. And there will be no rain to extinguish it—only the echo of blood falling in the kennels, of blood spouting and dripping, of an ocean and deluge of blood—spilt that such a world as this might be built.

Chapter II

THE FADING light of the full moon drifting over the fields, a strange still light spilled on the leaves, was like a sound heard within the mind, a sound remembered. But Anna's window was in shadow, the moon spilled only faint chilly sparkles on the dark leaves growing around the sill—a faint radiance, a glitter, and then all was dark again, though the roofs above were like the clear silver floor of the strawberry beds in spring, before the frost has faded.

Anna, looking out of her window at the stretch of countryside under the calm full moon, the light on field and tree, thought to herself: "It is nine years ago that Jonathan asked me to come to Ireland, and it was on such a night as this that I sat for hours, at my window, wondering what my future life would be?"

The years that followed the war had brought but little change in Anna's days; only the story of her life seemed like a book that has lain in the long wet grass all through a moonlit summer night. The light of the moon had been there, but the pages were a little darkened. The shining rich dyes on the moth's dusky wing, the radiance of the hour, the flashing sheen on the bird's plume, the light on the leaves; all these, that had seemed unfading, were a little dimmed.

Anna said to herself: "Yes, I am changed." Life grows slowly and imperceptibly like a tree, ripens and withers. But the changes are so slight that until the final withering it seems as if no change could ever come. You are young, and then suddenly, before you had perceived any difference, you are old—you look in the glass and see that the summer is over and that the white frosts have begun. "The frosts are not yet," Anna said to herself, "but they will come."

She was altered, and so was Jonathan, to whom the years had brought fame.

He was no longer the obscure young man, poor and without prospects, who had been the butt of Mrs. Linden and her younger daughter—the young and unknown writer whose shabbiness and unusual appearance had aroused the derision and all the latent impertinence in the circle of young people who came to the Lindens' house. He was, by now, one of the most famous of men. Not only the rank and terrible upheavals of his genius, but his strong and awe-inspiring appearance—his face with its strange mixture of ferocity, sensuality, and tenderness, its look of ungovernable pride, of power and of intellect, his piercing blue eyes, his thick long eyebrows and full and sensual mouth—these were known throughout the world. . . . Fame, and power. They were his at last.

But he never forgot the days of his poverty. Nor did he ever forget the feeling of helplessness and humiliation he had endured in the Linden household.

Mrs. Linden, however, looked back on the past with different eyes. She was never tired of telling her acquaintances—or such of them as had not known her at the time—the story of how Jonathan had wanted to marry Lucy. "Oh, yes, my dear, he was always at my house." He had been, it seemed, almost like a son to Mrs. Linden, and invariably consulted her about his work. Never a week passed but that he brought manuscripts to her for her criticism. And Mrs. Linden had always been perfectly frank with him. When his work was bad, she told him so, and he would cut out the offending part, or alter it to her taste. She had always known that he was a young man of genius, and had done her uttermost to encourage him. Indeed, it was largely owing to her encouragement and advice that he had begun to write. But, of course, when it came to a question of his marrying Lucy, that was a very different matter. For Lucy could never marry anyone whom she did not love, and although Jonathan, as soon as his fortune was assured, had written begging her to reconsider her decision, she had felt it would be doing him a wrong, as well as herself, if she held out any hope that she would ever change her mind.

The young people, the frequenters of the house, would, on their side, tell amusing little anecdotes of the great man's eccentricity and absent-mindedness, and every story showed the confidential terms on which he had been with the teller.

Sometimes the echo of these reminiscences reached Jonathan, who, on hearing them, laughed.

It was sad, they said, that people, when they became famous, forgot their old friends, those who had helped them most. . . . Oh, no, they never saw him now! He was too occupied, no doubt, with great people!

Famous men from all over the world did, indeed, come to visit him in Ireland, and, as well, hordes of persons wishing to interview and photograph him. And these last, when their written applications for an appointment were not granted, would appear in person, hoping by this means to wear down the great man's resistance. He was, too, bombarded with manuscripts, for it is an accepted fact that writers have nothing to do excepting to read the works of the unpublished and to find them publishers. And with these, and with the would-be interviewers, Anna dealt, for the most part. She would be sent for, and, on her appearance: "Dear Anna," Jonathan would say, "dear good Anna, see this poor man for me. I can't, I really can't be interrupted just now. But don't let him feel hurt. Don't let him feel humiliated. Only try to get it into his head that even a writer has, at moments, work which cannot be put aside." For he, who had drunk the deepest dregs of humiliation in the past, could not bear that even the slightest taste of this should fall to the lot of another.

Yes, great and enduring fame had come to him at last, and with it, a certain amount of money. "Poverty!" he had said once, long ago, to Lucy Linden: "One is in prison if one is poor. Behind iron bars, condemned to watch suffering in helplessness." For this had been, to him, the most cruel rigour of all, that he had seen the wretchedness of those who were even poorer than himself, and had been powerless to do even the smallest thing to relieve them. But now all was changed: he was no longer powerless in the face of these miseries.

His generosity had not, so far, taken on the eccentric character it assumed in later years. It took various forms. By this time, he had considerable influence over the government in London, and would often make use of it for deserving persons. Or he would, anonymously, send gifts of money to people whose pride prevented them from taking it openly from him. He was particularly generous in this respect to the poorer clergy. But a strange trait in his character, that of being, as one who knew him well has said, "A hypocrite reversed," caused him to disguise his kindness under such a harsh aspect, to speak so much of economy, and to pay out money with such an appearance of reluctance, that he was thought by the outside world to be both avaricious and cold-hearted. This hatred of hypocrisy, this dread of showing his good qualities, affected every rule of his life, so that, as one of his biographers wrote, "No mortal ever took more pains to display his good qualities and appear in the best light to the world, than he did to conceal his, or even to put on the semblance of their contraries. . . . His very civilities bore the appearance of rudeness, and his finest compliments were conveyed under the appearance of satire."

For he must at all costs conceal the tenderness of his heart, lest the world should guess at its suffering.

So he lived, than whom no man was ever more loved by his

circle of intimate friends, no man more hated and feared by the crowd, the generality of mankind.

The routine of his life was never disturbed, excepting by his periodical visits to London. It was given over to work; but once a week, regularly, he would give a dinner or luncheon party, and then Anna would walk over to his house on the morning of the party, would make all the arrangements, order the food, decide where the guests were to sit, arrange the flowers. Then Becky and she would take their places among the other guests.

The parties were gay; Hare and the famous men gathered about him were good talkers, and their conversation had a scope, a depth and breadth that would have been impossible in a larger company. Their talk ranged from philosophy and literature to politics, now light and gay, now grave. Sometimes Hare would tease Anna and Becky, who were as a rule the only women present, since Hare declared that women interrupted the talk too constantly with trivial questions, and made conversation difficult.

This was the even tenor of his life. And an ordinary observer would not have known that a shadow haunted the great, the famous Jonathan Hare. . . . But those fits of giddiness, from which he had suffered from time to time, had increased in frequency. . . .

Anna had known that these had caused him, as it seemed to her, an unnecessary fear, though he tried to disguise it from her. But one day, coming into his sick-room, and bending over him, she had seen such a look of dread, of childlike loneliness and despair in his eyes, that it had wrenched at her heart. "Jonathan," she cried, "what is it? . . . *Jonathan!*"

He could not reply, the silent, watching world into which, one day, those fits of giddiness would hurl him, lay below him, waiting, waiting. In silence he lay, looking at a sight that Anna could not see. At an old man sitting in a chair, in an empty room. Years ago now, years. . . .

It had been a clay-cold day on which he had last seen the

old man his uncle, just before the end; and the very darkness of the house seemed as if it had been created by the winter mists. There was no colour, there was no sound. Only the cold seemed to him like a cracked bell. The old woman had opened the door to him in silence, a candle in her hand: beckoning to him, she led him along the passage, up the black yawning stairs that seemed to him only another gulf into the ice-bound arctic cold. And then, stopping before a door, she opened it. There, sitting on a chair in the middle of the room, sat the bulk of emptiness. His white hair, crested like a wave over his mindless face, was thick as a seagull's bosom. . . . Mindless, empty. . . . By his side, a little way removed from him, was another chair, and on it one candle, with a small aguish beam, shaking in the cold that was like a mist.

Jonathan Hare stood there, looking at him, at the small brumal light. For a moment he stood looking. Then he turned and walked out of the room.

The door was shut. The future was not yet.

.   .   .   .   .

. . . Giddiness. . . . Then the appalling orang-outang roar of black and raging madness. . . . Then the hulk on the chair.

.   .   .   .   .

The great, the famous Jonathan Hare lay there, silent. And it was not until next day, when the long spell of giddiness had passed, that he spoke. Then, wiping the sweat from his clay-coloured face, looking at her with those despairing and lonely eyes, he had said: "Anna, promise never to leave me."

She said: "Never. I promise you that I never will."

She was there, a part of the fabric of his life. If he was ill, he sent for her, if he was angry, she must soothe him. It was to her that he went when he was in pain or when the world had disappointed him. But he was never entirely hers: there must always be a shadow between them, a shadow that he had created.

146

Now, looking out of the window at the dying light of the moon, she remembered the day, not long after her arrival, when she had realised what were to be the terms of their companionship. The heat had been so great that it seemed that all the moisture on the leaves, the sap in the trees, her own blood, must have dried. But now the evening had come, and Jonathan, sitting with her in her drawing-room, that was darkened against the heat, had suggested it would be agreeable to drive into the country. Agreeing, she went upstairs to get her cloak. But when she returned, he asked with surprise: "Where is Becky?" "Becky has a headache, she is lying down," she answered. "Then if she can't come, Anna, I am afraid it will mean that we shan't be able to go." "Not be able to go for a drive, Jonathan! Why? What *do* you mean?" "Well, Anna——" and he hesitated. "I want, as far as possible, not to give any opportunity for foolish ideas to creep into people's minds. And they are beginning to talk, I am afraid. . . . I have to think of you, Anna. I *must*. We shall have to avoid this in the future. So I intend that from now on, Becky shall always make a third, so that nobody *can* link our names together."

So she fell into her place in the background of his life, a constant attendant figure, as necessary to him as the bread he ate; but he never saw her alone again. Never, in all the long years of their life together—the long years that led from her youth to her fading—that slow fading that was like the dimming of the sheen on the bright bird's plume, of the light on the leaves, of the hour of afternoon.

Chapter III

JONATHAN HAD been away now for nearly three months, and it seemed to Anna that every acquaintance she had made in Dublin and the countryside had found it necessary, on one pretext or another, to call upon her at this time; and each visitor had only one subject of conversation—the reason for Jonathan's repeated visits to London. Old Mrs. Ainworth, for instance, waddling towards where she sat under a tree sewing a blue muslin slip, had hardly seated herself before she announced her theme and developed the fugue. Did not Miss Marton agree with her that Mr. Hare had been strangely restless lately, for the last few months? Oh yes, no doubt there were ministers to be seen and publishers to be interviewed, of course there were! They all knew *that*. But—and Mrs. Ainworth looked arch—she was sure there was more in it than *that*. Everybody was saying that Mr. Hare had found a nice young lady in London, and that was why he went there so often. It was quite time that Mr. Hare found a nice young lady and married. He ought to have a wife—someone quite young and who would take an interest in his work and be a real help to him. Did not her dear Miss Marton agree? And she peered into her dear Miss Marton's face in a purposely short-sighted manner, with eyes a little too full of kindness. Miss Marton felt she did not want Mrs. Ainworth to be quite so kind to her.

Letters arrived from Jonathan, and they were full of the records of small happy moments, of passing people. He was keeping some sort of a diary for her, but not for her alone, for Becky also, because Becky must always be there, be a guardian, a shadow between them. Yes, the letters were not really Anna's. Yet it seemed to her that she could see all his companions, knew every moment of each hour he spent. He had made a new friend, for instance, young Mr. Weston, the great poet, who was many years younger than himself. Poor Mr. Weston was a cripple—he was scarcely more than four feet high, a hunchback, and in constant pain. Jonathan loved him. He was one of the best of men, he said, and one of the most generous. Then, too, there was Mr. Jarvis, the dramatist, whom Jonathan teased because of his smart ties.

It was very hot in London, and Jonathan declared that the heat made him feel peevish, but Anna knew that he was glad to be in London, in spite of all his protestations. He seemed to be seeing a great many people, never to have a moment to himself. And she could imagine him expanding in this company; for he was by no means devoid of vanity. The people with whom he mingled were, for the most part, worldly and gay, and they made small absurd jokes which he chronicled for her and Becky. The Duchess of Brighton, for instance, had clapped his hat on another lady's head and she in fun put it on the railings. And in a few minutes, by a miracle it was transported still further along the railings until Lady Strawbridge showed him his hat out of her window which was five doors away, so that he was obliged to walk and get it and pay her and old Lady Shropshire and some other old beldam a visit. Yes, it was very hot in London, and he was distinctly discontented. He longed to be at home again, sitting with Anna under the trees.

Anna wrote to him nearly every day, and he received, too, several letters from Becky, who was much concerned lest he should forget a message she had entrusted to him, which she wished him to pass on to one of her friends, if he should happen to meet her.

To these reminders, he returned evasive answers. With the result that Becky, deciding that it would not be wise to rely upon his memory, decided to invoke the aid of her friend Mr. Henry Debingham. Would her dear Henry, she enquired, help her in this exceedingly *delicate* matter, go and see Jonathan

149

Hare, and, in some way or other, get it into his head that this was *really important*? She added that she was worried about Anna, who seemed to have lost all her spirits. "You know, Henry," she continued, "that since I have got to understand Jonathan better—(and I really become more and more attached to him every day)—I have always hoped that one day he and Anna would marry. He sees her continually—I might almost say every day—but any question of *marriage* between them seems as far off as ever." She often wondered if there was *nothing* she could do. Oh, how she wished that Henry was *near* her to *advise* her. A man's advice, with his broader knowledge of the world, was *so valuable*.

Mr. Debingham was alone when he received Becky's letter, a sitter having just left the studio. This was situated in a piece of waste ground haunted by pallid hens, squawking desolately and prophetically; and the appearance of Mr. Debingham's hair aroused in some observers the conviction that the feathers of these had sought within its shades a safe refuge from the general confusion. Another school of thought, however, ascribed the alien substances by which it appeared to be bestrewn to a different cause, believing them to be a sprinkling of the snows of Time. For the nature of his toilette, and his general appearance, undoubtedly aroused attention and gave rise to speculation. His complexion, always dark, was at moments darker than others; and this phenomenon was due to no freak of nature or change in pigmentation, but to habits and chance. His clothes seemed as much a refuge as a covering, and when fully equipped to face the world and the weather, he presented much the same appearance as that which we are privileged to see in photographs taken of certain brave men at the very moment of their rescue after six months spent among the Polar Wastes and the blubber.

Now, giving a savage kick to the warring and varying objects which hid the floor from view, and which seemed to spend their whole time in clamouring for his attention, so that he frequently presented to sitters the appearance of a harassed
150

mother returning home with her wearied and quarrelsome offspring after a particularly noisy Bank Holiday—he re-read Becky's letter.

He grinned. And as he grinned, his personality underwent a lightning change. It was as if you had been looking at a lantern-slide. . . . A click, a fade-out, and another slide totally unconnected with it, and equally unreal, had taken its place. He was no longer the simple-minded artist, sunk in an abstruse meditation (a role in which he had appeared in his sitter's presence), but a rather sinister, piratic, formidable Dago. For this remarkable man, who was a sculptor in those moments which he could spare from thinking about himself, and from making plans to confute his enemies, had a habit of appearing in various roles, partly as a disguise (for caution was part of his professional equipment), and partly in order to defy his own loneliness. For in this way, so many different characters inhabited his studio (all enclosed in his body, so that they had no opportunity of contradicting him or paying him insufficient attention and homage), that he had scarcely any need of outside companionship. Actually he was nothing but a great blundering, blubbering Big Boy, craving for Home and Mother; but he had to appear in different characters for the reasons already stated, and, also, in order to impress himself and, if possible, others.

There was the Spanish role, for instance, in which he would assume a gay manner, very masculine and gallant, and deeply impressive to a feminine observer. When appearing in this character he would wear a sombrero, would, from time to time, allow the exclamation "Carramba!" to escape him, and would build castles in the air (or prisons for the objects of his affections) with square blockish movements of his thick meat-coloured hands. (Foreigners gesticulate.) Then, when, as was invariably the case, the castles in the air and the prisons did not materialise, he would abolish them again with a single stroke. He would too, when out of doors, draw his stick along the railings, with what he hoped was a flash of teeth. But

151

always, just as the teeth were about to flash, the sun went in, so that the phenomenon was not discernible, or his bootlaces came undone and he was forced to do them up, so that the people on the top of the passing omnibus, who had been intended to witness and to admire the flash, could not see it. His life was full of little disappointments of this kind.

At other times he would appear in a nautical part, shooting short sharp sentences through his clenched teeth in a bluff hearty voice, much as the captain of a whaling schooner would issue commands in the teeth of a gale to his crew—rough diamonds to a man, but with hearts of gold, and obviously adoring their skipper.

It was in the Spanish role that he read Miss Mintley's letter. Oh, ho! So Anna's friendship with Hare was not leading up to the desired goal. Well! It would take that conceited, cold, unwomanly creature down a bit. (For Anna had snubbed Henry; she was obviously blind to his charm, his roles left her unaffected, and this must obviously prove her to be cold and unwomanly.) Then suddenly, a brilliant idea struck him. He could be the means of bringing her down still further. Why should he not take Hare to see Mrs. Vanelden! She would do anything in the world—would stick at nothing—to get a husband for that girl of hers, and if he knew anything of her and of Miss Essy, the daughter in question, once they had got their nicely padded claws into so distinguished a man as Hare, they would keep them there. Anna was in Ireland, there was nothing she could do. He could be taken from her, and she could do nothing about it. She would not even know it was happening. And Mr. Debingham grinned again.

The only woman in Hare's life, was she? Well, we should see.

Chapter IV

Mrs. VANELDEN's house was situated in one of the moon-coloured crescents, or circuses, bordering the edge of Regent's Park. Two crescents, one on either side, overlooked large gardens full of huge purring leaves and great bright flowers, pale yellow begonias that made you think of South America because of their Creole complexions; and here, shrouded by the great leaves of trees and bushes, the young people played tennis; from the windows of the houses, or if you sat beneath the awnings that sheltered the balconies, you could hear their voices calling to each other, although you could not see them, you could only, at moments, see a white dress, a glint of gold or bird-dark, bird-glossy hair as they passed among the trees. No old people ever walked in the gardens, but sometimes a dark foreign-looking woman would pass by, like a sudden patch of shade, and with her a child, looking like a tired August moon in her white dress.

The crescents and the gardens alike had a faint Regency character, partly, perhaps, because they faced remote light blue distances, such as one sees in water-colours of the period. Mrs. Vanelden's house looked light and temporary, as if it were a house in which one lived for the summer only; as if, when at last the summer was over and the voices and the white dresses flashing among the leaves in the gardens were gone, the house itself might crumble into a little moon-coloured dust, or be packed away with the muslin dresses. The feeling that it must always be summer in the crescents was increased, too, by the fact that nearly always a barrel-organ seemed to be playing in one or other of the crescents, light tunes, dropping like water, that one could imagine being played on xylophones and queer wooden instruments and guitars and flutes in Mexico

153

and Peru, under a huge tropical parrot-feathered sun, or waltzes that were fashionable fifty years ago and that were bright-coloured and waxen as the begonias in the garden.

The house in which Mrs. Vanelden lived had a double personality. The door and the windowsills were painted a sharp and chattering white, a striped curtain, the colour of a negress's head-handkerchief, bright as the summer weather, sheltered the door from the heat, an awning of the same material covered the balcony, and suspended from the latter were baskets of geraniums, and also of large flaunting marguerites that had a hard, boastful innocence and were as shining and glaring as if they had been painted. Everything in the rooms on the ground floor and first and second floors was very bright and happy and summery, it spoke of ease and of optimism; but on the top floor, or, as Mrs. Vanelden persisted in calling it, "the nursery floor" (she had never brought herself to remove the small gate on the landing which had prevented her four children from falling downstairs), where the girls shared a sitting-room, all was dinginess, all was dust and confusion. It was crowded with half-finished occupations, taken up because there was nothing more amusing to do at the moment, and forgotten before they were completed, dog-eared books left open on a table, pieces of soiled embroidery thrown down on a chair, a half-darned stocking, an unfinished letter, a half-filled cup of tea that had gone cold. It was a room in which something was always being lost—a handbag or a heart—and recovered again in a slightly dilapidated condition from under a little drift of dust.

The household, too, seemed to have a double personality, and to be divided into two sections. Mrs. Vanelden's section was the antechamber to a discreet paradise, to a heaven that made allowances. She was a woman in late middle age, whose clothes bore a close resemblance to an untidy nest, in the midst of which a musty density, a wingless but feathery entity, brooded over nothingness. The nest was covered with mossy velvet, fronds of feather, tinkling bright objects that looked as
154

if they might have been stolen and made use of by a jackdaw, and pieces of dry and withered narrow ribbon that gave the impression of being pieces of straw. In colour and consistency, her hair was like sodden autumn leaves, and this, again, added to her nest-like appearance. It was drawn back in such a way that her face wore a look of innocent surprise, and wherever she might be, she gave the impression that she had found herself there inadvertently, and had reached the spot by some unexplainable means. Her eyes, which were round and shaped like those of a goose, were left deliberately vacant of thought, in order that occasionally an expression of great tenderness towards the whole world might spring into them. But this, again, would be quickly withdrawn as soon as it had served its purpose by striking the right note, much as a cuckoo will spring from the clock, strike the hour, and then return to its seclusion. For Mrs. Vanelden, who prided herself on the possession of a good heart, was careful not to make much use of this, for fear of ruining it by an overstrain.

She had spent much time in Switzerland, patronising the mountains, praising their stature and grandeur with an amused, light and summery laugh; and into this laugh she had carefully instilled the echo of the mountain bells. It had been trained to move in silvery arpeggios, going first up, then down. At moments, however, when she was tired or was, for one reason or another, intending to show a particular amiability to somebody, a more natural laugh sounded, and this was strangely reminiscent of the sound made by a cuckoo when considering the means by which its offspring might most safely and unobtrusively be placed in another bird's nest. Her voice was deliberately simple, it was designed to show that she was a simpleton, and she was in the habit of retailing stories which showed her in this light, which exhibited her utter unworldliness. She was always, it appeared, being cheated and deceived, and for some reason this seemed to give her a great deal of pleasure. "You know what I am," she would say, and would laugh at herself affectionately.

She had but little money, but owing to her simplicity and unworldliness, had laid up for herself, as it were, much treasure in heaven. Her most worldly friends—and she had many—prided themselves on the fact that they could set store by such a simple-minded creature. That she should take it for granted that they would appreciate and value at its true worth such simple-mindedness, was an obvious tribute to the often unsuspected goodness of the hearts that lay within them, and it was rewarded by loans of villas on the Riviera, boxes at the opera, motors, and by scores of invitations. Nobody was more surprised than Mrs. Vanelden when these blessings were showered upon her. But though, as she explained, she cared little for these things, indeed, they took up much of the time which she would have far preferred to spend in reading quietly—("you know what I am")—it would have seemed ungrateful, almost churlish, to refuse them.

She would frequently lament the constant calls on her time made by these invitations and by her hosts of friends, saying, with a little resigned laugh: "Mais que voulez-vous? I suppose it is a duty like another, to give sympathy, or advice, or the support of one's presence. But people spoil me too much, and I must confess that there are moments when I would like to have a little time for reading, for my own thoughts, for self-development."

To Mrs. Vanelden, self-development meant an increase of cosiness, an added certainty that she was right in every action, every thought. She lived for the comfort of the mind, and the whole of existence seemed so dependent upon her convenience, that you felt she had spun the world out of herself, as a silkworm spins silk—or a spider her web—to form a cocoon, a place of warmth, a surrounding, a nest for herself, or a trap for others; and this impression was increased by the fact that she spent a great deal of time in knitting, weaving webs of soft wool to protect herself from the blasts from heaven. When you were with her, your inner world died, and the outer world seemed as opaque and as familiar as the pale blue china that

Mrs. Vanelden's mother had brought back from Cannes in the eighteen-eighties.

The society in which she mixed was very varied. As I have hinted, the nest (and she brooding within it) was situated in the shade of many powerful and protective persons, eminent and accommodating divines, sleek and pouting, filling their coats and their own spiritual needs as compactly and fully as a neatly rounded potato fits its skin, celebrated and acquisitive divorcées who, during the reign of King Edward the Seventh, had cast their hearts about as if they were nice hard tennis balls; and leaders of society, some with voices like the bellowing of the Golden (or Brazen) Calf, others like a tunicate, possessing, to quote the scientific description of this elementary form of life, a preference for dwelling amidst mud, a stomach and a mouth, but neither nerves nor a heart. There were, too, a good many elderly peers and a few cleanshaven American, or pseudo-American, business women, possessed of large salaries and immense competence, who carried huge and expensive bags, with gold fittings, from which they would produce what appeared to be time-tables, and whose voices, movements, and general habits gave the impression that they had portable homes situated on the platforms of Victoria station.

Nor were these all. For in the shadow of these magnificent figureheads of various kinds could be discerned a dim and amorphous undergrowth, persons useful but not powerful, discreet sycophantic and anonymous women, the ghosts of fashionable restaurants, pondering and pandering, waiting and watching, to discover, chronicle and hymn the praise of the newest fashion in behaviour, customs, and persons.

Such was the background against which the simplicity of Mrs. Vanelden showed in such admirable relief. She was much blessed, also, in her daughters, and especially in the eldest, Esther, or Essy, who, an admirable stage partner, never forgot her cue, her entrances, exits, and supporting by-play.

Essy had inherited much of the innocence and unworldliness of her mother, but she differed from her in appearance, and,

157

excepting when these two qualities were particularly in evidence, in manner. She was twenty-four years old, but her mother alluded to her persistently as "my little girl," and Esther lent all the support in her power to this presentation of herself, by childish mannerisms, such as tossing her head and throwing back her masses of curls, and by the use of such phrases as: "I feel so terribly old, you know, I shall be *twenty* in January."

She was a plump young woman whose whole appearance and manner, when she was standing or sitting still, gave the impression that she was on the point of slipping down a hill. Her face, which was round and deliberately puckered into an expression of childish mischief, had a small snout, and she was in the habit, if she found herself near a looking-glass, of making a little pig-like grimace. She had small fat feet in gaudy down-trodden shoes, and when she moved she seemed to overflow every constriction physically; as she walked, each overflow seemed to lap lazily upon an unseen shore.

Though Esther had this overlapping, unrestrained appear-ance, her woman friends seemed, for the most part, geometrical cyphers, sexless figures of indestructible, highly varnished Birmingham hardware, but with a Metropolitan polish, and turned out according to the latest international taste in hard-ware. Their faces were like the definition of Zero . . . "Nothing —nought—duck's egg—goose's egg—cypher—none—no-body . . ." and from these epitomes would issue the new fashionable voice, deliberately colourless and wooden, or tinny and tiny and as circumscribed and meaningless as if it issued from an inferior and worn-out musical box, or rich and artificially hoarse. It might be said of these ladies that Respectability was the only outcast with whom they were not on speaking terms. They could bear neither her nor her votaries, making an exception, however, in favour of Mrs. Vanelden and her daughters, for the reason that "their house is *too* amusing, my dear. You never know who you may find there." To these were added a crowd of young men, screaming about "chic" and "the latest thing, my dear," in voices high and shrill as

158

those of parrots or of peacocks. Their costumes were as striking as the feathers of these birds, and they had attained to a certain gossip-column fame because of their schemes of interior decoration, walls covered with boot-buttons or straw, or furniture made of steel. Amongst these sophisticated persons there were, however, a few girls whose youthfulness, even childishness, equalled Esther's. And two of these latter examples now rushed into the room, clapping their hands and screaming in high childish voices.

This outbreak occurred at a moment when Mrs. Vanelden, her daughters, and a select company of greater and lesser friends were seated round the dining-room table, having nursery tea, as the hostess called it. For Mrs. Vanelden had never quite grown up, as she confessed, and nursery tea was one of the simple pleasures to be enjoyed in her house. As the young girls burst into the room, Mrs. Vanelden, who was in the habit of taking her guests on a personally conducted tour of her principal characteristics, acting as guide and showman, and pointing out, with a gentle, half amused, half affectionate laugh, the less easily discerned treasures of the collection, was descanting on her love of flowers, a passion that was amongst her prettiest originalities. But her voice was drowned by screams.

"Oh," shrieked the girls in a chorus. "You *must* come out and look at Peter's new motor. Oh, it's so *huge*, big as a house! We've just come up from Wiltshire in it. Oh, it goes so fast! And all the way up we screamed to Jackson:

" 'Faster! Faster! Faster! Faster!

" 'Faster! Faster! Faster! Faster!' "

Mrs. Vanelden shut her eyes. She wore a patient smile, waiting for the clamour to cease. Then her eyes opened again, the cuckoo sprang from the clock, struck its note, and disappeared once more.

How young they were! *How Young!*

She continued the tour. "You *know* what *I* am."

("Faster! Faster! Faster! Faster!")

Mrs. Vanelden looked at the girls. She ignored the interruption. "I *adore* flowers. I can't live without them. It is my way, I suppose; I am like that."

("Faster!")

"And the simpler the flowers are, the more I love them. Primroses are the flowers I really love the best, dear *soft* things." ("Faster!") "How I should love to wander out into the woods now, yes, at this moment, and pick some."

"But you couldn't pick them now," said a young man. "Primroses in summer!"

"For me," said Mrs. Vanelden quietly, "there are *always* primroses. I adore them! Lord Sunningdale—dear naughty thing, he is always spoiling me, he knows what I am, and says someone must take care of me, for I never take care of myself— sent me such a huge box of orchids this morning, out of his greenhouses. I suppose they are very magnificent really, people who know tell me they are. Still, I shall always love primroses *best*, though of course I love these flowers too, because they come from my dear old friend."

A middle-aged man, raising his eyes from his plate, said with a nervous titter: "*I* love pansies! I always talk to them if I can. They say such a lot to me, with those lovely black-fringed eyes of theirs. You have no idea of the things one can say to a pansy."

"Dear innocent things!" said Mrs. Vanelden, whose face bore a slightly vexed flush. She changed the conversation.

But she was to be interrupted for a third time. A bluebottle, rushing into the room through the open window, produced, with extraordinary virtuosity, first an accurate sound-picture of a Bishop exhorting his flock to prayer, and then, hurling itself against a window-pane, a spirited imitation of a 'cellist executing a particularly difficult pizzicato passage upon the C string. Tired of this performance it then soared into the air, whirled round and round, in a frenzied dervish dance, falling finally in what appeared to be a dead faint on the floor.

"Oh," screamed the young girls. "Oo, the horrid thing! Do put it out of the window, somebody!"

160

This was too much. After all, the bluebottle was in Mrs. Vanelden's house, and therefore there must be something to be said for it.

"Rather a nice summery sound!" she said, and gave her light laugh.

It was at this point that Mr. Debingham appeared, with Jonathan Hare in his wake. Advancing towards his hostess with a business-like abstraction, totally ignoring his feet, not in the least rudely, but as one ignores old and tried friends who can yet be trusted to do their best for one, Mr. Debingham shunted his right arm towards her as if it were a set of trucks, and thrust his hand in hers with much the same movement one might use in disposing of an unwanted parcel, liable to come undone at any moment: "Well, Mollie!" he shot at her, from behind clenched teeth. "I have brought Mr. Hare to see you."

He then withdrew to the other side of the table, this time in the Spanish role, and concentrated, for the rest of the afternoon, an intensive stare upon Esther and Hare. For he had a confirmed habit of staring, with eyes that bore a melancholy blink of yearning and reproachful affection, extremely disconcerting to the object of the gaze. He succeeded, indeed, in concentrating upon this sufferer a look which combined the expression worn by a returned and travel-stained wanderer, seeing from afar the old Homestead, and the look of the canine worshipper in the well-known advertisement of "His Master's Voice" gramophone records.

Mr. Debingham had taken the precaution of warning his hostess that he was bringing Hare to see her. "He is a very famous man, you know, Mollie," he had said. "Famous! " echoed Mrs. Vanelden. "But, Debingham, *how exciting*." For she was far too unworldly to distinguish the famous from the obscure. "But then, so many distinuished people come to your house, Mollie," continued Mr. Debingham. "*Do* they? *Are* they distinguished, Debingham?" Her eyes were overflowing with the milk of human kindness. "You know what I am!

I never know these things. But from what you tell me, Mr. Hare must be such a *delightful person*. My little girl and I will welcome him for himself." She added, "As a matter of fact, Debingham, I believe I did meet him, a year or two ago, and thought him charming. It will be nice to renew the acquaintance."

Therefore, on the day when he was scheduled to appear— quite by accident, it seemed to him (and nobody was more surprised than Mrs. Vanelden, although Mr. Debingham had telephoned in the morning to tell her he was bringing him) —the tea was even more nursery in character than usual. It is well known that great men love simplicity. And Esther, tossing her curls in and out of her eyes, making her fascinating little pig-like grimace, was more childish than ever. "You must sit next my little girl, Mr. Hare," said Mrs. Vanelden; "she has been plaguing and plaguing me, because she had found out that Debingham knew you. 'Mumsie,' she kept on saying, 'tell Debingham he *is* to bring Mr. Hare to see us.' She is *so* impulsive! (My precious, you have got some jam on your finger. Wipe it off, pet, or you'll have it on your pretty dress.)"

Later: "Essy seems to be getting on very well with your new guest," said Mr. Debingham, all joviality and goodwill.

Chapter V

ESSY VANELDEN thought that she had never been so happy before, in all her life. The summer days and nights seemed to her like falling stars, a flash of light, and they were gone and others as bright had taken their place. Every morning she woke to new happiness; she had not a moment, now, for moping. The sulkiness to which her younger sister Molkins was accustomed, and which was reserved for the Sluttery (as Mr. Hare called the sitting-room on the "Nursery" floor)—for it must never be allowed to show downstairs—this had been thrown away altogether, like an old dress.

She, who had never taken any interest in clothes, now spent hours in trying on dresses—(muslins, light and flashing as the summer air, silks dark and rustling like leaves)—and all because she was so happy. Was it *possible* that she, little Essy Vanelden, of all people in the world, could have attracted this man of genius, this great writer of whom the whole of London was talking. For he *was* attracted—he made no secret of it. He came to the house every day, and sometimes more than once a day; he who knew all the important people in London, the secretaries of State, the writers, the hostesses.

She was so happy, that in the middle of the night, sometimes, when the moonlight was still falling thick as curd, or just before the dawn was grey, she would jump out of bed and, drawing the flowered curtains of her window, look out at the sleeping crescent, thinking, "Another day. Soon it will be another day." She would sit there, in her muslin dressing-gown, with the cool airs blowing through the open window, and then she would go back to her bed and lie there sleeping or half awake, with the dawn flowing over her like thin lapping water, till the growing light, piercing through the curtains, strewed pale flowers upon her bed. Then, at last, there would be a tap on the door, and in would come Mary with her early morning tea, and Essy would have to pretend not to see what was lying on the tray beside it. For every morning, without fail, there would be a note, sent by hand and addressed to "Little Missessy," in which plans were suggested for the day. The notes ended, as often as not, with some reference to having coffee in the Sluttery, which Mr. Hare declared was the most agreeable room in the world. And sometimes, too (for little Missessy loved to feel the importance of being the only confidante of the great man), Mr. Hare, laughing at her childish ways, would enclose with the note a letter written to another

163

person, which he wished her to see before he posted it. Then, one morning, came a letter enclosing one to her cousin Mrs. Long; and the note to Essy contained these words: "I have written three or four lies in as many lines. Please seal up the letter to Mrs. L. and let nobody read it but yourself. And please let the outside starched letter to yourself be seen, after you have sealed that to Mrs. L. See what arts people must use, though they mean ever so well."

Essy lay in her bed reading this letter. She read it with care, three times. Then, getting out of bed, she locked it up in a box that contained her jewellery. She did not quite know why, but she had a feeling that in the future she might be glad that she had kept that letter. And then another thought struck her. If it came to that, why should she not keep all Mr. Hare's letters to her? How interesting that would be!

He went with her everywhere. Often, in the late afternoons, when the street with its dark branching shades seemed like a dwarf Japanese forest, with the gold light quivering like sand under the large black leaves and branches of the shade, they were seen coming out of a picture exhibition in Bond Street. He would be one of a happy, laughing, luncheon party in a fashionable restaurant; or, when a friend lent Mumsie a motor for a few days, Mumsie and Molkins and he and she would make up a party with some of Mrs. Vanelden's friends and go for a picnic in Windsor Forest. There, sitting on the grass, they laughed and talked nonsense till evening fell. Once they drove down to Brighton, and Mumsie and Molkins rested in the hotel while Mr. Hare and she walked by the sea. The airs were like great rainbows, and on the pale waters the gold spangles were like the freckles on the summer strawberries. And Essy thought that the day would never fade, and that the summer and her youth would last for ever.

Often, too, in the warm summer evenings, they drove down by moonlight—a whole crowd of them—into the country, and did not return to London till very late; and they would play hide and seek, he chasing her, a dark sylvan lady, along

164

the moonlit paths. And the moonlight and the sunlight seemed to have been created just because little Essy Vanelden wanted to walk and to drive with Jonathan Hare. And though they were with so many friends on these expeditions, nobody ever laid claim to one moment of Jonathan's time, nobody ever hoped for any attention from him. He was Essy's property. That was understood.

He came and sat for hours in the Sluttery, with her and Molkins, and drank coffee she had made, while she, with the funny childish proprietary airs she always adopted towards him, scolded him for not drinking it while it was hot (this was a great joke between them, and often, after he had returned to Ireland, he reminded her, in his letters, of her constant exclamation: "Drink your coffee! Why don't you drink your coffee?"), and then he would turn the tables on her and tease her about being nothing but a brat, and about her lack of learning. He was going, he said, to constitute himself her tutor. . . . She must really learn to read. . . . What? She *had* learnt to read? Then she must learn to read properly. She must learn to read the right things. She must stop being such a little ignoramus. He was going to begin the arduous work of teaching her when he was next in London. And when he *did* return, he promised that if she was good and didn't quarrel with him, he would come to dine three times a week, and would tell her a thousand secrets—affairs of State, what this writer and that were up to—oh, all kinds of things.

And Essy wondered, was it, *could* it be, that he wanted to come back, because he had a new interest, a new *friend* in London? She could not, she dared not, believe that it was so; and yet, there was the fact that he came to the house every day. Oh, how sad it was that he must go back to Ireland. But he would return. He had promised that.

Intensely amused by the way she had taken possession of him—(it never entered her head that he could wish to speak to anyone else, or to spend his time in any other way than in her company)—Jonathan told himself that this was a pleasant

165

interlude. After all, she was scarcely more than a child. He was so much older than Essy: why should he not have this charming friendship with a little girl who might almost have been his daughter? . . . And then, too, everybody needs a change at times, needs, also, a little uncertainty. Too much safety is wearying. And Anna's companionship, after all these long years, almost resembled a marriage, after passion has died. He was too sure of her, too certain of her devotion. His dear good Anna!

He knew that when he entered the house for the first time after his return from London, he would feel that he had never been away. Everything would be unchanged, familiar. She would be sitting sewing under a tree, just as he had left her; and though she would look up at him with happy laughing eyes, with the expression he knew so well, he would see the marks of fatigue on her face. She had grown to look much older, lately. . . . He thought: "Nothing ever happens there!"

Nothing. Only once in all her letters, which were filled with questions about his doings, with anxiety about his health, did he find one piece of news, and that was not of a nature to interest him. "Becky had a letter from Susan Daw yesterday," she wrote. "And would you believe it, she is *married*. She has been married for four years. And her husband is, of all people in the world, a *German*: Becky and I are thinking of taking them as servants; we need someone to run the house, and Susan says they can get no work anywhere. His people will have nothing to do with him because he has married an Englishwoman; her people and the French (she met him in France) will have nothing to do with her because she married a German. She says they have been treated as outcasts everywhere, and are now half starved."

His good Anna! He wrote to her nearly every day, and in one letter he told her, casually, that he had met a charming woman, a Mrs. Vanelden. He had been taken to her house by Debingham. But he blamed himself for this impulse, as soon as he had posted the letter. Women are so unreasonable, the

166

most inquisitive and acquisitive creatures in the world, and she would, no doubt, jump to the most absurd and unfounded conclusions. And, wearily, he sat down to write to her again. The Vaneldens, he explained, were kind, if rather worldly people. Mrs. Vanelden was a widow, a middle-aged motherly sort of woman, with two sons and two daughters, the latter scarcely more than children.

He did not mention them again for some time. But Anna did not forget, and after a little while, asked Jonathan who were the people who boarded near him, with whom he dined now and then. "What do you mean?" he enquired. "I don't dine with boarders. . . . You know whom I have dined with every day, better than I do." And he added: "Well now I'll write a little, and think a little, and so to bed and dream of Anna."

For his letters were as full of tenderness as before. She had been suffering from some trouble with her eyes, and in one letter he wrote: "Pray don't write, Anna, until you are mighty, mighty, mighty, mighty, mighty well in your eyes, and are sure it won't do you the least harm. Or come, I'll tell you what. You, Miss Anna, shall write your share at five or six sittings, and then comes Becky all together, and then Anna a little crumb towards the end to let us see she remembers." Nothing, he declared, gave him any sort of dream of happiness but a letter now and then from his own dearest Anna. And his letters, which were usually written at night, just before he went to bed, always ended with some expression of devotion: "God Almighty bless and protect dearest Anna," or "I have no room but to bid my dearest little Anna good night."

But his friendship with Essy progressed.

Mrs. Vanelden, in conversation with her friends, was not very communicative on the subject. There were moments, in the last few weeks, when the finest bloom in her simplicity would appear, to an acute observer, to have become a little dimmed, although nursery tea was, if anything, even more in evidence than before. "Early days, my dear," she would say.

"Early days. *Chè sa?* Yes, he certainly *seems* to be attracted by her! But then, he is so much older than her, and a *very* important man." ("*Important* man!" thought the bewildered listener. "A few months ago Mollie would never have said that. I doubt if she knew that importance existed!") "And really Essy is nothing but a child. No, she has no idea of anything coming of it. *Of course* not: it has never entered her head. And then there is this woman in Ireland that they talk about (one has heard rumours). The daughter of the agent at that place where he was secretary years ago, or something of that sort. Followed him to Ireland, so they say." She shrugged her shoulders, and gave her light summery laugh. "Oh, no, my dear, I have made no enquiries. Why should I? One takes that sort of thing for granted—I mean that there has been something of the sort in a man's life. After all, we *do* live in the world, don't we?" ("*Live in the world! Mollie!*") "Oh, my dear, why *should* she make a fuss? And if it comes to that, what can she do about it? What else can she expect? After all, it happens to them all, sooner or later!"

"Them?"

"Well, that sort of woman."

Chapter VI

SUSAN ORTHOVEN, sitting sewing in the window-seat of her room in Anna Marton's house, thought of the few years that had passed since Mrs. Sinding's death, and her own marriage, of the hatred that had grown into love, the hatred and love that had sprung from the love of a dead man. She thought of the two outcasts, herself and Hans Orthoven, who had faced starvation rather than deny the power of love and of forgiveness, who had pledged their word to each other on the grave of the man they both loved, and had then gone out into a world which rejected with loathing the woman who had married the man who had killed her lover, the man who loved the enemy he killed. But now they had won through to peace, it would be theirs for ever, in this quiet house in which their lives would be spent in giving their faithful service to the only beings who had befriended them.

Mrs. Sinding had gone to the north of France, taking Susan with her, to stay in a house that had belonged to her husband, whose mother had been French. And it was there that she had caught influenza, and, after only five days' illness, had died.

For weeks afterwards, Susan could not believe it was true. She had not lived through those five days, she had not seen Mrs. Sinding's dead face, she had not followed the coffin. She would have liked to cry, but she seemed to have no tears left; tears, like everything else in the world, had deserted her.

She did not care, now, what became of her. She had nowhere to go, and there was nobody to whom she could speak. She had no money, and she saw herself faced with starvation, but she was too numb to remember with any force the night she had spent among the beggars on the benches, to realise that this would probably be her fate again, only this time she would be amongst people to whom she could not speak because she did not know their language. And then, one day, three weeks after Mrs. Sinding's death, an old lady whom Mrs. Sinding had known slightly took Susan to be her servant.

Madame Herbin seemed to belong more to the crustacean species than to the human. She had very bright beady black eyes, and wore always a shiny black silk dress that looked as if it were so hard that nothing could penetrate it, and she had a way of scuttling sideways as she walked, looking very cunning as she did so, as if she had been visiting some secret hoard.

She lived in a tall narrow sly-looking house which seemed to have grown sideways in an attempt to economise its own space, and at the same time to take up as much as possible of the space that should have belonged to its neighbour. Everything in the house seemed hungry or cold or both—the dusty sunlight, stretching out its thin furry life in the half-empty rooms, the moonlight that was harsh and white as brine or as a disused salt-mine. Hunger gave inanimate objects a positively living look, the shadow waiting to swallow the sunlight, the curtains trying to swallow the air. The only thing of which Madame Herbin was lavish was Susan's work: she was never allowed to rest for a moment, at 5.30 she must be downstairs and lighting the meagre kitchen fire, and then she must work without stopping till it was ten o'clock and time for her to put her candle out, for on no account must an inch of candle be wasted. Food and drink and fire and sleep were cut down to the smallest shreds and given out in parings, and Madame Herbin had developed a system by which she was enabled to supply herself, without cost, with various necessities: with tea, one day; with milk, a second; with the couple of eggs which must serve her and Susan for dinner, as a third; on a fourth, with coal; on a fifth with sugar that would be made to last for the whole week. This she effected by remembering that she had run out of these commodities, and sending Susan to borrow them from a neighbour, promising at the same time to repay them next day. Then her poor old memory, as she called it, would fail her, and nothing more would be heard about the repayment. Susan wondered what would happen when all the neighbours rebelled against this system: for the last time that she had been sent to borrow sugar, she had been unable to do so, and as a result, there had been none in the house for days.

Always hungry, and always tired, Susan lived through the days with only one thought: that if ever she succeeded in extracting a holiday from Madame Herbin, she would visit Jim's grave, which was at no great distance. Jim . . . he had been dead, now, for over three years.

But it was not until Madame Herbin wished to pay a visit of a fortnight to her married daughter that Susan succeeded in getting a holiday, and then it was only because Madame Herbin was glad of any excuse not to pay for her food during that

170

fortnight. Susan, as she set out, thought: "If only I had the courage I'd die where I'm going. Die, and never see that dreadful house again."

.   .   .   .   .

It was two days before she came to the grey land, the land of the dead, scarred and pitted as if it had been laid waste by an earthquake. It should be rich, should it not, that land, with so much treasure laid below; so many millions of hearts that once held the world and the hope of great adventures, so much youth? But even the air that brooded over it was smirched and sullen, the sun seemed a candle-end, waning, melting, in an endless waste of shade.

Her heart in her seemed dead. She thought: "If I hadn't a heart in me, I'd be much lighter. What's the use of it now, anyway?"

Then, late on the second day, she saw the wooden cross that bore Jim's name.

As the light died, Susan said to herself, "I must have been sitting here for hours," but then, time meant nothing to her now, so actually, she might only have been sitting there for quite a short while. She had waited for some sound, for some sign, but there had been none, so she thought: "Perhaps it is all a mistake, perhaps he is not really there at all." And then, when it was nearly dark, she saw him standing at the foot of the grave that bore his name. She had been sitting with her head in her hands, so she did not see him come: but there he was, her Jim for whom she had waited for so long. Only she wondered: "Why does he not take me in his arms? Why does he not kiss me, as he used to do? Does he think I am frightened of him, of my Jim, because he has come back to me from *there?* . . . Oh, can it be that he does not know me? Has he forgotten me, in all that long time when he was lying there, alone? Jim, Jim, I never thought it would change you like this! You didn't come to me, Jim. So I have had to come to you. You see, I have come to you at last."

171

But he made no movement. He did not come towards her. He only stood looking at her. And then she saw that it was not Jim; it was a stranger who stood staring at her.

It was a long time before he spoke, and then he said: "Who are you? Why are you here?"

"My lad is here," she said. "He has waited for me a long time. But I have come to him at last. I shall be with him now for ever."

"Your lad? So it was you whom I must find!"

"Find *me*?"

"Yes. I told him I would find you. In that long night, before he died."

Chapter VII

IT WAS early next day when they met again, in the grey land, in the world of the dead; and he found her sitting in the same place, as if she had never moved from it, she saw him standing looking at her as she had seen him standing the night before. She wondered now that she saw him in the lack-lustre twilight that haunted the land, how she could have thought it was Jim. He was of the same build as Jim, but this man could never have been young and gay. His face was hollow and filled with a shadow that seemed an echo of that twilight; it was grey and hard as the rocks.

Day after day they met, and he hardly spoke to her. Then one day, standing beside her, he said: "My name is Hans Orthoven. I am a German. Here lies the only friend I have." There was a long silence, then he said: "And I killed him."

Susan stared across the waste of silence, the stricken world that lay between them, at the man standing there. Then from the black hole between her lips came a strangled sound:

"Murderer!"

"Yes," he said. "I am a murderer. Like all men on earth. But must hate be born again?"

She cried: "It is *you* who have stolen him from me!"

In a low voice he said: "He would never have come back to you. He had gone, and in his place was some dreadful ghost that had arisen from this soil—a murderous ghost, hating, fearing the light, creeping, revengeful. His soul had been lost in despair, and this thing had come in its place. But on that last night, it came back to him, the soul that had loved you, the soul that you knew. Death has given him back to you."

He was silent. Then he said: "He forgave me. He said: 'I should never have gone back. I could never go back to life after this. I was dead from the moment I began to kill. And now you have saved me.' He told me that I must write to his father and tell him about that last night. So, when the war was over, I wrote to the old man. I asked him, too, where I might find you. But he replied: 'What does that matter? She will get another man. All women are alike. She cannot use my son. A dead man cannot give her a new life.' "

Conception. Breeding. Generation. The building of new worlds. What else do they need—all things that flower and bear fruit? Yet, in the centre of all, is a dark seed—death.

"And then," he went on, "one day he came to find me and to kill me." He stopped dead. He was looking back on the day, a year before, when, turning away from the window out of which he had been staring, he saw the old man standing in the doorway. There, crouching as if the structure of his bone had been changed by hate, until his skeleton leaned as if it thirsted for some dark stream of blood, with his head bent from the light as if he no longer had a part in it, the old man stood. He was a patch of thickened black shade, excepting for the gleaming thing in his hand.

Crouching there in silence, he waited. There was no sound in the room excepting for a drumming noise that might have been the ticking of a clock, or the beating of a heart, then the German spoke:

"Well. Why don't you shoot? Is it because you know that you can't kill a dead man? That's where I have the advantage of you. You can still feel pain."

His voice died away. From the old man's lips came a hoarse animal sound.

"I am an old man. And my only son is dead."

"Yes," said the other. "You are an old man. You have lived more years than I. Yet I am a thousand years older than you. All the wasted years that lie under the earth—those wasted years since Christ died—all the future that lies murdered, all the years in which the children who will never be born might have walked in the sunlight, all the years that my child might have lived, and his child after him. They are piled on my shoulders, and are dragging me down. I breathe, so I know that I am unburied. But I have no place in all the world. When I walk in the sunlight, people do not see me. I have no place in the light. I get up in the morning and I lie down at night, but no part of the earth belongs to me. I have no country. It will not have me. My mother bore two other sons, and the English killed them. So my mother cursed me because I love the enemy I killed. He is my only friend, and where he lies is my only home."

Standing at the window, he waited. Then, as he looked at the doorway, he saw that the black shadow crouching in it was gone.

Now, speaking to the girl beside him, he said: "There were so many millions of us, happy in our small lives, we had homes and were warm.

"Once I, too, loved. I had a wife. I had a child.

"Then one day, a man, harmless as any other, came to visit the place where we lived, and in his honour, because he was the Governor of the Province, there was a procession. And my little son, my Hans, four years old, went to watch it. Why should we care who has the power and supremacy, who has the money and the great possessions, or which nation is to rule? Are we not all alike, made of flesh that is a pitiable thing, that is born and dies in pain?

174

"My Hans went to watch the procession. And a man who thought this nation or that, this political party or that, must or must not rule, threw a bomb at the harmless old man who was a Governor, and he killed my child, and he set the world on fire. And my wife, my girl, the woman who was half my heart, who was the life in my blood, who was my pulse, she died. The nations that should have been one nation, they killed her, and they killed our child, with their greed, their fear, their blindness and hate. And they gave me hate in the place of love."

Hate, a monstrous sun that dissolves the bones in the body till the soul creeps in the dust like a serpent dragging its dark slow dull weight along. Hate, a sun that darkens the blood into blackness, thickens it into a morass. Hate that melts the flesh. Hate that fuses the hater, with the hated till they are one being and indissoluble, indivisible, till through the days and the nights the hater and the hated are one.

He said: "I was blackened by my hate. But then, in that long night, when the hating men and the men who were mad with fear had retreated, and we were left on the field, the boy who was dying and I with my wound that was less than the wound in my soul, hate died—died as if it had never been born, and love came in its place. I loved and forgave mankind. For this boy whom I had killed, as he lay in my arms, suddenly it was my child that lay there, my child that was murdered by a man as foolish and as blind as me. He had come back to me out of all this terrible welter, this muddle and waste that we have made of the world, come back to forgive the man who had killed him in his blindness. And I saw that we are all equally guilty, and all equally pitiable: small creatures afraid of the darkness, yet pulling it down upon our world.

"Yes, it was the boy I killed who gave me back love.

"We had delivered each other. And as he lay dying, he kissed me."

Chapter VIII

Anna had thought that darkness could never overtake her; but this year, the whole of life seemed changed, even the summer was dimmed—was only the mechanical dull action of the light and shadow over a dark world. Grief is like this, meaningless light and shade, light without warmth, shade without coolness, but sometimes, too, it is a sleep, in which we float and drift aimlessly down a long river; or it is a slumber from behind lidless eyes.

William, who had come over to see her from his parents' house, was sitting with her near the open window, looking out over the world of buttercups. Field after field of shining living gold, with sometimes a tree casting a water-dark shadow. But there was one field where there was no shade excepting the sedate dark shadow cast by Becky as she walked along in her bunched gown made of some country stuff that was the colour of the honeycombed hen-brown wild columbines that grew at the edges of the fields. There was a density about the shadow that she cast on the golden fields: seen from far away, with no wind to blow her talk over the buttercups, she was like a dark grave nun, a Sister Tabitha or Sister Dorcas, or like a ghost lady walking alone in the fields. There was no other living creature in sight, excepting a cock whose shining water-dark feathers, golden feet and five-pointed crown, could be seen moving among the buttercups.

A world of shining living gold, but, for Anna, the shade of winter had fallen. William looked at her. She was sitting with her face half turned away, but he could still see the small scoring of new lines near her eyes. She had not been looking well lately, and had been troubled by a little cough which often, she said, kept her awake at nights.

Now she turned her face towards William, and in her eyes was a frightened look. She said: "Something is wrong, William. Something is very wrong with Jonathan. Oh, I don't mean his health. I've been dreadfully worried about that too. But there is something I don't understand in his letters. It is not what he says. But one feels—one feels there is silence underneath every sentence. Silence, and something hiding beneath that. Sometimes I feel as if I were in one of those deep sleeps in which one dreams that one is bound hand and foot, helpless, unable to move, with the danger coming ever nearer and nearer, a danger that one cannot see, but knows is there."

He had changed. And Anna, wandering in darkness, had no certain knowledge of the true reason. Only she knew that it was winter, and that the long time of cold had begun.

On his homecoming to Ireland from London, he had seemed restless; but Anna had thought this was the result of fatigue, and his eagerness to return to London she ascribed to his new friendship with Weston the poet. It was dull for him in Ireland; she recognised that, and she noticed with an amusement in which there was a touch of pain the excuses he made for his short stay in Ireland, the pretence that there was a great deal of business that he must transact in London. He seemed, even, to have succeeded in believing this.

Now that he had gone again, his letters arrived as regularly as before, and they were as long as ever; but they were changed. He no longer said that whenever he wrote to her, he felt his lips forming the words as if he were talking to his dearest little Anna; he no longer said: "Oh, faith, I should be glad to be in the same kingdom as Anna."

The letters were full of excuses for remaining in London.

But there were moments when she almost felt his physical presence, as if she might hear a door open and, raising her eyes, see him before her, smiling as he used to do before the winter had begun. She could, she thought, see his daily life, the people he knew. . . . But there was one person whom she did not see.

He had taken lodgings, he told her, a few doors away from Mrs. Vanelden's house. He thought he had mentioned her to Anna when he was in London before, had he not? A kind, motherly woman, if a little too worldly. He had not been well lately, so he had found himself dining very frequently at Mrs. Vanelden's house. He could venture as far as that, but would not care to go farther. It was really very convenient to have near neighbours whom one knew, and who would look after one if one was ill. And then, too, interesting people went to her house. Yes, she was undoubtedly a valuable acquaintance.

And Anna was glad that his lodgings were close to the house of a kind motherly woman, who would take care of him, if he was ill.

So time drifted on, and winter melted into spring, spring changed to summer. And nobody in the world had ever been so happy as Essy Vanelden.

He was hers now; she told herself that there could no longer be any doubt of it: he was hers and hers alone. Now that summer had come, he had moved away from his lodgings near the Crescent; but he left his best clothes in Mrs. Vanelden's house, and twice a day he came there to change. When he wished to receive friends, it was to Mrs. Vanelden's house that he came; his wine was kept in their cellar. He often played cards there with Mrs. Long, Essy's cousin, who from time to time would try to arouse his jealousy by mentioning other possible suitors for Essy's hand, or to make him uncomfortable by enquiring why she was so melancholy. Their house was, indeed, practically his home. He spent all, or nearly all his time with Essy: he introduced her to all his friends. For she was, after all, a young woman of fashion, used to the world and to meeting people of importance. She was quite different from his dear Anna, so good, so reliable, but a little shy and gauche, a little behind the times. His kind, good Anna. Yes, it was undoubtedly a pleasure to be seen with Essy.

And he told himself that it was perfectly safe; had he not made it clear to Essy from the beginning, or nearly from the beginning, of their companionship, that both were perfectly free—free to move away from each other if they chose?

But Essy did not want to move away. She was perfectly happy, and her heart swelled with pride at the thought that she, little Essy Vanelden, was the confidante of the great man of whom the whole world was in awe. Not only that! Mr. Weston and all the other famous men by whom he was surrounded, indeed the whole of London, *knew* it. They all knew that the great man was her captive, was utterly under her spell.

Then one day, something happened that was to change the whole of Essy's life.

It was two years after they had met for the first time; and it was just such flashing summer weather as that in which he had been brought to Mrs. Vanelden's house. Jonathan was staying in Windsor, and letters, as usual, passed between him and Essy. He could not imagine, he told her, how she would pass the time in his absence, excepting by lying in bed till it was twelve, and then having all her followers about her till dinner time. What did she do all the afternoon? She and Moll must walk as much as they could in the Park, and not sit moping, for he knew that they could neither work, nor read, nor play, and that they did not care for company. He longed to drink a cup of coffee in the Sluttery, and hear her dun him for a secret, and bully him because he did not drink his coffee while it was hot.

And then came this sentence: "How comes it that you have all decided to come to Windsor? If you were never here, I think you all cannot do better than come for three or four days."

For this was his way of suggesting that they should pay him a visit. It was then that Essy took the step that was to alter the whole course of her life. She wrote saying that she would come alone, excepting for her young brother. She would bring no mother, and no sister.

Essy Vanelden was going to make her proprietorship evident to the whole world.

.   .   .   .   .

Essy Vanelden sat in the Sluttery, sulking. Her eyes were red from weeping, and she had relapsed into her old down-at-heel, tumbling-down-hill appearance. She said to herself: "He *asked* me to come. He *asked* me. After all, I know perfectly well that it was not for Mumsie's and Molkins's sake that he suggested our coming. And then, when I make it clear that I am willing to come, he puts me off, by pretending he is coming up to London. And does not even take the trouble to do it himself. He sends his friend Smith to do it for him. That horrid Mrs. Hendry is there, of course, and I suppose he is seeing *her* all the time."

Mrs. Hendry was a lady who, recently, had been trying to distract the great man's attention from Essy.

She took up a writing pad: "Mr. Smith tells me," she wrote "you have made a solemn resolution to leave Windsor the moment we come there; it is a noble resolution; please keep to it."

Biting her pencil, she added: "I *shall* go to Windsor, and to be revenged, I shall stay there as long as Mrs. Hendry does, and if *that* is not long enough for you, I shall follow her to Hampton Court, and then I shall see which makes you the most furious, seeing me, or not seeing her. Besides, Mr. Smith has promised me to intercept all your letters to her, and hers to you, so that I can read them."

Then, going into her bedroom, she walked over to a table where, by a vase of pale roses, a box stood. It was a gaudy painted box, and looked frail, but it was stronger than it seemed. Opening the box, she took out a large bundle of papers. Some were written in a small scholarly hand, others in a large sprawling untidy handwriting. And as Essy looked at these, her expression changed. She smiled.

Chapter IX

As soon as she had posted the letter, Essy would have given a world to get it back. What could have induced her to do such a mad thing? He would be angry, and Essy knew what his anger could be like! At dinner that night, Mrs. Vanelden saw that something had happened to disturb her little girl, but, with her usual airy tact, she disregarded the signs that this was so. They drove down into the country after dinner, and, walking in the calm moonlight, Essy's terror grew. What *had* happened, she asked herself, that she was walking here without Jonathan—she from whom he was inseparable?

She hardly slept, but next day, the glamour of the sun, the warmth, the summery sounds, brought her comfort. Nothing had happened: her happiness was safe. Indeed, she was glad now that she had written that letter, for she had at least shown Jonathan that, whoever else stood in awe of the great man, she did not! She would do as she liked, and the sooner he realised that, the better!

Mumsie was going to be out to lunch, and would not be returning till late, and as she did not want the car that Lady Mickleover had lent them, Essy and a girl friend drove down to Windsor, to take Jonathan by surprise. But when they arrived at Jonathan's lodgings, they were told that he could not see them. He was ill, it appeared. . . .

And so she must drive back to London.

She was furious. He thought he could treat her like that, did he? Well, we should see! And as soon as she heard that he was going to Oxford, she announced her intention of following him there, adding that she hoped it would be more agreeable there than at Windsor. In answer to this announcement, she received a short note saying that he would not see her for a thousand pounds; that he had no time to write to her at length, for he was in his dressing-gown and writing a dozen letters and packing up papers—and, as for her complaint about her visit to Windsor: "Why, then, you should not have come, and I know that as well as you." He thought it was wrong of her to come to Oxford, but he supposed that if he did not look up any of his acquaintances, but let somebody from the hotel show her round the colleges, she might not be known.

Reading this letter, a gasp of anger escaped her—of anger mixed with fear.

But when he returned to London, and dined at their house as usual, she felt reassured. And in her renewed assurance, she talked a great deal too loudly. She had an ugly voice. More than once, too (so anxious was she to hold his attention), she repeated a trivial remark twice or thrice.

Several times she caught Hare looking at her. And she could not interpret the look.

Then, next morning, almost for the first time in all their friendship, there was no letter for her lying on the tray with her early morning tea. However, as she told herself, he had left their house very late the night before, and probably had not had time to write. But that afternoon, he did not come to the Sluttery to drink coffee, although this was his daily habit. Something must have kept him, she supposed. Still it was strange; she would have thought he would have telephoned. She waited for him until half past six and then, very bright-eyed, told Mumsie she thought she would go and see Alicia Long. When she returned to the Crescent, there was still no message for her. Yet, even then, she was not really frightened. She knew that he had a great deal of business that had to be done at the moment, and, too, he was seeing more people than ever.

Next day he came to luncheon, because he had an appointment with the Duke of Brighton, and after lunch he took the Duke into the sitting-room that Mumsie had lent him—(it was his, Mumsie declared; for the house was as much his house as it was that of her little girl's: he was quite another son to her)—and after the Duke had gone he came and sat for a little while in the Sluttery. But soon—he could not have been there for more than three quarters of an hour—he looked at his watch and said he must be going.

And so it went on, day after day. He still teased Essy about her laziness and about her jealousy if he talked to Molkins, poor Molkins, who was always ill now, who always looked frightened. But he was no longer so attentive when she spoke; when he had an appointment to take her out, he was nearly always late; several times he telephoned to say that he could not come at all; and once, he even went so far as to put Mumsie off when she and Essy and Molkins were to have come to tea in his rooms. Summer faded, and winter took its place; then winter melted into spring, but the glamour of spring seemed to Essy to have died.

Shadow had fallen. At morning and evening, walking in the dews or standing with her hand upon a door, hesitating whether to close it, you saw an immense black shadow like a pillar or monument behind her, until, as she grew older, she would seem but a shrunken emblem of that shade.

But still she said to herself: "Everything will come right, it *must*!" He was going to Ireland in a few days time, travelling by slow stages, and she would write to him just as if nothing had happened, they would continue their correspondence throughout his stay there, and when he returned to London all would be as it had always been in the past.

She was confirmed in this belief when she received a letter from him, written the night before he left London, in which he said: "I promised to write to you. It is impossible for anyone to have more gratitude at heart for all your kindness and generosity to me. I will write to you all from some of my stages, but directed to you. . . . I have hardly time to put my pen to paper, but I would make good my promise. May God bless you, and make you happy; and so good-bye, brat."

Comforted and happy, she went to bed, locking away this letter with the others in the painted casket. She had had one moment's unreasoning fear when he did not come to say good-bye before he left London, but how foolish that had been. After all, he could scarcely have had a moment, there must have been so much to do. And another letter, a letter written to them all, but addressed to her, would arrive to-morrow, or on Thursday at the latest. She must not be impatient.

But it was a week before the letter came, and then it was addressed to Mumsie. And the letter spoke of Molkins just as much as of Essy—as though she were equally important to him—and contained, too, a great deal about Essy's scolding and grumbling! He supposed (he said) that Essy would grumble because he spoke of Moll. Well, he was away now, and who would Essy find to scold, and who would Moll find to tell her stories and give her chocolates? He thought he would send Essy a letter in print from Ireland, because she always declared she could never read handwriting. He had looked in the chimney at Dunstable, where he had stayed for a night, for marks of the coffee Essy had spilt there, and he had wished he had a diamond ring with him to write their names on the window. . . . And he added, that he could hear Moll laughing at what he was saying, and Essy scolding and grumbling. And that Mrs. Vanelden must be sure to write and tell him who visited Essy when she was lying in bed in the morning, and all the other news.

The letter caused a great flutter, and Mumsie and Essy counted the number of times that he mentioned Moll and the number of times that he mentioned Essy, and they laughed a lot, and Mumsie teased Essy, for the numbers were even.

Essy wrote and told Jonathan about the counting and the teasing, and reminded him that it was now three long weeks since he had written her a single word. "Oh, happy Dublin," she cried, "that can occupy all your thoughts." She was uneasy, but she told herself that all would come right. It *must*. One's life does not fall into ruins just because one has given way to a momentary foolishness.

For her letter, the mad escapade of her visit to Windsor, *had* been a mistake. She would admit it now. What had caused her to make those fatal mistakes, the heat of the summer, vanity, a wish to prove to herself and to others that Essy Vanelden was sure of the great man? ". . . *Fatal!*" What was she saying? *Of course* they were not fatal! Everything would come right, be as it had always been. Only she must be more careful in the future, not make these mistakes.

And then came the news, quite by chance, that he was ill. Distracted with fear, and with the worry caused by his silence, she wrote to him a second time, though it was only four days since she had written him her last letter: "Who is your doctor?" she asked. "For God's sake do not be persuaded to take too many slops. Satisfy me so much as to tell me what medicines you have taken." It must be, she said, the journey that had upset him, and the sooner he went into the country the better. She added: "If I talk impatiently, I know you have goodness enough to forgive me, when you remember how great a comfort it is to me to ask these questions, though I know it will be a long time before I can receive an answer. Oh! What would I give to know how you are at this instant. My fortune is too hard, your absence was enough without this cruel addition. But I must confine my thoughts, or at least stop from telling them to you, or you will scold me.

"*Don't* be angry with me for writing. I did all I could to prevent myself from doing so till I heard you were better, but it was useless. I had to write. I beg you to make Parvisol write to me and tell me what I wish to know. I am impatient to the last degree to hear how you are. I hope I shall soon have you here."

Every dawn, she, who had watched the growing light, thinking: "Another day of happiness!" would creep like a sick animal to breathe in the air through the open window.

Four o'clock. Only another four hours, and then there would be a letter—there *must* be. Every time during the day when there was a knock on the front door, she would rush past Mary and pick up the letters. But no. There was not a sign. Not a word.

'Then, three days after she had written this expression of her anguish, she heard, through a casual sentence let fall by a friend, that he was well again. He was well, and he had not written. Her agony now had gone beyond control; she was blind and deaf to all but this. Throwing all caution, all restraint to the winds, she wrote to him again, and this time it was not possible for him to misunderstand her letter. The little Missessy, the brat, the child of the pleasant companionship, had fallen violently and irretrievably in love with him.

And silence fell.

If she walked in the streets, she saw him beside her. If she sat in the Sluttery, she heard the sound of his voice. The barrel-organ in the Crescent, playing its little light happy tunes, added to her anguish by reminding her of the days when she was young and it was always summer. It was summer still—but everything was changed.

Everything around her. There was no one to whom she could speak. Molkins was not well: she had a cough and always seemed despondent, she crept about, her head bowed, her face yellow and anxious-looking, she paid no attention to Essy's misery. And Mumsie: she too had changed. Several times since Jonathan had left she had spoken quite sharply to Essy, though never, of course, in public, for when other people were present no flaw was to be detected in Mumsie's surface. Yet Essy could not help feeling that something had happened to annoy Mumsie, even that she was angry with her little girl.

And then a second change happened in Essy's life, and this time it was something that happened to Mumsie. It could scarcely, however, be said to affect Mumsie, as she knew nothing of it.

It was a very hot afternoon, and Essy and Molkins were going for a drive in the country in the borrowed motor. Passing the door of Mrs. Vanelden's sitting-room on their way out, they looked in. Mumsie was sitting on the sofa with a book in her hand (You know what I am, reading is my passion!), and a sweet smile on her face. She did not look up as Essy and Molkins put their heads in at the door.

For some weeks now, Mrs. Vanelden had complained even more frequently than usual, that she had no time for reading. Her friends, dear naughty things, took up the whole of the day. They *would* insist on her going to luncheon parties and dinner parties, theatres and the opera; they *would* drive her down into the country; they were always running in and out. But this afternoon, for once, her time would be all her own, excepting for a visit from Lord Sunningdale, her *dear old* friend, whom she was expecting at about four o'clock.

Her old friend would like to find her reading. "How like Mollie!" he would exclaim. And Mrs. Vanelden wondered which was the most suitable author for the occasion. Molière, she thought, for Lord Sunningdale was an admirer of the French classics. Mrs. Vanelden did not care for Molière, because, as she said frequently—though not in Lord Sunningdale's presence —he wrote about such pretentious people. *Les Précieuses Ridicules*, for instance, seemed to her to be dead people, pretending to be alive. But on this occasion, it would be a pretty, suitable touch, as she told herself, if she were found reading this work, which was among Lord Sunningdale's chief favourites. Yes, Molière was undoubtedly right. And taking down *Les Précieuses Ridicules* from the bookshelf, she draped herself on the sofa, arranging her smile.

It was a very hot afternoon, she thought. Quite breathless. And the canary was making a lot of noise.

.   .   .   .   .

In an hour's time, Lord Sunningdale, making his way up the stairs unannounced, thought: "How quiet the house is: not a sound excepting for that bird singing." And opening the door of Mrs. Vanelden's sitting-room, he looked in. . . .

Yes, there was Mollie, sitting with a book in her hand, and a wide smile on her face. She did not look up from the book as he approached.

"Molière—what!" said Lord Sunningdale, advancing towards her. "Molière—what!"

There was no answer. Only the wind from the open window blew a few letters from the writing-table on to the floor. "Unopened bills," Lord Sunningdale said to himself. And the canary continued its song, a flimsy sunny bridge over darkness.

Chapter X

LETTER AFTER letter, letter after letter. They fell upon Jonathan as monotonously and as pitilessly as the rain. The world seemed to be filled now with nothing but rain, and Essy's letters that fell like rain, and the wind that haunted the outside of the house, like the ghost of a living creature, hunting for any crevice through which it could creep, shaking the doors, crying at the windows. Sometimes the wind and the rain sounded like a ghost, but at other times they had a curiously animal sound, barking and yelping, growling and grunting, neighing, braying, mewing, purring, bleating, lowing, croaking, crowing, cawing, cooing, gobbling, quacking, cackling, among the thick fleshy leaves and along the lanes; the wind and the rain seemed to be the only live things in the world. Those, and his thoughts. And, of course, the letters.

There was no end to them. She would clutch at any excuse to extract a reply from him, so that she could feel that he moved still in the same world as that in which she walked. And her mother's death, the fact that she had left her children up to the eyes in debt, gave her an admirable excuse for writing to him. Would he not give her advice? He *must*, for to whom could she turn if not to him. Mumsie's old friends seemed so changed since her death; they were not interested in Essy's troubles— they did not even pretend to be. Yet those troubles were heavy enough to have aroused their pity. Essy was afraid to go out, lest Mumsie's creditors should be waiting outside—angry people who talked in rough voices—she was afraid every time that the bell of the front door rang. Every morning she woke up with a feeling of dread, wondering what fresh blow the day would bring, wondering if the creditors would carry out their threat to put the bailiffs into the house.

By this time, the repulsion Jonathan had felt when she first revealed her love for him had, mingled with it, a real pity for her circumstances. He would not leave her to her fate without making an attempt to help her. And he wrote, telling her that if it was necessary for her to borrow money, he would guarantee the loan. But this again only fanned her hope that by one means or another she would succeed in reviving in him the feeling he had once had for her.

He could do nothing with her. When the first repugnance had worn off to some slight degree, and he was able to remember that he had once felt affection for her, he who had hoped to restrain her, first by silence, then, when that failed, by a cold and severe letter, now tried to restore some kind of normal relationship between them by teasing her, by affecting to believe that her declaration of love for him had been written as a joke, or that her love was a hallucination that, born in a moment, would vanish in a moment, without pain. It was useless. She was beyond his control or her own. And his pity began to give way to anger.

He was, at the time, a paying guest at a vicarage in Berkshire, the house of an old acquaintance, the Reverend John Geree, who, melancholy and thoughtful by nature, had become even more so by reason of the solitude in which he lived. In this retreat, Jonathan, who was angry with the government because of their failure to keep one of their promises to him, revenged himself upon the world in general by boring himself into a state of mulish muteness. Mrs. Geree was paying a visit to her father, and of this Jonathan was glad, for he had conceived the idea that her return would only add an increased weight of dullness. He was, therefore, alone with his host, and Mr. Geree and he would eat their meals in silence, or, if

189

conversation became necessary, Jonathan would pretend to an increased deafness in order to make this as difficult as possible. For days at a time he would refuse to speak. Nor did the actual routine of their life add to the gaiety, for out of consideration for Mrs. Geree, Jonathan had insisted that he should not change the habits of his life, so that they dined between twelve and one, at eight o'clock had some bread and butter and ale, and at ten, went to bed. There was nothing to do but to read and to walk: the empty hour, that drone-sound striking, was struck by dullness alone.

It was, therefore, a relief to him, in spite of his self-imposed silence, when his friends Mr. Weston and Mr. Jarvis invaded this hermitage, one Sunday morning at church time, and announced their intention of staying with him for a few days. This invasion had not been carried out without some misgiving, for none of Hare's acquaintances, however intimate their friendship with the great man might be, could be certain how they would be received. His eccentricity, slight to begin with, had increased of late, and he had strange habits which had grown odder as his years increased. He had been known, for instance, when his friends visited him, to add up the cost of their entertainment in a loud and rather grumbling voice, though with no real appearance of regret, for he was anxious to be generous with his friends and wished to show them that he did not grudge the sum of money that was spent in offering them entertainment.

No contretemps of the kind happened, however, on this occasion; they escaped with the usual scolding, to which they were accustomed, and Weston, whose temper was not so curmudgeonly as that of his famous friend, was more amused than stunned by the Tartarean gloom in which he found himself.

The rain had stopped, and a period of intense dryness had set in; Weston, walking with Hare and Jarvis in the fields, thought that the dust might have been the dust of all the dead philosophers of the world. . . . The Martha-coloured scabious waved aimlessly, and from time to time, from beyond the cotton-nightcap trees, there came a sound of crazy hen-coop laughter, cackling at Jonathan Hare and raising the black anger that was lying like a well in his heart.

For, although the rain had stopped, the letters, that mimicked the rain, had not. Still they fell upon him, pitiless drop after drop. She was threatening him, now, that she would invade his retreat in Berkshire; and this must be stopped at all costs; he had better, he supposed, go to London to see her. And still the letters came, and each letter was a ghost come back from the dead to haunt the great, the famous Jonathan Hare in all the walks of his life.

And then one day she fulfilled her threat: she came. A cab drove up to the door, there was a ring at the bell, and he was only just in time to tell Amy, the maid, that he would not see her. She had to go back to the station in the cab that had brought her. Jonathan, sheltering behind the curtain of his bedroom, saw her drive away: he caught one glimpse of her face. She was so changed he would scarcely have known her.

Chapter XI

WOULD HE never be free from these entreaties, these attempts to force herself on him through his sense of pity. She was now completely beyond control, she had thrown all restraint to the winds. She followed him now wherever he went, and he would see her piteous look bent on him from afar: for she did not dare to speak to him. He was sick of her look of misery, of mute reproach imputing to him a guilt of which he was innocent, since he had made it clear to her from the beginning, or *almost* from the beginning, that she had no rights over his life. He had been, it is true, amused by her proprietary ways, but that had been only play, and as soon as she tried to exercise them seriously, he had shown her the truth. She was a pleasant extraneous thing whose life had been sacrificed because he had chosen it as food, as material to feed his own. She was part of his existence, then, like the food he ate. But has the food that nourishes us any rights over us?

He told himself that he had had to make this clear in self-defence. If she could have imprisoned him, she would have buried him beneath a world-fall of feathers, of soft and cosy sleep, so that he might live no more under the pomp and splendour of the black sun that ruled over his universe. "A friendship like ours," he had said to her, so that she might have no excuse for misunderstanding the nature of it, "is the best human relationship that exists, because it leaves us both completely free, and yet at the same time it binds us more closely together, is more lasting, than any other." And he told himself that in saying this he had given her, as well as himself, the chance of freedom. Was it his fault, then, that she had refused to take it?

When Essy laid no restraining hand upon him, he neither loved nor hated her. He had never loved her, but there would be moments in the future when, fearing that she might escape from him, not into a freedom that would leave him also free, but into some refuge that would exclude him, that she might develop interests apart from his, in people other than himself, his vanity would masquerade as pity. Then pity, as he told himself, and not a love of power, would urge him to retake her, to prevent at all costs the flight of this helpless creature into some unknown and dangerous future. And at these moments he could even feel a transitory tenderness for her. She lived but in his life, and she was more malleable than Anna. But the tenderness soon died under the flood of entreaties it let loose, the reproachful letters, the solicitous enquiries about his health, fluttering about him like scared hens, dropping feathers in all directions, musty, cloying, and suffocating.

Unutterable weariness. He would never be free from her, even if she died, for he knew that in spite of all her promises, she had kept every letter, every record of their companionship.

The little Missessy with whom he had thought to find freedom in treachery, had now become his doom. Yet who could have believed that this figurehead, with its overlapping mouth and breasts and hips, the mouth that overlapped the face, the breasts that overlapped their constrictions, the voice and sentences that overlapped their meaning, the fat little feet (with always one small hole in one stocking), overlapping the downtrodden gaudy shoes, could have become this grey and prison-worn creature?

Now, with dread and repugnance in his heart, he climbed the narrow stairs to the Sluttery, to find her, standing like a ghost, upon the landing. She could not even have the decency to wait for his hand upon the door, to pretend that she had any other interest in all her life but him. She could not even pretend to read a book or to sew while she was waiting for him, a pretence of indifference that would have aroused, once again, his vanity and acquisitiveness. She must stand there, like some harmless creature who has been wantonly murdered, forcing him, who in spite of his ferocity hated the sight of pain, to see that homeless face he had drained of all meaning, that body whose life he had taken for food.

Her aspect was so changed that he looked at her with a half-repelled pity. Could this be the gay, careless, down-at-heel Missessy of the Sluttery, the brat who, at twenty-four was still pretending to be nineteen, with her tossed curls and her pouting mouth—(stealing behind her, he had, with amusement, watched her practising these habits in front of the mirror) —her perpetual agitation and animation, and her silly childish voice reiterating "Nobody wants poor little me!"

Seeing him, she gave a gasp, and drew him away from the dusty sunlight, which fell through the skylight on the top landing, into the Sluttery.

If she could only learn to be silent. But the words, the entreaties, broke from her mouth, hesitating and lame, and at moments her voice sank into a dreadful muttering, like that of an animal trying to learn the speech of men in order to tell

Gs   193 them of its pain. "I have tried," she whispered, "to keep my promise, not to write to you, not to reproach you. I have tried so hard not to write you an angry letter."

"Reproaches! There is never anything else. I have come to dread the sight of your letters."

Raising her eyes from the floor to his face, with the look of hopeless appeal he had come to know so well, raising them for a moment and then dropping them again, she said: "Oh, Jonathan, how *could* you have been so cruel as to leave me without a word, in that terrible anxiety, knowing you were ill, and not knowing if you were better or worse. Waiting all day in anguish and then waiting all night for the next day which might bring news—and none coming."

Oh, those long nights of waiting, and then seeing the first light cut into the room. . . . She paused, remembering. There had been dawns when she had felt that blood must ooze from those gradual slow cuts of light. . . .

Looking at the chilled and repelled face of the stranger into whose polar waste she had intruded, her voice grew dulled as if she had been stricken with a deadly sickness, or had been imprisoned for so long that speech was a rarity to her. She muttered: "Oh, *why* did you not make Parvisol write to me a word to tell me if you were better, when I begged it so much. Why could you not write or say one word to please me? I have often heard you say that you would willingly go to a little trouble and inconvenience, if you knew it would give another person a great deal of pleasure. And if you were able to write yourself, how could you have been so cruel as to wait so long before telling me the thing I wished most to know. If you thought I wrote to you too often, your only way was to tell me so, or at least to write to me again so that I could know you don't quite forget me. But I know now that you never think of me, that you put me entirely out of your mind excepting when you get a letter from me and so can't put the thought of me away from you. If you were happy, it was cruel of you not to tell me so"—she paused, choked by her dread, and then,
194

in a strangled voice, said—"unless your happiness would mean my misery."

There was a silence, and she looked at him with terror. Oh, what *bad* she said? She thought: "I must stop, I must stop," but a voice she scarcely knew as her own, that seemed not controlled by her, went on: "You never answered my first letters, but they must have reached you, for I sent them, not through the post, but by people who were going to Ireland, and so they can't have been lost."

He looked at her with curiosity. Any other woman in the world would have understood the letter he had written to her, after weeks of silence, in answer to her anguished entreaties, the pages that fell upon him day by day.

She had waited, for one word, for one sign, not only for days, but for nearly five weeks, creeping down the stairs like a frightened animal every time that she heard a knock upon the door, with the drum in her heart increasing its speed and the sound of its beat until it seemed as loud as the knock upon the door. So it went on, day by day. Not a word, not a sign. And then, one hot summer afternoon, after weeks of waiting, the letter came. It was just after Mumsie died, and before the worst trouble with the creditors began. He had not then heard of her death. Essy stood in the passage, listening. Molkins was out, the servants were at work, and it would be safe to pore over her treasure, she would not be disturbed, or her happiness spied upon. A faint chopping noise, a pleasant summery sound, rose from the kitchen, together with the sound of a distant voice, dropping like water. In the crescent outside, a barrel-organ was playing a happy South American tune. You could imagine the dark-faced, grave family, dressed in black, bending over their instruments among the enormous purring leaves under the tropical sun. The tune said: "You will never grow old. The summer will last for ever. Other women will grow old, and their faces will become lined, and love will fade. But for you, happiness and youth and the summer will last for ever."

She forgot Mumsie and the troubles brought about by Mumsie. She was so faint with joy, her hands were trembling so much, that for some moments she could not undo the letter. But she did so at last, standing under the skylight to read it.

At first, she could not understand its meaning; the words seemed to her to have been written by a foreigner in a language that was unknown to her. Then the dusty sunlight shone down on the handwriting and it came alive with a pang.

"I have received your last bad-tempered letter." So it began. "I told you when I left England that I would try to forget everything and everybody there, and would write as seldom as I could. I did, indeed, mean to write one general round of letters to my friends, but my health has made it absolutely out of the question. To be frank, unless the Government sends for me, I have no intention of ever seeing England again." With this, and a few sentences about his walks by the river, and watching the trout playing in it, the letter ended. There was not a word of tenderness, there was no answer to her wild reproaches, her accusations that he had forgotten her for another woman.

She stood for a moment in the dusty sunlight, and then went into the Sluttery and sat down on the sofa where she had so often sat beside him while he drank the coffee she had made for him. She still held the letter in her hand.

She knew, now, that she *dared* not show that she understood its meaning: for if she did, she would be forced to face the truth that either he or she was dead. Dead, or had never been. So she continued to write him imploring letters, as if they were both still living beings. And he, looking at her now, on their first meeting after the writing of that letter, knew only that he could kill her time and time again, but she would come back from the grave in which he had buried her in order to plague him. She had changed from the little Missessy of her own creation and his into something as uncombatible and terrifying as a ghost.

At first, under this change, she had been only a shadow,

varying in depth and length and darkness, a grey and feathery shadow waiting near the banisters on the top landing to envelop him if he should walk up the stairs; but then she had changed again, and had become the cold menacing and lengthy shadow that is cast at evening, a shadow that at times was thrown right across his path, so that he must crush it into the ground if he made a step forward, while at other times it built itself into a huge high threatening catacomb, out of which issued a clanging, menacing, cold and prophetic voice.

But that voice was dulled now, under her deadly sickness. For she had changed again, and had become the Seven Plagues of Egypt, desolating the whole of life until nothing was left but a desert.

He said: "Your letters were not lost. Naturally I received them. But there was only one thing which any friend of yours could do, having read them, and that was not to answer them, in the hope that this would restore you to some sense of self-control, of"—he hesitated—"well, pride."

"Pride?" in a desolate whisper.

He said: "I can't understand you. I cannot understand why you won't be content with what I can give you. But no; you become more indiscreet in your behaviour, in your letters, in your very looks, every day. It seems as if you were incapable of caution, incapable of consideration for me. You knew perfectly well that you ought not to have come to Wantage, knowing that I was there. Then why did you? And you, who used to brag that you were so discreet! Where has your discretion gone?"

"Oh, Jonathan, is it really true that you are going away? Will you be gone for long? Oh, tell me you will be back before another winter comes. I do not know how I shall endure the cold without hearing your voice, without the touch of your hand. There are times, long deserts of time, when I feel I shall die soon, die and not know any more sun, never hear the sound of your voice again. I cannot bear the time of cold. It is too like cold people who hold a little drift of dust to their

197

hearts and who have never known love. It is too like dead people, among whom I must go. I have suffered so much. But it will be still colder there. Only say something to comfort me. Don't let me be afraid."

Putting out her hand timidly, she tried to take his, but with a look of repulsion he withdrew it, saying: "You are far too physical. I have told you that over and over again. Yes, in spite of everything I may have done in my life, my nature is purer than yours."

Her empty hand fell in her lap again, and then, with a slow gesture, she raised it, wiping her lips. She said: "Only tell me you will come back."

He hesitated, then, in a chilled and misted voice said: "Essy, you have begun to develop misery as a habit, you have allowed it to grow on you, developing it of your own free will until it has become a necessity to you. It is no longer an emotion or a feeling, but something you indulge in as the poor indulge in sorrow because it is their only luxury. "

So walled up in her misery that she could scarcely hear what his real voice was saying, because it was a sound from the outside world, and she was alone with misery and the idea she had created of him, she cried once more: "Will you be gone for long?"

This endless scene. These unceasing reproaches. Looking at her with distaste, he said with a patient slowness, as if he were explaining something to a child or a foreigner: "I have told you already that I have not the faintest idea how long I shall stay in Ireland. It is quite possible that I shan't stay there for long; I may even be back in London before the winter. But it is impossible to say for certain. When I am there, I will write to you as soon as I can spare the time, but I want you to understand this, once and for all. I shall never write to you excepting through a third person, I shall never address a letter to you at your own house. It is far too dangerous. And Essy, if you insist on writing to me, I must really ask you to get somebody else to address the envelope. I cannot have these

198

interminable shoals of letters addressed in your handwriting—you do not know who may see them. And for heaven's sake, avoid saying anything private or particularly important. You can never be sure that the letters may not be seen, and then you can have no idea of the appalling misunderstandings and inconveniences, the unending trouble and complications that would be caused."

Pressing her wretched face against the window frame, a face so empty of all but misery that it seemed like a crumpled piece of paper that had lain in the rainy streets, had been blown through the streets all through the night, she said: "You are making me desperate. Now you won't even let me write to you. At least, I mustn't say anything private, I must behave as if I were a stranger to you. Very well, then, I shall come to Ireland. Yes, *I'll follow you wherever you go*, and then I shall know who has changed you towards me, who is keeping you from me. I shall know with whom I have to deal. You can't deceive me, Jonathan. I know now that there is another woman, that you are trying to get rid of me because you want to go to her. But you will not rid yourself of me so easily as that!"

He said: "I have told you over and over again that there is no other woman. But if there were, you would not have the slightest right to complain. You have no rights over me. I am neither your husband nor your lover." Then, in a voice charged with a hatred so patient that it seemed as if it had existed long before his birth, before his conception, before the first man walked upon the earth, he said: "I have told you before, that if you will insist upon coming to Ireland while I am there, you must not expect to see me often. I shall only be able to come and see you very rarely. The place is a hotbed of gossip, and one can have no freedom of any kind, because everything that one says and does is known all over the town in a week's time. We should have to be most careful about meeting." He paused, then added: "And Essy, you must really try not to leap to all these ridiculous conclusions and make these appalling scenes. If you could only realise how irritating it is to be

199

bombarded with endless insinuations and reproaches, to be spied upon and have every movement watched, every word pounced upon and distorted!"

The hatred had frozen now, and a wintry indifference had taken its place; his voice was like a small cold wind. He said: "For all I know, we may meet again this winter. I can't say for certain, but it is quite likely. If we don't, we can only trust to chance. Essy, I am saying all this simply out of friendship for you. It is of *you* I am thinking when I say we must be careful, because it is you who will be injured if there is gossip—not I. And, once and for all, do stop asking me these interminable questions. If you only knew how much they, and the reason that lies behind them, revolt me!"

As he spoke, his feeling of power increased, and he added: "I have thought, now, for some time, that it would be better for you and better for me if you never saw me again, if I went completely out of your life. You seem unable to make the slightest effort to control yourself, and now your lack of self-control has reached such a pitch that really something will have to be done. If you are truly unable to control yourself in such a way that scenes like this do not occur, I shall have to take matters into my own hands and do what I think best—that is, go away for good."

"Oh, Jonathan! Not see you again? Not ever?"

She remembered a small dog she had seen once in the city— a little untidy dog running through the streets between crowds of tall remote people, looking piteously and imploringly up in each face as he passed. He would never again find anyone whose face he knew, or whose voice he knew and who would speak to him kindly. His master had lost him on purpose, had taken him out into the streets and had given him the slip because he was wanted no longer; and now he would go on running for ever, until his feet were worn to shreds, he would lie down in the unfriendly night under the shadow of a doorway or a railway arch, perhaps, or in the yet more uncaring air, and he would steal a bit of food here, a bit there, out of dustbins.

200

But then would come a day, and then another, when he could find nothing to steal—not even a scrap, and when he would be too worn out and bewildered by that endless running through the streets, that search for his master, beginning in the early morning and pausing only for a little while at night, to continue it any longer. He would find nothing to eat, and so, in a very short while, that pursuit would be over.

Pressing her handkerchief to her lips, she thought of that small dog and the pursuit that would end only when he died. Then, turning her grey, prison-face away, the face of one who has been so long in prison that when released into the free and uncaring air she could only feel the terror of homelessness, of having nowhere to go, she said: "Have mercy upon me!"

Chapter XII

HE WAS gone again. Casting a half curious, half contemptuous look at Essy, he had gone, not speaking a word. He had simply opened the door and walked down the stairs, not once turning his head to see what she was doing. And at first, remembering that look, she was alone with shame; the world was a desert, it had no other inhabitants but herself and shame, a humiliation so burning that she wondered her body did not crumble, slowly, piece by piece, into ashes. It was a long time before pain returned, and with the pain, a full realisation of all that had been said, and of the equally murderous silences.

That day, the whole of her past existence, consisted of one hour alone, and that hour would last for the rest of her life; she was clothed in it as if it were her shroud; it was the beat of Time within her heart, and would be till she was dust. This alone had been real in all her life, the hour in which she knew, beyond any doubt, that he did not love her, had never loved her. Yet, though the anguish was not to be borne, at those times when it ceased from sheer weariness, and numbness invaded her body and her soul, that foretaste of death was more terrible still. So, as ghosts haunt their murderers, so that, reviving the memory of their agony, they may believe themselves still to be living, she resolved to see him again, to be in his presence, hear his voice.

There was the house at Allbridge, near Dublin, that had belonged to her mother. She would go to that, taking Molkins with her—poor Molkins whose cough was getting steadily worse, day by day, and who might feel better in the country air. It would be wiser to go there, in any case, for, at Allbridge she would not be afraid to open the door for fear of finding her mother's creditors standing there, waiting for her. There was one man in particular who terrified her, a very stout man with a face the colour of a November fog and black glasses. Even in dreams she could see that fog-coloured face, those black and airless dummy windows. And there would be nobody to miss her in London; for it was strange how completely Mumsie's friends had vanished. You would believe, almost, that they had not been real people at all, that they had just been something that Mumsie had invented.

Essy and Moll packed their belongings as quickly as possible, and it was not long before the house in the moon-coloured crescent, that house that could only exist in the summer and when people were young, that would crumble into a little moth-bright silvery dust when the summer was over, when youth and hope were over—this was wrapped in dust-sheets as if a dead person stayed there.

It was a very hot day when they set out, and everything was very light and glazed and loud—but she was like a black tunnel hollowed out by her anguish and stretching for ever, empty excepting for the steel threads of her misery, tearing through nerve after nerve, making a jagged tear, and then tangling the nerves together again as with a giant shuttle.

Near where they embarked there was a fair, and the band

was playing a Waldteufel waltz that had often sounded from the barrel-organ in the moon-coloured crescent; "Estudiantina" was its name; but now it was no longer light as the happy summertime, bright like a great flower, one of the huge waxen begonias that grew among their furry green leaves in the gardens of the crescent; it belonged to the world of machines and of cruel necessity. Even the heat seemed part of a man-made force, steam, perhaps, from the band's machinery, and the noise seemed as if it were dragging the streets after it, round and round, with the tramways chasing them in vain. The chattering crowds, walking through the purring greenery, were only jarring threads of the light; plush mantles seemed to purr in the heat, black crustacean silk gowns shone from an occasional hollow, braying, blaring shade.

Blindly she made her way to the ship, and it was not until she was sitting on deck, that the bright colour of the sea, and the glittering sea-breeze, awoke her. Until then, only pain had existed.

They had a long time to wait for the train, and Molkins said: "You must try and eat something." So they followed the metallic waves of people that were jarring through the firework-spurting greenery into the little restaurant. There, sitting down at a little table, Molkins asked for the menu and ordered something which Essy ate mechanically, staring straight in front of her. She did not speak. It seemed to her, as she sat there, that the noise and light of the jangling heat was more intolerable than ever, the heat and light that seemed out of tune and out of time to her misery, having sometimes a quick and terrible beat, dragging sometimes as slowly as Time would drag for the rest of her life—Time that for the nine years that still lay before her, would consist of one hour alone. Everything seemed changed by the heat; even the elaborately-done black hair of the barmaid, blue-ribbed by the light, seemed breaking in waves as noisy as the sea. And sitting there, watching the sharp drinks upon the chattering white tables quarrelling with the light, Essy thought, "Hell must be like this—noisy light piercing to one's bones, picking them clean through all eternity, discovering all one's secrets, while one is walled up, alone excepting for the light, alone in the midst of an endless crowd."

At last the train came in, and Essy and Moll took their seats. In the highly varnished heat of the afternoon, the faces of the people opposite were shining as if they were encased in glass, everything seemed much too close, and as if she were looking at it through a lens that did not fit; and when the train halted at a wayside station, the trees, the flowers, the advertisements, the people on the platform, looked curiously solid, anchored, as they were, against a puff of breeze that was dark blue and shallow as the sea near the landing-stage. At one station Moll leant out and bought some brightly varnished woollen buns, and some dark brown tea. Then she and Essy listened idly to a man and woman talking on the seat opposite them. The man wore a rather sanctimonious look, he had eyes like triangles of thin slate, and his nose, which was thick at the end, had a deep centre parting. The woman was highly glazed. They did not, apparently, know each other well—Essy thought that the man was probably a business acquaintance of the woman's husband—but each was evidently anxious to impress the other. To Essy, listening from the centre of her misery, it was like listening to the speech of an animal; the words came from a different state of being. Now the man was saying, in his droning bagpipe voice: "The Englishman is not sufficiently clothes-conscious. His clothes fail to arrest and to hold the attention." And he added: "I am one of those rare beings that is called an Idealist. I want the best of everything."

But his companion had not been listening, for she was busy with producing a bird's-eye view of her own character for his benefit; and now she said (in reference, perhaps, to something that had gone before), "I am not one of those girls who don't mind if they know what they are looking at or not, when they go to the Pictures. They don't mind what they are looking at as long as they are looking at something. But *I* like *knowing* what I am looking at."

Knowing what I am looking at. Knowing what I am looking at. . . . The numbness had descended upon Essy again, a feeling as if she were about to sleep. If only she could sleep for ever!

But that was not to be yet. Not for nine long years.

Chapter XIII

JONATHAN KNEW now that, even if she died, he would never be rid of her, but would still hear her voice, like the wind under the door. He would hear it crying round his windows, sobbing in the trees. And the sickened feeling came to him that she was indeed the wind, seeking always and circling round, listening if he spoke with another person, carrying away his words and storing them in a mad transformed scattered memory. She would creep through the crevices of doors and of windows, she would come from the other end of the world to chill his heart, unthinking and mad as the wind. Sometimes with violence and abandon, sometimes with a hopeless dead sound, weary from the long search, sometimes fallen and sunken till she was no longer the wind, but a cold air of desolation, drifting homelessly through some gap in door or window—only to find nothing, nothing again—sometimes dimmed and dulled like an air from the grave. And always at the back of his mind was the fear that one day, walking in the street, Anna would see that homeless face, and would read in its lines the history of her own betrayal. Essy might even try to speak to her; she was quite reckless enough. Or Anna, passing, might see Essy waylay him, and then, seeing those desperate and uncontrolled gestures, would learn the truth. The fool! She was for ever waiting in the street, in the hope of forcing him to speak to her, for ever sending her manservant to stand in the lane that led

205

to his house, until he should pass. "I met your servant," he wrote to her at last in despair, "when I was a mile from Trim, and could send you no other answer than I did, for I was going away; besides I would not have gone to Kildraught to see you for all the world. I always told you you are wanting in discretion. I have promised to pay a visit to a friend for a fortnight, and shall then return to Dublin, and will call on you as soon as I can."

Was that too rough, he wondered, for he must not drive her to desperate measures, and, too, he must not make it impossible for himself to advance from this position, if he should wish to do so. He added, therefore: "I am afraid you had a very tiring journey. Do take care of yourself in this Irish air, to which I am afraid you are a stranger. Does not our Dublin look very dirty, and the country very miserable?"

She had always been swayed by his opinion in the past, had based hers upon his, and now, perhaps, if he declared that he found Dublin dreary, she might even take it into her head to return to London. It was a forlorn hope, but it was worth trying.

It was at this point that she sent him a letter which, though it distracted him, touched his heart. He had never loved her, but he had once felt affection for her, and it was impossible, now, not to pity the desperate situation into which her mother's death had plunged her.

"You cannot but be aware, at least to some degree," she wrote, "of the many worries I am slave to; a wretch of a brother"—(the brother who, in six months' time, was to die and leave her and Moll the whole of his fortune, the brother who had always shown her tenderness! But what did she care if she blackened him in Hare's eyes, if she could by this means revive some feeling for her in his heart?)—"cunning executors, and importunate creditors of my mother's, worries which are heavy enough to sink greater spirits than mine without some support. Once I had a friend that would see me sometimes, and either tell me I had done right, or advise me what to do.

206

But now when my misfortunes are increased by being in a disagreeable place, among strange prying deceitful people, whose company is far from an amusement, you avoid me and give me no reason, but that we are amongst fools, and must submit. I am perfectly well aware that we are amongst fools, but know no reason for having my happiness sacrificed to their caprice. You once had a maxim, which was, to act what was right, and not mind what the world said; I wish you would keep to it now. Pray what can be wrong in seeing and advising an unhappy young woman? I cannot imagine. You cannot but know that your being angry with me makes my life insupportable. You have taught me to distinguish, and then you leave me miserable. Now all I beg is, that you will for once counterfeit, since you cannot otherwise, that kind friend you once were, till I get the better of these difficulties for my sister's sake; for were she not involved, who, I know, is not able to manage them as I am, I have a nobler soul than to sit struggling with misfortunes, when at the end I cannot promise myself any real happiness. Forgive me; I beg you to believe I cannot help complaining as I do."

Poor girl, poor helpless pitiful affectionate Essy! It was true, she had no one on whom to rely save him, and he could not desert her now. He must keep her infatuation for him within bounds, for her sake as well as for his own, but it would be nothing short of cruelty to refuse to see her under these circumstances.

He was about to ride over to tea with Anna and Becky, but he found time to write a short note to Essy, and this had all his old tenderness. He would see her in a day or two, he said, and she must believe him that it went to his soul not to see her oftener. He would give her the best advice and assistance in his power. He would have been with her sooner if a thousand impediments had not prevented him. He had not realised she was in difficulties; he would willingly give his whole fortune to remove them. It was not possible for him to see her that day, as he had an engagement, but she must not think it was from any want of friendship or tenderness, which he would always continue to the utmost.

Then, having given this letter to be posted, he rode over to tea with Anna.

It was a numb autumn day, and the wan, sallow light, the dull listless wind, added to his general feeling of despondency. He knew, too, that he would find Henry Debingham at tea, for Henry was spending some time in Dublin, for the purpose of executing certain portrait busts that had been commissioned from him. And Jonathan asked himself if anything could possibly be more ill-timed than Debingham's visit. Sooner or later, he was bound to see Essy's wretched stricken face, as she stood waiting, watching in the hope of seeing Jonathan, and if he did, he was quite capable of telling Becky the whole story. Or would he keep silent? Jonathan was not quite sure. Debingham's manner was curious, had been for some time, and Jonathan was beginning to believe that he had had some secret ulterior motive in introducing him to the Vaneldens; he even wondered at moments if Debingham had not foreseen the outcome, had wished to bring it about.

Now, sitting at tea with Anna and Becky and Henry Debingham, he noticed Henry's eyes bent on him with a curious stare, and his sense of discomfort increased. Anna was looking tired and was rather silent, and presently Henry commented on this, shooting the words at her from behind closed teeth: "Well, Anna!" (he was, at the moment, appearing in his nautical role) "What's the matter with *you*?"

"Nothing is the *matter*," she replied.

"But, you are not your usual self."

She did not answer for a moment, and then said, slowly: "Well, I have been having a very odd experience lately, for some weeks now, and—though it may sound absurd—it is beginning to get on my nerves. For weeks, whenever I have been into Dublin, I have had the impression that somebody was *watching* me, that I was being followed wherever I went. At first I could not conceive who was doing this, for often there was nobody in sight, and I began to think I must have imagined it. But a week ago, I found it was *not* fancy. I was walking along, when a young woman came towards me, exactly as though she were going to speak to me, and then at the last moment, she changed her mind, and fled. There is no other word for it. That has happened twice since then. It happened this morning. I do not know what it is about her, but she gives me a feeling of terror; there is something desperate about her whole appearance—I have never seen a face which had despair written on it before. And then, when she changes her mind, she gives a gasp and looks frightened. And she is gone before I have a chance to speak, to ask her what she wants."

She stopped dead. Then: "She is like something blown along by the wind," she said. "You cannot imagine her having a home, or a resting-place of any kind; she is like a piece of paper that is blown along the streets, that will be blown along for ever. But something desperate is written on it.

"It is having a strange effect on me, this haunting. I ask myself, is she mad, or does she take me for somebody else? I have not the faintest idea who she is. All I know is, that I have never seen her before in my life. What *can* she want from me? Has she a message that she must deliver? And if so, from whom, and why does she not give it?"

"Oh," said Mr. Debingham, very blunt and manly, "you ought to ask Hare. He can probably tell you who she is, and what she wants." And he winked at Jonathan.

Jonathan looked at him gravely. He did not reply.

PART III

Chapter I

THE YEARS were drifting on, and it seemed to Anna that they had been blown along by the wind, but aimlessly, hither and thither, not like the homeless ghost that had haunted her, the piece of paper on which something desperate had been written. That, though it had no resting-place, had an aim: the years, blown onwards, blown hither and thither, had none. Only the greatness of Jonathan's work remained, but it was a fifth element which seemed a quintessence of the other four, it was outside and above the years, remaining steadfast whilst the small human events beneath were blown along by the cold and uncaring wind towards some unknown goal.

It was eight years now since Anna had seen the despairing ghost, eight years since the last haunting; but she did not believe it was laid, she waited for the moment when it would rise up in her path and confront her. She had never found out what was the ghost's name when she was living; no whisper of this had ever reached her. Only of one thing was she certain: that Jonathan knew that name, and that he knew what the ghost wanted.

And round and round in her head, as if this, too, was blown by the wind, went the question: "What is it that he is hiding from me? Can it be this that has changed him?"

She thought of the time, long ago, long years ago when she was young, when she had first noticed a change in him. She had said to herself: "What shall I do, where shall I go, if I should ever cease to love him, if even that is taken from me? If he leaves me nothing to love, nothing in the world? How homeless I shall be. It must be the last death that one can endure—but a death without a home—to look at the face that we have loved, and not to know it for that face, to ask oneself: 'How did I come to love him.' "

Thinking of this, she remembered how, when he had left her before, in her early youth, it was as if she had been blind. He had left Rotherham Park, and it seemed to her that there was no light, there was no colour, there was no shape in the world. Only the blind can feel shape with their fingers, they can feel, by the faint differences in the air, if they are passing by a bush with leaves or a wall made of stone, they know if it is the light of the sun or the moon upon their lips and foreheads, they know when the dark changes into light. And she had said to herself: "He is about to leave me again. But this time it will be different; he will walk in his accustomed places, but I shall know there is no Jonathan, that there never has been. And this time I shall not be like the blind, for I shall not feel the heat of the sun or the warmth of the moon or the light of the stars. I shall be dead."

Years ago. Long years ago.

Now, when she tried to remember her youth, it was only this that she could recall. The rest of that part of her life seemed to have happened to another being. Yet her childhood was real to her. The thin child with straight black hair cut in a fringe across her forehead, with the lion-like eyes and the face that looked as if it had been powdered by the sun's gold motes through the branches of a forest glade—the child who seemed always dressed in black, like a little foreigner mourning for someone she had never known—she walked with Anna always in the silent rooms, lay down by her side in sleep. But the young and radiant girl with whom Jonathan had driven in the forest never came to visit her now.

Her health had sunken, and she felt, at times, weighed down with care. In the last few years, the scandal that had grown round her name when she first lived in Ireland, and which had dissipated after a while, had reappeared, with the result that

212

she saw but few women, and had little companionship excepting from the men who frequented Hare's house. And her sadness grew; it was like a mist hiding the world from her.

Night by night, Susan was awakened from her sleep by hearing a strange sound. It was a weary, hopeless sound that rose and fell as if it were too tired to go on. And yet all night long that sad small sound continued. Susan thought: "It must be a child crying; it sounds as if it were lost." And getting out of her bed, she drew the curtains and looked out, but there was no one to be seen.

Then, one night, as dawn grew nearer, and the sound still went on—the small, unfriended, lost and helpless sound—Susan said to herself: "I believe it is in the house!" And opening the door, she listened. It came from Anna's room. Hastily putting on her dressing-gown she crossed the passage and opened Anna's door. "Why, Miss Anna!" she cried: "Miss Anna!"

She was lying with one arm flung across her face, and she did not answer. Only the sound continued. It was the sound of Anna crying in her sleep.

. . . . .

The year wore on, and now it was no longer possible for Jonathan to remain blind to the change that had taken place in Anna. Her face, when she thought that he could not see her, bore a tired and hopeless expression that he could not quite read; there were moments when, with a pang, he thought: "Those eyes have a humble and patient look, like the eyes of one who is about to die." Yet Anna was still of this world, death was to her a far shadow, a winter whose cold she need not fear for many years; there must, therefore, be some other reason for that look. And he, dreading to ask her the cause, lest he should read the truth in her face, asked his and her old friend William Ayrton to question her—Ayrton, who was, by now, a Bishop, and married to a small plump good-natured wife—a very different woman from Anna whom he had once loved.

When William married, two years after Jonathan had become attracted by Esther Vanelden, Anna, groping in the darkness, had thought, with pain, "Even William is deserting me now. There must be something about me that cannot hold love!" Then, remorsefully, she said to herself: "Can it be that I want a sacrifice to be offered up to me? That my life has so sunk my nature that, knowing that I must go sunless, I would have William live without any human warmth? Or, worse still, is it that my pride, my vanity, are crying out for food?" And she thought: "I shall be happy, soon, that William has married and has forgotten me."

Now, when her old friend asked her the reason for her sadness, she thought: "I have never, excepting for that hour of black blind selfishness, kept anything from William; we have always been perfectly truthful with each other." And she answered that she knew, only, that Jonathan had changed and was now indifferent to her, that she knew, too, how she stood in the world's eyes, and that the sacrifice of her innocent reputation had been in vain, since she now meant nothing to him.

And darkness, drop by slow drop, fell into Jonathan's heart, as he thought of the waste of the years in which happiness might have been, the waste of his own heart and all its tenderness—the doom cast by the ghost that waited for him—waited till he should join it and be its companion for ever: his own phantom, his *Doppelgänger* . . . an old man, a mindless hulk, sitting motionless on a chair in an empty room.

Tenderness for Anna filled his heart; was she not his friend of friends, the woman who had devoted her life, her heart, and all her thoughts to him? Yes, she had suffered; nor did she know the reason for the cold and empty years.

Should he break down the barriers of his pride, and tell her all . . . that he had sacrificed her happiness and his, and all the years of her youth, in order that she should not, in the end, fall victim to the terrible and silent ghost that waited, remorseless and inexorable, for its hour to strike?

Never. She should never know. For he could never, either

in his healthy moments, or in those moments of madness that had the grandeur and the vastness of years, or in those years in which he lay buried in a huge and polar silence, acknowledge the cracks and fissures which foreran the breaking of his heart.

He would never tell her that with each return of his deafness, his giddiness, he moved nearer, step by step, to the room where the ghost waited. For his illness had increased: and in every five or six weeks he was deaf and giddy for three or four days together.

What could he do that would in any way comfort her? His heart that had been anguished with tenderness and pity now grew ice-bound with pride as he thought of the step he must take. It was his duty to take it, and Anna could bear the truth, she was not like Esther Vanelden. A half-truth is less easy to bear, but of that Jonathan did not think.

He wrote that he had resolved not to marry until he had a sufficient income, and to marry only at a time of life which would enable him to live long enough to see his children settled in the world. With regard to his monetary affairs, he was still in debt, and he had now passed the time of life which would make his second intention possible. But he was ready to go through the form of marriage with Anna for the sake of her peace of mind, and to reassure her that his old tenderness for her was unchanged, on condition that the marriage was kept a secret from the whole world, that it was a marriage in name only, and that they should continue the habits of their lives unchanged. She would remain in her house, he in his, and they would continue to meet only in the presence of a third person.

When Anna received this letter, she sat for a long time holding it in her hand. So it had come at last—the letter for which she had waited through the long years—through her youth and her youth's fading! She knew, now, that she had waited for it as we await the moment when we shall be laid in the grave.

It was very late when she was aroused from her thoughts by a strange sound. What could it be? It seemed to be in the room itself. Then she realised from whence it came. It was the sound of her teeth chattering.

Anna had not known the night was so cold.

As she brushed her hair and made ready for sleep, she looked curiously at the reflection of her face in the glass. As, many years ago, Lucy Linden had looked at the stranger in the mirror before her. Anna knew now, that the young girl in the forest would never return to her, that it was true that she was dead, or had never been. Perhaps it was the death of that girl that was causing such anguish to her heart. . . .

Nothing mattered now. Only the years were passing, and perhaps this empty ceremony might lay the ghost that Anna knew was waiting in her path, until the hour struck and it could rise and strike her down with its stone-cold shade.

So, one day in November, Jonathan Hare and Anna Marton were married, by William Ayrton, in the presence of Becky Mintley and Susan and Hans Orthoven.

This was the happiness that had awaited her, which she had seen in the grey dawn, and in the moonlight, and in the glamour on the leaves, which she had heard spoken of in the whispering sound of the growth of trees.

The day for which she had waited had come.

It was a listless and numb grey day, like all the other days of the years that still remained to her.

Chapter II

THROUGH THE long days and nights, the misery fell, black, drop by drop in Jonathan's heart, until that heart seemed a fathomless well which would be filled with darkness. And each drop struck a deadly chill. Wherever he looked, there was ruin: there was Anna, whose life had been laid waste; there was Essy.

How was it that this wreckage had been caused? He had thought to extract a little happiness from life, both for himself and for Anna, his beloved friend. It was not he, but the waiting ghost, the old man in a chair in an empty room, who had turned her to stone. And Essy . . . the wretchedness that had come to her was the result of an accident which he should, perhaps, have foreseen, but for which he could not consider himself to blame. It was not *he*, Jonathan Hare, who had struck at her heart; the pain from which she suffered had been inflicted by fate. Poor little Essy, he pitied her, and pity revived some of his old feeling of tenderness for her. He would, he told himself, do his uttermost to soothe the pain. It was thus that Essy recovered him.

Their old companionship was resumed. Twice or three times a week he would ride over to see her at Allbridge, letters were exchanged between those times, and hers to him would be signed by the name he had given her: "Your own Skinage," for, by now, partly for the sake of secrecy, partly out of a playful affection, each had invented a name for the other. Sometimes the letters were written in French, in order that their respective households should not read them, and in one of these, he congratulated her on her mastery over the language; but then, as he assured her, "one must know you for a long time in order to know all your perfections, for always, on seeing or hearing you, one discovers new ones. For elegance, sweetness and wit, no one can surpass you, and I am a fool to write in the same language to one who is incapable of foolishness, if one excepts the esteem you have for me. For it is no sign of merit, nor any proof of my good taste, to find in you every quality that nature could give—honour, virtue, good sense, wit, sweetness, agreeableness, firmness of character; but in hiding yourself as you do, the world does not know you and you miss the praise of a million people. During the whole time that I have known you, I have never heard one word from your lips that could have been expressed better, and I swear to you that, severe critic as I am, I could never find a single fault with your actions, nor with your conversation; coquetry, affectation, prudishness, I have never known in you.

"And with all that, do you believe it would be possible not to esteem you above the rest of the human kind? What animals in skirts the most excellent of other women seem beside you. Is it possible that they can be of the same sex? It is unkind of you to make one despise so many human beings who, if one did not think of you, would seem supportable." . . . "Above the rest of the human kind . . . the most excellent of other women . . ." But Anna would never see that letter. How should she? For who would show it to her?

Not Essy, now, for she was happy again, and sure of him. She no longer dreaded the power of Anna Marton. The only thing that would make Essy show that letter would be if she should ever come to hear of his marriage. But that, he told himself, was impossible. Anna would never betray what she knew must be for ever held secret: she would never break a promise she had made to him. His faithful Anna!

He was beginning too, to teach Essy to exert a little caution, and this he had done by putting into her head the idea that a secret between them was not only fun—a great joke—but that, in some way, it bound them more closely together by excluding the rest of the world. That Jonathan shared a secret with her alone, showed that he had, in truth, returned to her, that he was *hers*. And Essy clapped her hands with joy. In her renewed happiness she was reviving all her former little-girl habits.

It seemed to her that she was back in the days of her youth, in the Crescent, when happiness had first come to her. Only now, there were no city sounds to wake her from her long dream.

In the calm days of the late summer, in the grey dawn, she would sit at her window as she had done when she was a young girl, thinking: "Another day of happiness, soon it will be another day"; but this time she was not looking out over a crescent in a city, but over fields of waving corn. She thought of the day, earlier in the summer, when walking with Jonathan

218

in the green darkness of the garden, she had pulled down bunch after bunch of the old cherry trees—the sweet vermilion flames that have at their hearts the coldest snows. Moll had said to her: "Be careful, Essy, you are playing with fire." And Essy had called through the branches: "Who cares?" Then Jonathan had pretended to scold her: "You are always playing with fire, Essy; and another thing, anyone would imagine you were in love. You dated your last letter to me a month before it was written." Looking up at him from her hiding place among the flames and the flickering leaves, she cried: "Tell me, is my dating my letter wrong the only sign that I am in love. Is it? Is it, Jonathan?"

She had never been more happy, and Jonathan too, was glad to have returned to their former relationship. He found his visits to Allbridge agreeable, for Essy had regained her old gaiety—it was fun to be with her, and her liveliness was a welcome change from Anna's silence—which, always a habit with her, was now growing deeper. In the atmosphere of laughter and chatter he could forget, for a little while, his own wretchedness, and the remorse that he buried in his heart. He told himself that all the old nonsense was at an end, that Essy had recovered her balance, and they could both, now, afford to forget what had been, at most, an unfortunate outburst of hysteria. She had suffered from a temporary hallucination, that was all, and now she had recovered from it, and there would be no further scenes and reproaches.

He teased her about her quarrelsomeness, and called her "Governor Huff"; he declared that she must have come scolding into the world and would scold until the moment she left it. Now he was in trouble, according to himself, because he had written to Moll and she had shown Essy his letter: and he swore that he would never write to Moll again, if she could not keep secrets better than that! It was the first love-letter, he said plaintively, that he had written for a dozen years, and as it had had so little success, he should never write another. Never was a *belle passion* so defeated, but "the Governor," he

219

heard, was jealous and seemed to have a great deal to say in the matter. Essy had better mind her nurse-keeping—for poor Moll's illness was growing worse day by day—do her duty, and leave off the huffing. Now she complained that she could not read his writing; he was glad to hear it, he said, because her time would be taken up in puzzling it out; and he had done everything he could to make it difficult. He only wished that hers was as indecipherable as his, for then it would not matter if her letters were dropped by a careless messenger.

And Essy asked herself if it were possible that those terrible months when he had been so angry with her could have been anything but a bad dream, a black dream in the dead of night? She was awake now, the sun was shining, and he was beside her.

He wrote to her saying: "What would you give to have our history exactly written, through all its steps, from the beginning to this time. It ought to be an exact chronicle of twelve years from the time of spilling of coffee, to drinking of coffee, from Dunstable to Dublin, with every single passage since." Then she found that he had remembered everything, their conversations, the little intimate details of the days he had spent at her mother's house, the time when her brother went to France, "fifty chapters of little times," the time when she had visited him unexpectedly. He went over them all, and swore that he would make a chapter about each.

She said to herself: "He must have a little love for me, or he would not remember. Only one who is a little in love would keep such trifles in his memory." "Tell me sincerely," she answered, "did these circumstances crowd on you, or did you recollect them to make me happy?"

So it went on, day by day. And day by day, Anna, his wife, walked from her house to his, settled the affairs of his household, arranged his dinner-parties and his luncheon-parties, took her place as one of his guests, and then returned once more to her silent and shadowed house.

The gusts of fury to which Jonathan's illness made him liable were growing upon him, and often Anna was obliged to smooth down the servants who had suffered from these, or to interfere between him and them.

It is strange how what we most long for in youth loses its shining. There were moments, now, when she was glad that she did not share Jonathan's home.

Chapter III

TEN LONG despairing weeks. . . . Every morning, Essy had run down to the door, hearing the postman's knock. No letter. . . . It would come, then, in the evening. But still there was not a word. Essy said to herself: "I am reliving those terrible months in London, in a black dream. The dream has been long; but soon I shall awake."

Every afternoon, as soon as luncheon was over, she drew up the chair to the window, never taking her eyes from the road along which he would ride, until it was so late that she knew it was no longer possible that he would come. Then rising dumbly, not even looking at Moll, who was lying now, helpless and uncomplaining, on a sofa near the window where she might get a little air, Essy would drift out of the room.

Night and day, in the dawn as she looked out over the fields of corn, in the day, walking in the green darkness in which she had walked with Jonathan, she thought: "Why *could* I not have been content with the little I had: why must I have pulled down this ruin upon myself?"

She had broken her promise and had begun to importune him again; she had written to him, and the letter had arrived in the middle of one of his dinner-parties, with Anna sitting at the table. He had thrust the letter hurriedly into his pocket, but he could not hope that Anna would not have seen that the letter was in a woman's handwriting. Essy's script was typical of her—uncontrolled and unformed, it seemed always to be rushing to an unforeseen goal, like Essy herself.

She would have to be restrained again, there was nothing else to be done; for only that morning a woman who worked for him had told him that she had heard he was in love with a Miss Vanelden who lived at Allbridge, and she had even given him details about his visits and said that she heard Miss Vanelden was very witty. Soon it would be all over the town, and it would only be a matter of time before it reached Anna's ears. He groaned.

At first, he had tried to restrain Essy gently, telling her she must not make herself and him unhappy by vain misgivings, that she must try to understand the situation and to have patience, for soon, if they exerted caution, gossip would die down and all would be well again. But it was useless; she would not listen to reason, she had, once again, lost control over her actions and her speech, and when, as a result, he stayed away from her house altogether, her letters fell upon him day by day, hour by hour, until it seemed to him, too, that he was reliving in a dream the days six years ago, when she had first declared her love for him.

He dreaded every knock on the door, fearing that it would bring him one more despairing letter or message. Yet even so, he still felt some tenderness for her; it was strange, he thought, that passion and misery should have given this careless, unrestrained creature such nobility of utterance as that to which she, at moments, attained.

"I must either unload my heart," she wrote in her wretchedness, "and tell you all its griefs, or sink under the inexpressible distress I now suffer by your great neglect of me. It is now ten long weeks since I saw you, and in all that time I only received but one letter from you, and a little note with an excuse. Oh! how have you forgot me. You endeavour by severities to force me from you, nor can I blame you; for with the utmost distress and confusion I see myself the cause of uneasy reflections to you, yet I cannot comfort you, but here declare, that it is not in the power of time or accident to lessen the inexpressible passion I have for you.

"Put my passion under the utmost restraint, send me as distant from you as the earth will allow, yet you cannot banish those charming ideas which will ever stick by me whilst I have the use of memory. Nor is the love I bear you only seated in my soul, for there is not a single atom of my frame that is not blended with it. Therefore do not flatter yourself that separation will ever change my sentiments; for I find myself unquiet in the midst of silence, and my heart is at once pierced with sorrow and love. For Heaven's sake, tell me what has caused this vast change in you, which I have found of late. If you have the least remains of pity for me left, tell me tenderly. No, do not tell it, so that it may cause my present death, and do not suffer me to live a life like a languishing death, which is the only life I can lead, if you have lost any of your tenderness for me."

She would, she *must* receive an answer to this. In two days at the uttermost, his letter would reach her. But the night of the second day came, and there was no sign from him. The last knock on the door sounded . . . the footsteps retreated. Essy wrung her hands; it was as if she were wringing her heart out of her fingers; she looked at them, feeling a dull surprise that blood was not oozing from them.

She said to herself: "Anna Marton has renewed her power over him. It is she who has taken him from me."

There were moments now, when she saw herself as if she were a separate being, noting the lines on her face, the movements that suffering gave her. She felt little at those times, excepting a kind of wonder that this separate being whom she was observing, could suffer so much.

At other times she felt nothing at all, as if she did not exist, and then she would begin to see herself as a character in a play.

It was a very hot summer, and in the burning weeks of late

August and early September, while the nasturtium-coloured sun flamed outside the house, Essy drifted like a shadow in her long black dress through the rooms where the other shadows were so tall and grey that they might have been the romantic English-Gothic imitation ruins in her garden, she drifted along the paths that led to the gate, and sometimes she said to herself, apathetically, as if she were reciting a part: "Long after I am dead, I shall haunt these paths, sit in these arbours —I shall stand by the gate leading to the path along which he used to ride when he came to see me. People will see me drifting along under a sun like this, and they will say: 'There goes Shadow.'"

She knew by now that he did not intend to answer her letter, so there was nothing for it but to write to him again.

"Tell me sincerely," she cried, "if you have once wished with earnestness to see me, since I wrote last to you. No, so far from that, you have not once pitied me, though I told you how I was distressed. Solitude is insupportable to a mind which is not at ease. I have worn out my days in sighing, and my nights in thinking of . . . who thinks not of me. How many letters must I send you before I receive an answer? Can you deny me in my misery the only comfort which I can expect at present. Oh! That I could hope to see you here or that I could go to you. I was born with violent passions, which all terminate in one, the inexpressible passion I have for you. Consider the killing emotions which I feel from your neglect, and show some tenderness for me, or I shall lose my senses. Surely you cannot possibly be so much taken up but you might find a moment to write to me, and force your inclination to so great a charity. I firmly believe, could I know your thoughts, which no human creature is capable of guessing at because never anyone living thought like you, I should find you have often in a rage wished me religious, hoping that I should have paid my devotions to Heaven; but that would not spare you, for were I an enthusiast, still you would be the deity I should worship. What marks are there of a deity but what you are to be known by? You are
224

at present everywhere, your dear image is always before my eyes. Sometimes you strike me with that great awe, I tremble with fear; at other times, a charming compassion shines through your countenance, which revives my soul. Is it not more reasonable to adore a radiant form one has seen, than one only described?"

Creeping along in the grey shadows cast by that brilliant sun—the shadows that were like the English-Gothic ruins in the garden—waiting at the gate, to see him if he should come, she said to herself: "Perhaps he will pity me if Moll dies—seeing me alone."

For Moll was coughing her life away, day by day. Her face wore that humble deprecating look that is borne by those who are about to die—who have no place in this world, and who must not disturb those who must still live. Sometimes Essy would awake with a start from her stupor of misery, and would look at Moll with terrified eyes. But for the most part she was apathetic. She knew that she would soon be alone: that was all.

Yet she had loved Molkins—did love her still. Only she could feel nothing. At times, when Moll could bear it no longer, she would whisper: "Oh, Essy, I am feeling so ill, so dreadfully ill." And Essy would answer: "Poor Moll. Yes, go on, Moll; I am listening." But all the time her eyes would be fixed on the window, and Moll, after looking at her humbly for a moment, would let her eyes drop again, and would fall silent.

Yet there were moments when a pang of desperate sadness, of almost intolerable pity and love would invade Essy's heart. It was *Moll* that was dying! Oh, it was not, it could not be true! But it was. It seemed as if some cool breeze floating through the window had awakened her from some deep sleep to reality. And at those times she would realise that Moll was suffering—even that she was afraid—that the sadness that overhung everything was not only because she, Essy, was going to be alone for ever. Misery lay beyond and outside that.

Hs

The days drifted on, and now Moll was no longer frightened; she was just tired, that was all. The last few weeks, in which she had known that she was dying, and had nobody to whom she could speak, had been terrible.

It was on a very hot September day, late in the afternoon, that Moll died. Essy had been sitting by her side, and Moll looked at her. She tried to raise her hand and to take Essy's. She tried to speak: but all she could say was: "Poor——"

And her voice died away again. Moll was trying to tell Essy that she was sorry for her.

An hour later, when the shadows were growing longer on the grass, Essy looked at Moll again. Her face had lost that lonely, humble look it had worn of late. There was no movement under her breast.

"Moll—Moll," Essy cried. "Oh—Moll!"

But Moll did not answer. Her loneliness was at an end.

Then Essy said to herself: "*This* will bring him back to me." She had sunk to that.

Chapter IV

THE LETTER which reached Anna Hare, on a hot afternoon in September, was in an unfamiliar handwriting, of a large and sprawling, formless character. You would not have thought Fate wrote with such a hand.

It lay at the bottom of a small pile of business letters, bills, and circulars that had been readdressed from Jonathan's house to be dealt with, in the course of the day's business, by Anna, his wife. There were more letters, Anna noticed, than arrived, as a rule, by the 3.30 post.

She was alone in the house, excepting for Susan and Hans, for Becky Mintley had gone on a visit to a friend in London.

There was not a sound to be heard. Taking up the letters she walked into her sitting-room and opened them at her leisure.

When Anna, having read the other letters, came to that which was written in a large uncontrolled handwriting, she looked at it, for a moment, with a half-interested curiosity before she opened it. A woman's handwriting, evidently. And she did not receive many letters from women nowadays, for they avoided the mysterious Miss Marton, who had such a strange relationship with Mr. Hare. This letter, too, was from a woman she did not know.

She opened the letter, and for some moments, stared at it uncomprehendingly.

It had no formal beginning; the words, sprawling across the page, ran thus:

"I can bear it no longer. Tell me: you must. Are you the wife of Jonathan Hare? If you are, then he has betrayed both you and me.

"ESTHER VANELDEN."

Anna Hare sat looking at this letter for a long time; she was still holding it when the light died.

It was quite later in the evening when she moved again. Then, walking over to the writing-table, she addressed an envelope to Jonathan Hare, slipped the letter into it, and, on another sheet of paper, wrote these few words:

"I send you this letter from a woman to whom you have presumably given the right to ask this question.

"Do what you please in the matter. I shall not answer, for I do not know her.

"Do not try to see me. I am going away.

"ANNA."

The next day, when Essy Vanelden woke, she had a strange feeling of peace and happiness, mingled with excitement. It

227

was one of those days in early autumn when the gold light, sinking deep into the earth, penetrating into the heart of the trees, is like those dreams we have in youth and know will never fade, and looking at the glamour on flower and leaf Essy knew that something would happen to-day which would change the whole of her life, which would bring back happiness. If she had not known that it was not possible, she would almost have believed that Jonathan would come to see her to-day, and that everything would be as it had been before, in the days when she had deceived herself into thinking he loved her. She realised now—as she had done long years ago, after he had come to rebuke her in the Sluttery, in those dreadful days of her first loneliness—that he did not love her; but she intended to deceive herself again, if it were possible, if, by coming to see her without reproaches, he gave her the slightest chance of doing so. Only thus would life be bearable. And she said to herself: "I won't bear such suffering again. One can always die!"

How free we are, if you come to think of it.

She was glad that she had written to Anna; for she knew, beforehand, what the answer would be: "I am not his wife." And her letter to Anna might, and surely would, separate Anna from Jonathan for the rest of time, for Anna would know, now, that if she, too, had believed that Jonathan was hers, she had been deceived. Essy no longer hated Anna, she felt almost sorry for her, felt a kind of pity as well as satisfaction when she thought of the stroke that she, Essy, had dealt her. But that sense of numbness in her feeling towards Anna would, she knew, soon give way to another form of bitter hatred—a different hatred, a changed bitterness from that which she had formerly felt for her, but none the less violent. Those whom we have killed we hate even more desperately than those who are yet alive and have it in their power to return an injury.

Perhaps, she thought, Anna would come to see her, and Essy would be able to read on her face the signs of the death she had inflicted. Then if she still, having received Essy's letter,

228

tried to cling to the belief that she had any rights given her by Jonathan, Essy would show her some of the letters that Jonathan had written. "Do you think it would be possible not to esteem you above the rest of the human kind? What animals in skirts the most excellent of other women seem beside you."

And, thinking of that letter and of Anna, Essy smiled.

At twelve o'clock that day, from her window that overlooked the road that led to her house, she saw Jonathan riding along just as he used to do in the days of her happiness. He was coming to see her, she had recovered him and all would be as it had been in the days before this trouble came to her. She waved her hand to him from the window, but he did not look up.

She brushed her hair hastily, and then ran down the stairs to meet him. Should she open the door to him, she asked herself? No, because he hated any signs of impatience, of impetuosity. So she walked into the morning-room, and stood there, with her back to the window, her heart filled with happiness, her hands outstretched to meet his.

He walked into the room and stood, for one moment, looking at her; his face was so terrible that she thought she had never seen it before, it was not the face that she knew; this man was a stranger.

Then he threw down a letter at her feet, and turning without one word having crossed his lips, he left the room.

It was the letter she had written to Anna.

She knew, then, that she would never see him again—never, in all the long moments of the few months that remained in which she must still live.

She did not watch him ride along the road that he would never cross again.

Chapter V

I<small>N AN</small> arctic universe of wind and rain Esther Vanelden rushed round and round as if it were a gigantic wire cage, her thin muslin dress clinging to her skin, her hair, black from the wet, dripping down her cheeks, as if it, too, were a part of the black flaying rain, and as she rushed, she muttered sometimes, sometimes screamed at the polar waste of rain and wind, defying it to do its worst, howling with laughter that had a noise like the storm, mocking at this pitiful cold that was so much less than that of her eternal night.

"Wind, you are not cold enough for me. Pierce me to the blood! Turn me to a pillar of ice! Tear the flesh from my bones! Devour it like wolves. All the sooner will my heart be laid bare. Freeze it! Freeze it! Where is the polar night of ice to hug my soul and blot it out? Where is the polar darkness to blot out the world?"

So she wandered over boreal plains whose mist seemed as if it must change to ice at any moment, by lakes like Stygian marshes of blackness, by marshes that would never suck down misery, that left misery to stand upon the earth, but unconnected with it, like a half-formed being of black stone, a monument of a civilisation that has never been; so she strayed, a waif of death; but not even the mists through which she rushed could numb her hatred.

Sometimes people from the cottages laughed at this mad, dying creature rushing by, who seemed tall as the trees, dashed by and swaying in the wind. The rain lashed at her with steel whips, tearing at her cheeks that were now so thin they seemed nothing but red rags. Moll, before she died, had done the one act of friendship that then lay in her power, and had given Essy her disease, so that she too, would not be alone much longer.

And Essy, in her frenzy, was laying her muslin-clad body bare, to be annihilated by the cold, by the lashing flaying universe of the rain, in order that her sufferings might be over more soon, her revenge be the more near.

"And when you've laid my heart bare," she shrieked, "and washed all the blood away from it, and when you've buried me beneath your mountain heights of rain, there's another will be laid bare. I'll show the earth and the light the great man as he is."

In the box in which she had for twelve years hidden his letters, she held his doom. It was not Esther Vanelden alone whom she was murdering in this polar cold, it was Anna Hare and Jonathan her husband. It was a slow fate, to have the flesh torn from the bones and from the heart by the wolfish winds of the plain; but though she must endure it first, then it would be theirs.

For her dead hand would strike: no sooner was she laid in her grave, than his letters to her, the poem he had written to celebrate their friendship, would be published. Then would come, first a gathering murmur like darkness falling, followed by the noise of the howling winds of laughter that would arise from all the cities in the land, and then, a death in life.

For Anna and he would both be alone, like Esther Vanelden. The whole world would separate them. They would be alone for ever.

Chapter VI

THE HAND of the dead woman had struck its blow, and Anna Hare now knew the truth.

At first, she had refused to read the book that contained the story of her betrayal, she had refused to recognise that Esther Vanelden's life or death could, in the remotest degree concern her. But in the end, the events that followed the publication proved too strong for her.

She had tried to be alone, but even that comfort was denied her, for the women who had avoided her in the past now intruded upon her misery, spied upon every mark of the ravage it had wrought upon her, condoled with her, rubbed vitriol into the wounds. Dressed in black as if they were wearing mourning, they sidled into the room on tiptoe, as if she had been stricken by some deadly sickness; they spoke in hushed voices, quoting passages from the letters that Hare had written to Esther Vanelden; with hypocritical faces of grief and pity they sympathised with her. And it was useless for her to attempt to avoid them, for if she did so, they wrote to her. She was defenceless against their letters, which were even harder to bear than the wounds made by their voices.

At length, she decided that it was necessary for her own protection that she should know the worst pain that the book could inflict.

She had been in a state of strange calm, like a ship that is becalmed under a tropic sun, with no water but the salt sea, no air but that which has been killed by the sun; but now, as she turned the pages of the book, that state was at an end.

The knife tearing the membranes of her body, she read passage after passage.

"What would you give"—these were the lines that first met her eyes—"to have our history exactly written through all its steps, from the beginning to this time?

"It ought to be an exact chronicle of twelve years, from the time of the spilling of coffee, to drinking of coffee, from Dunstable to Dublin, with every single passage since. There would be the chapter of Madame going to Kensington, the chapter of the blister; the chapter of the Colonel going to France, the chapter of the wedding, with the adventure of the lost key; of the sham; of the joyful return; two hundred chapters of madness; the chapter of long walks; the Berkshire surprise; fifty chapters of little times; the chapter of Chelsea; the chapter of swallow and cluster; a hundred whole books of myself, etc.; the chapter of hide and whisper; the chapter of one who made it so." . . .

"Twelve long years." During that time they had enjoyed a thousand secrets, a thousand small intimacies that she had never known, she who must starve in silence, must ask nothing, must submit to see him only in the presence of a third person.

Her eyes fell upon another passage:

"Do you believe it would be possible not to esteem you above all the rest of the human kind? What animals in skirts the most excellent of other women seem beside you. Is it possible that they can be of the same sex?"

Anna Hare covered her grey face with her hands. It was some time before she continued to read.

. . ."You need make use of no other black art beside your ink. It is a pity your eyes are not black, or I would have said the same of them; but you are a white witch, and can do no mischief."

There was nothing more that could happen to her ever. The twenty years of her faithful love had been annihilated, crumbled to dust, not by the hand of the dead woman, but by that of Jonathan Hare.

You would have thought, looking at her, as she sat with her arms leaning upon the table, her head propped between her long hands, that she no longer lived, that she had suddenly died in an attack from some illness of the heart, had it not been that from time to time her eyes moved, there was a faint pulse beating in her throat. The pupils of her lion-like eyes were distended so that those eyes looked black. They fell upon another letter. . . . "So good-bye, Brat."

Ah, yes, twenty years of faithful devotion, of self-abnegation, dull the eyes and the hair. After twenty years of starvation, we are no longer young.

There could not, now, be much more time in which she must suffer. She turned the pages. "Mais soyez assurée que jamais personne du monde a été aimée, honorée, adorée par votre ami que vous."

233

Anna Hare looked through the open window.

The earth was so wet that you would almost think that all the multitudes of the dead that lie beneath it had been weeping— that those who had once been warm and now would be cold for ever, had been weeping hopeless tears. If she were to walk in the fields now, her feet would sink so deeply into the wet earth, that the holes they made would seem like waiting graves.

She remembered a day in summer when he had said to her: "It will be hard for you to some degree. . . . There are many things you must put behind you, that you must renounce. But you are the only woman in all my life whom I will call my friend."

In the nights, fiery with spring, that followed the long day on which she had first known of her betrayal, in those nights when young leaves lie upon young leaves, young breast upon young breast, the dead man lying in the tomb of Anna's heart as the child dies in the womb, changed suddenly to a living but unborn child, brought to her the anguish of impending birth, plunged towards the light, clutched at her heart with imploring hands, only to sink back once more into night and the desolation of the tomb, bearing her heart with it.

After such nights as these, she lay with the sweat cold upon her brow as if it were the thick dews broken from the earth. But now those nights were forgotten; it was autumn, and soon the winter would come, and the rays of her long sun would be but winter branches, ever darkening.

On a cold and listless day of autumn, numb and uncaring, Anna, her black gown waving emptily as if no body were within it, wandered over fields hallowed by the seed and the light. Drifting brokenly across the fields, at length she came to the ploughed land where, yesterday, she had watched the rooks mocking at a scarecrow. "No bread will come from that field," she thought. "They have ploughed, but forgotten to sow."

Kneeling on the wet earth, as if she wished to press her dead weight deep, deep into it, so that at least the earth would keep the imprint, the memory of her when she was gone, the woman who was soon to die watched the torn and unmeaning creature waving to her hopelessly in the wind; and through the emptiness within her dress a sudden shaft of anguish pierced like a dreadful light. She knew now that it was not herself that she was watching, as, at first, she had thought; it was not the woman who was about to break her promise for the first time in her life, that promise she had made long years ago, when she was young, and he had said to her: "Anna, never leave me." It was not the woman who was about to break her promise that she was watching. It was Jonathan.

Soon she would be gone, and his existence would be like that of the lifeless creature before her, blown by every wind, waving with his empty arms that had once grasped the whole world, over a field that had never been sown. No warmth anywhere, no light anywhere.

That night, the first hæmorrhage burst through her lips.

Anna had not known so much blood could come from her deadly wound.

Chapter VII

I N THE great man's house there was silence. Esther Vanelden was dead, the letters and the poem he had written to her had been published, but no one should know whether he had suffered, whether he had felt humiliation or anger. He withdrew into the country, remaining there, in complete solitude excepting for the presence of his servants, for three months.

Only once, when a friend, knowing that the publication of the poem was imminent, suggested that Hare should, himself, publish an authentic version, for fear that scurrilous alterations might have been made in the original, had he broken his vow of silence.

"As to the poem you mention," he wrote, "I know several copies of it have been given about, and the Lord Lieutenant told me he had one. It was written at Windsor nearly fourteen years ago, and dated. I wrote it as the result of a joke with some ladies, the one it was addressed to died some time ago in Dublin, and on her death the copy was shown by her executor. I am very indifferent what is done with it, for printing cannot make it more public than it is now; as for my own part, I forget what is in it, but believe it to be only a cavalier business, and those who will not make allowances may choose; and if they intend it maliciously, they will be disappointed, for it was what I expected, long before I left Ireland.

"Therefore, what you advise me, about printing it myself, is impossible, for I never saw it since I wrote it. Nor if I had, would I use shifts or arts, let people think of me as they please. Neither do I believe the gravest character is answerable for a private joke, which, by an accident and the baseness of particular malice, is made public. I have borne a great deal more, and those who will like me less, upon seeing me capable of having written such a trifle, many years ago, may think as they please; neither is it agreeable to me to be troubled with such accounts, when there is no remedy, for it only gives me the ungrateful task of reflecting on the baseness of mankind which I knew sufficiently before."

So did the great man proclaim his indifference, though the world was darkening around him, into a strange and sinister-hued gloom like that of a gathering storm.

He was, by now, on a visit to the house of James Weston, the great poet, outside London; but the visit was a torment to him. He was suffering increasingly from the terrible giddiness and deafness which, in the end, would imprison him, now in the maelstrom whirl and heat of Hell, now in the silence of the polar wastes.

At this time, by an effort of will, the magnitude of which can be gauged only by the power and blackness of his subsequent madness, he was still a visitor to our human world; but he knew that one swirl of the giddiness might hurl him into the other, over that red brink, into something that he could not see clearly; and he needed to avoid that brink by the effort of a terrible caution, which could only be exerted in silence. This was not possible at the house of James Weston. It was invaded by so many of Weston's and Hare's acquaintances, chattering like monkeys, talking like philosophers, that he was drawn nearer and nearer to the maelstrom, hearing in the innocent voices which penetrated the thick mist of his growing deafness, some hint of the appalling roar of the world which would so soon claim him as an inhabitant.

There were other and slight troubles, but all of these increased his uneasiness. Weston, in his kindness and solicitude, fluttered like a little white moth round and round him, increasing his giddiness, while the poet's voice penetrated that black fog of deafness like an insect's voice, so tiny and so warning did it sound. Hare, in those hours when he was not half in communication with the waiting, watching world into which the madman crashes, tried to keep a hold upon himself. In a letter to one of his friends, he complained of this giddiness and deafness, as though they were not a preparation for that other world that would so soon envelop him, but only the symptoms of an ordinary illness; but he said that if they continued, he must leave Weston's house, for "Weston is too sickly and complaisant, and the acquaintances were too many." He complained also, in some verses, that he was too deaf to hear the weak voice of Weston, and that after looking at each other for a moment, they had to return to their different occupations.

And all the while, he was weighed down by the misery in his heart. At times, that heart seemed heavier than the stone of Sisyphus, and he, the giant, must bear it up the steep slopes of the day for ever, only to have it sink back into a fathomless night. What was it, what could it be, he asked himself, that Becky Mintley's letters were designed to hide from him? For it was obvious that the foolish good-natured creature, every time she wrote to him, wrote only that she might hide some truth from him that silence would have revealed. She made constant references to Anna's state of health, which, it seemed, had grown worse: she coughed, now, constantly. And then Becky would seem to be on the point of withdrawing that statement. Anna was a little better, she said, to-day. . . . And with each semi-withdrawal, the anguish in Jonathan Hare's heart deepened.

It was two long months before he learned the truth, from his old friend William Ayrton. . . . Anna, his friend of friends, his unacknowledged wife, was about to break, for the first time in all her life, a promise she had made to him. Anna was about to leave him. He would be alone, save for the ghost of the old man, waiting for him in the darkened room.

And as he read the letter, he felt that he was enclosed for ever in a world of polar silence. No sound from the outer world could ever reach him, nor could his voice penetrate through those world-walls of ice. Yet, with some hopeless effort to warm himself by the memory that there had once been human warmth, that there were still beings moving outside that wall of ice, even though his cry could never reach them, he wrote to William: "My heart has been so sunk, that I am not the same man, nor ever shall be again; but drag on a wretched life, till it shall please God to call me away."

His heart anguished within him, he thought of those days in which he might have lived by Anna's side, looking into her eyes, hearing her voice, touching her hand, those eyes, that voice, that hand, that the earth would so soon hide from him for ever. Instead, he had been at the side of Esther Vanelden.

He could not, he would not, be present when the darkness took her from him. It was strange that William, who usually understood every state of feeling, seemed unable to realise the impossibility that he should be asked to endure this anguish. William had written, it was true, with the greatest tenderness, with every appearance of understanding the unspeakable grief that Jonathan would suffer, and yet, it was evident that it had never entered his head, that Jonathan would be utterly unable
238

to support the agony of being with her during the last weeks of her life, and when she died.

And besides, Anna herself must be considered. His presence could only add to her suffering, for how would she be able to endure his grief, she whose life had been spent in shielding him from any wound that the world could inflict!

He must make it clear to William that for her sake, as well as for his, he must not come.

He wrote: "I must tell you, as a friend, that if you have reason to think that Miss Marton cannot hold out till my return, I would not think of coming to Ireland." He would, he explained, remain in England for another six months, until he could bear to face the world "after an accident that would be so fatal to my quiet." He added that he wished that she could be induced to make her will. "Think," he continued, "how I am feeling while I write this, and forgive the inconsistencies. I would not for the whole world go through the pain of seeing her death. She will be among friends, who for her own sake will take the greatest care of her, whereas I should be a torment to her, and the greatest torment to myself. In case the matter should be desperate, I would wish you to advise them, if they come to Dublin, to stay in some airy healthy part, and not in my house. For leaving everything else aside, it would be a very improper thing for her to breathe her last there.

"Please write to me every week, so that I may know what steps to take, for I am determined not to go to Ireland, to find her just dead, or dying. Nothing but extremity could make me so familiar with these terrible words, applied to so dear a friend. Tell her I have bought her a gold repeating watch, to be a comfort to her in winter nights. I had intended to bring it to her as a surprise, but now I would like her to know it, that she may know how my thoughts were always for her comfort. . . ."

To another friend, one who had often been a guest, in the happy past, at those parties that Anna would never arrange again, he wrote: "They have up till now written me deceiving letters, but Ayrton has been so just and prudent as to tell me the truth; which, however racking, is better than to be struck on the sudden. Dear Jim, forgive me, I do not know what I am saying; but believe me that violent friendship is more lasting, and as much binding, as violent love."

For her sake only, he said, was life worth preserving, that friend whose childhood he had trained, whose dear companionship had stood between him and the waiting ghost. How had he been so blind in the past, as to let anything come between them? But then he told himself that nothing had . . . certainly not Esther Vanelden.

Why was she so sunken that she could not fight against this illness? Had she suffered from that comfortless, that unacknowledged marriage? From his vow to see her only in the presence of another? From the misery caused by the ghost in the empty room, the ghost of whose presence she was unaware?

She knew that he loved her, and that, surely, was enough.

And he tried to see her, in his mind's eye, as she had been when she was young . . . the girl with the shining dark hair that held the sun and the moon and the glamour of deep waters captive in a net, the girl with the wide lion-like eyes that held the innocence of lost Edens. Why had he resolved that he would not return to Ireland? He *must* return, that he might gather up and enclose in his eyes, his mind, his heart, every memory of her, so that he might not be alone when she was gone. So, she would not have left him for ever; something of her would be with him still.

He would touch her hand, to keep the memory of that touch with him. He would see that trustful look in her wide eyes. . . .

No, better not that; it would be too hard to bear when she was dead. . . . But perhaps that look would have changed, Esther Vanelden would have struck it into the dust.

Chapter VIII

H E HAD returned, to gather each look, each word, into his
memory, that he might hold her for ever. When he saw
her, he felt as if the walls of his heart had crushed in, and had
crumbled, slow bit by bit, to dust. But every particle of dust was,
not dead, as dust should be, but a separate universe of
pain.

Seeing her touch the world that she so soon must leave, of
which she was no longer a part, putting the useless bread within
her lips, hearing her say: "Draw the curtains, the night is outside! Light the fire, I am cold." He thought: "Was ever sinner
condemned to such a torture as am I?"

The moments were flying and he could do nothing to hold
them back. He was a great man, but Time and Death would
beat him yet.

The days went on, and the life in Jonathan Hare's house
remained, outwardly, unchanged, for the world must never
know that the giant's heart lay in ruins. So he would ask the
Vicar and his wife to supper once a fortnight, and they would
play cards, there would be the usual dinner-party on Sunday;
but if the county families of the district called, he pretended
to be deafer than usual.

And all the time, beneath the moth-like frettings of such
trivialities, the dust into which his heart had crumbled was
blackened by the knowledge that Anna must die. There was no
help for it. There was no hope for it.

She was gradually growing weaker, but she did not complain.
Only once she told Becky that her heart had so sunk under its
load of misery, knowing that even now Jonathan would not
acknowledge her, that pride held him from her still, that she
had no strength left to keep her from the darkness.

Sometimes she would be carried into his house, and would lie there for a while, and he would speak to her with an anguished tenderness, he would touch her hand. Each day that she made a visit to him, he had a little claret mulled and kept near the fire, in order that she might be revived after her drive. He would hold this to her lips himself, and all the while, he did not know whether he dreaded most that her presence would leave him utterly and for ever, or that he would, for ever, be haunted by this changed ghost. A sick and changed ghost lying in a room behind him, while he advanced ever nearer and nearer down a long passage, to the room where the ghost that was his *Doppelgänger*, his other self, awaited him.

Then one day, when, overcome by a fit of coughing, she had to be carried upstairs and laid on a bed, Susan Orthoven, who was preparing restoratives in the next room, heard a curious sound. It was a creaking, hesitating sound—that of a human voice that was trying to express something from far away. The voice said: "If you wish it, my dear, it shall be acknowledged."

And a small sad sound answered; the faint and fading voice of the dying woman said: "It is too late."

Day by day he sat by her side, imprinting her features, her look, her smile, her voice, upon his memory. And it even seemed to him at moments that it was not true that she was about to leave him for ever—that Time and Death would relent, pitying him.

Then came a day in January, when it seemed as if the bells must soon sound among the leaves, and all old and outworn things would be put away—old leaves and dark beliefs and the mists hiding from us what we most would see—and on that day Anna could no longer be carried from her bed to the sofa near the window.

Now, as she neared the earthly end to her faithful love, she was surrounded by her friends, yet she was alone, since he was not by her side; but to this she had been inured by the other ⸱ʰs she had passed through.

She lay looking at the light, and on her hair was a darker dew than that which Jonathan had shaken from a branch upon her locks, long years ago, when she was young and they were driving together in the forest.

Suddenly she spoke, but as Becky bent over her Anna did not seem to see her. She whispered to herself. . . .

"Look, the ice is breaking. . . . Oh, the beautiful green rivers! How happy they are; they can flow at last. After long years. . . ."

    .   .   .   .   .

At eight o'clock that night, while Jonathan, as was usual on Sundays, sat surrounded by company at dinner, the news was brought to him, in a letter, that she was dead. He put it next to the hollow where once had been a human heart, and remained silent.

But at eleven o'clock, when the company was gone, he who knew that the being he most loved, and who most loved him, lay dead of the long misery caused by that madness in his nature that would not let him acknowledge her, or his love for her, began that moving funeral oration, that belated tribute of love, which breaks off suddenly in the middle with the words: "My head aches," and is continued only on the next day, like some stony and hopeless route march which had to be accomplished:

"January 30th. Tuesday.

"This is the night of the funeral, which my sickness will not suffer me to attend. It is now nine at night, and I am removed into another room, that I may not see the light in the church, which is opposite the window of my room. With all the softness of temper that became a lady, she had the personal courage of a hero. . . ."

Chapter IX

ALL WINTER long, the mountainous seas, now livid white with passion and roaring like a universe of lions, now swollen immense and black, thundering and boiling like a hell of lava-pouring volcanoes, vast as the maelstrom of madness that will burst the roaring, cracking world of a brain, the unavailing hell that had been a human heart, rushed onwards to uproot the universe of man, the civilisation founded upon a beast-world. Braying like a nation ruled over by asses, howling at the waves, chattering like a universe peopled by apes, the wind seemed the epitome of that civilisation that was to be destroyed, as it rushed to tear up the earth and, beholding the secret lying in that holy resting-place, to scatter the seed, that there may be no more life.

But now the wind and the sea had subsided, and the world was sunk in a numb mist like enveloping deafness, through which no sound could pierce but that of the rusty cawing bell of the Deanery, swinging its pendulum into empty space, like a brain swinging backwards and forwards into madness. Sometimes that bell had a human tongue: it said: "Too late."

Now that she had gone to warm the dead, leaving him sunless for ever, in a more endless cold than she could know in her grave's long night, she who had her deathless love for sun, for covering, for warmth, it was the living who seemed the dead, the living who should have sought the covering of the earth for shelter. He, who had hated calm, could cry now for the solitude and silence of the grave, for the lion-claws of his anguish tore him from that shelter, and he was exposed to the empty night—cast upon the desert of the night like a dead man in the sand. Then, bared to the uncaring light of heaven, from wind to wind like the scarecrow that Anna had seen waving to her over an unsown field, a dead man rose in the morning, dressed in the clothes that the living man had worn, and joined the company of those in whom the beat of Time still sounded. He who in the last years of his life had seen each stain of age, of fatigue, and of despair in her face, and had used them as a flail with which to flay her, that he might possess the secret of her nerves, that he might watch the pulse within her heart, he who had written: "I saw a woman flayed, and you will hardly believe how it altered her person for the worse," yet, knowing that her bones were laid bare by death, cried: "Come back. Come home. Whatever stains death has left upon your beauty, in whatever guise you are now, come back, I cannot endure my heart that has lost its beat, my bones laid bare to death by their deserting flesh. Come back."

But for answer, there was only the echo of those words she had said when she was about to leave him:

"Too late."

Every evening, when he returned to his house, opening the door, he half expected that he would hear a voice he knew. Surely it was only his deafness that hid it from him. For she would never leave him.

Never.

She had given him her promise.

Sometimes in the empty sunlight, he would see a little shadow moving towards him. And he would think, only for a moment, that it was a child, a small eager child with black straight hair and a fringe cut across her forehead. Where had he seen that child before? Years, oh, years ago, at Rotherham Park. Yes, that was it. A child whom he had taught. Who had trusted him.

But the shadow had gone. It would not stay with him. He was alone.

Yet one night, when she had been twelve months in her grave, he dreamed that she had returned to him, that she, knowing the coldness of the empty winds by which he was blown, in an endless waste, had cast aside the earth and the coldness of death for his sake. All the cathedrals of the earth might be build above her to press down the body that might not return, all the cities of the world, with their foolishness, and their turmoil, be piled there, all the black bells of the universe might toll the words "Dead . . . Dead . . . Dead . . ." but they could not keep her from him in his solitude.

The way was very long, and she must come alone, and lighted only by her love. But in the winter night, as he lay in his narrow bed, he saw her standing by the door; and her smile was sad and pleading, just as he remembered it. Perhaps she was begging him not to send her away, now that she was dead, and his pride could no longer be diminished by her love for him, nor could her reputation be harmed.

Humbly and pleadingly she crept nearer to him, she gave him her kiss, and, miracle of love, her lips were warm to his. But lips that come from the grave for our sake should be dust-dun, death-cold; and so he feared her, dared not touch and see if still her heart were warm. And she who had laid aside the coldness of death lest he should feel it when she came to lie beside his heart, giving him a sad and understanding smile, turned to the door and passed through it.

He who, whilst she was living, had torn down all the earth of the grave and laid it on her heart, now that she was dead had banished her to that company from which she could never more return.

Chapter X

H E WAS alone for ever. And in the years that followed, slowly, gradually, his flesh changed into stone, until he became like ~eless statue of a giant in an immense and tropical forest. ¹ish and volatile moth might brush against his stone, every songless bird build among his ruins—he heeded them not. Only, as the years passed, the stone grew more and more forest-aged, until the statue knew, at last, that it was stone, although it was made in the likeness of a giant.

He was sunk in a stupendous silence, and even when the news reached him that his beloved friend Jarvis had died, he refused to express his grief. "Upon this event I shall say nothing," he wrote to Weston. Yet he had been unable to bring himself to open the letter that contained the news of that death for five days, for although nothing spoke to him from the human world, yet some insect voice of warning had whispered to him that it contained something evil, something that plotted against the eternal stone. But he said nothing that might tell if any part of that stone could still remember the warmth and the sunlight.

Anna had been dead, now, for years, but he, who for eight days after her death had refused to touch a morsel of food, whose friends feared that her death would bring about his, could not bear, even now, to speak her name. Nothing remained to him of the mortal being he had loved, but, hidden away in a drawer, a shining dancing darkness, like a river or dark leaves on which the light will never be quenched, under a cover on which he had written the words: "Only a woman's hair."

So the years passed, and then, suddenly, the strange statue-like sleep was broken, the stone was galvanised into a terrible mechanism of movement. . . . It could be seen then that the giant had been fretted away by those trivialities that had passed unheeded.

Time had brought him an increased fame, but it seemed to him nothing but an empty sound that echoed down the long passages, and in the lead-cold darkened rooms. It was strange, he thought, that he had once longed for it, and that now it was his, he knew that it meant nothing. His eccentricity, which in his youth had been slight, had become more and more noticeable; even his appearance had grown stranger; his immeasurably black and deep eyebrows gave his gravity such an exact resemblance to the gravity of a raven, that one might expect a black and rusty caw, instead of a human voice, to issue from his lips. The thick fog of his deafness had increased to such a pitch that conversation was impossible, so that he was surrounded by a thick black half-mad silence like the plumage of the raven he resembled. One of his biographers tells us that "Having thus excluded conversation and desisted from study, he had neither business nor amusement, for having, by some ridiculous resolution or mad vow, determined never to wear spectacles, he could make less use of books in his later years; his ideas, therefore, being neither renovated nor increased by reading, wore gradually away, and left his mind vacant for the vexations of the hour, till at last his anger was heightened into madness."

Sometimes the house would be surrounded by a sea of rags; all the beggars of Dublin crowded round it, clamouring to see the man who had formed them into an army. For he had marshalled them, given them a badge to wear, and under his direction they had now what amounted, practically, to a trade union. He had, too, opened an office, which he placed in the charge of one of his underlings, where they might borrow small sums of money, the only condition attached being that the borrower must return it on the day stipulated. But this led, often, to a semi-riot. The sea of rags would flutter stormily, poll-parrot voices scream in anger. For the great man insisted upon his rights. If the beggars did not repay him on the day agreed upon, he threatened to sue them.

The crazy poll-parrot voices screamed, and the sea of rags stormed and fluttered, but these were almost the only sounds to be heard. The house knew no human voices, only echoes.

So the leaden hours passed in the gelid darkness of the rooms.

Sometimes the old man would sit and think about the past. Once, in a letter to Weston, he wrote: "I never wake without finding life a more insignificant thing than it was the day before. . . . But my greatest misery is recollecting the scenes of twenty years past, and then all of a sudden dropping into the present."

An old and lonely man, for whom a ghost waited.

But soon he was to have companionship. In the darkened rooms, suddenly, springing, it seemed, from nowhere, a minor host of small dark people appeared, all almost alike in appearance and manner, dressed in black and creeping sideways, scuttling like crabs, smiling and rubbing their hands together.

The great man was lonely . . . they had come to be his companions. And they would bear anything from him, his appalling outbursts of rage, his roars of fury that could be heard outside the house, the humiliating jokes he made at their expense, the tricks he played upon them. For were they not the natives of his lesser darkness?

One of these creatures, Francis Wilson by name, was found by Hans Orthoven (who, with Susan, had come to look after Hare's house since the death of Anna), importing his luggage into an empty room. When questioned, he smiled blandly. . . . No, the great man had not *asked* him to come and live there . . . but . . .

Time wore on, and sometimes Orthoven would see him slinking sideways through door after door, carrying a heavy bag. . . . The great man's library had gaps in the shelves now.

Then, night by night, as the creature from the room upstairs took his seat at the dining-table, a strange scene occurred. Jonathan Hare would drink glass for glass of wine with him, staring at him the while with those formidable and ferocious eyes . . . and the creature smiled back. It would not be long, he told himself, before the plot succeeded. . . . Yet night after night, it failed. He could not make the old man drunk.

For this he had planned to do. Drunk, Jonathan Hare would be in his power; he had the document ready, and all he would have to do would be to put the pen into the old man's hand and guide it, and then the property would be Wilson's for ever.

But time was passing, and if he was not quick, he might be too late. For what if Jonathan Hare should die without signing the document!

Then one night, as Hans passed the door of the dining-room, some instinct caused him to open it and look into the room. What he saw there made him rush forward.

The old man was lying back in his chair, his white hair tossed over the cushions, his indomitable and savage eyes staring into those of the creature who was bending over him and pressing his throat with his hands.

Orthoven flung Wilson out of the house, and soon Dublin was seething with the story he put about, that the great, the famous Jonathan Hare had been seized with madness, and had attacked him who was his greatest friend, whose life had only just been saved in time.

Then silence fell again, and even the sounds made by the beggars seemed to have died away.

But sometimes a clattering noise like the sound of hooves was heard in the sombre rooms where the cold seemed a mist, as Jonathan Hare passed up and down the stairs, driving two of his sycophants before him in harness, whipping them as if they were beings from his universe of horses, his white hair flying in the boreal air that haunted the house.

A gigantic burst of laughter sounded, echoing down the passages, from landing to landing, through the empty darkened rooms. Then came silence.

Chapter XI

IT WAS four o'clock in the morning, and the stealthy footsteps sounded on the deserted top landing, as they had sounded now for three mornings at exactly the same time. Someone who did not wish to be heard was creeping along. Then, as the footsteps grew nearer to a window, the grey furry half light fell upon a white crest of hair. . . . It was Jonathan Hare, going to keep his tryst at the secret meeting place.

It was strange that he had never noticed that empty room before, in all the years in which he had lived in the house; yet it must have been watching him from the beginning, waiting for its second inhabitant. The house was large, of course, too large for one person, and that was why he had never, until a few days ago, been aware of it. . . . Now he was approaching nearer and nearer to the room where the ghost waited for him. Only a little way remained. A few steps more, and the door would open. He would be within.

At four o'clock each morning, the room claimed him. And then there was the day to go through, in which he must preserve an utter secrecy, with the room drawing him—drawing him—trying to overcome his caution, trying to take him in an unwary moment.

He would look slyly at the few people with whom he was still in communion. . . . No, it was obvious that they had no suspicion of that meeting place, of the being whom he had gone to meet, and who had not yet kept his tryst.

At first, those furtive visits were a relief to him. He had waited for this so long, and it was not so terrible as he had expected. It is comfortable to fall into the depths, with no hope, so that one can lie at ease there.

Then fear fell upon him again, freezing his heart. What was it that was drawing him to that room—that he went to meet?

Sometimes he fell upon his knees and tried to pray. But the Lord's Prayer was all that he could remember. When his cousin came to the house and entered the room of this inhabitant of Death, he was met by a terrible sound like the clapping of a bell, issuing from the swollen and blackened tongue that could only utter the word "Go. . . . Go. . . ." And the sound was succeeded by a silence like that of the deepest forest, broken only by the sound of footsteps walking backwards and forwards, ever increasing in speed, the sound of Jonathan Hare trying to outstrip his fate.

Once a plea reached the outer world, a letter to William Ayrton that seemed almost a cry for mercy: "I have been

251

very miserable all night, and to-day extremely deaf and full of pain. I am so stupid and confounded that I cannot express the mortification I am under both in body and mind. All I can say is, that I am not in torture, but I daily and hourly expect it. Pray let me know how your health is, and your family. I hardly understand one word I write. I am sure my days will be very few; few and miserable they must be."

Then one midday, hoarse roars were heard, echoing through the house. Hans, running upstairs, heard that they came from an empty and shuttered room, a room that had never been used in all the years in which Hare had inhabited the house. The door was locked, but Hans, bursting it open, rushed into the room. It was completely dark, excepting for the fiery red eyeballs of the old madman, and those echoing them. He was threatening his image, his *Doppelgänger*, the ghost that waited for him, in a mirror.

A week afterwards, guardians were appointed to take charge of him, lest he should commit murder upon himself.

Nothing remained now, of what had been that great and awe-inspiring figure, but his terrible pedestrianism, which, after his madness had increased into the black, smoky, Tartarean fire wherein the last dust of his mind was consumed, kept him on his feet for ten hours a day; so that when his meat was brought to him, cut into mouthfuls as though he were a wild beast, he, having left it till it had stood for an hour, would eat it walking.

Only twice, during all the time of his raging madness, did he speak; when Hans was breaking a large piece of coal, a harsh voice said: "Fool. . . . It is a stone. . . ." And when Susan, seeing that a knife had been left in his presence, took it as he was about to snatch it, then a voice coming from the depths of unutterable misery was heard. It said "I am what I am. . . . I am what I am. . . ."

And silence fell.

But sometimes an appalling hollow booming noise echoed down the long corridors and in the empty rooms, a drumming like that which breaks the silence of tropical forests, a crashing,